Petunia 1949

Leah Brewer

In memory of my dear mama, Rose Holt Castleberry. Oh, how I'd love to hear your wonderful bedtime stories again.

Chapter 1

May 1949

Petunia Hollings couldn't remember a time in all her sixteen years when she liked her red hair. To be honest, she had despised it since she'd first looked in a mirror. Her family all had brown hair. So why was she the one born with the ghastly red hair?

Lloyd, her older brother, said she belonged to the milkman, which was ridiculous. They didn't even have a milkman. He was a year older than Petunia but acted like a child. Mama used to spank him until he got taller than her. Now, she just thumped his ears when he acted up, which was daily.

After spending too much time browsing at the only store within walking distance, she had to hurry, or she'd be in a pickle. It wouldn't have mattered if the dirt road to her house was two miles or a hundred. Mama waited at home, so Petunia trudged down the road like she was on a mission to save the world. She might've left home hungry, but not so much now, seeing she'd already choked down enough dust to make her own mud pie.

Flat land and trees lined the distance between Petunia and her house. Too bad all the creeks on the route had dried up, or she'd gladly drink the dirty water.

The darkened gray clouds boiling across the sky meant a storm would be rolling through soon. She stopped and scanned her surroundings. A quick jolt went through her. The chilly wind bit into her arms and legs, and she picked up the pace. She tugged on her brown dress. The course material scratched her thin legs even more, and the wind blew like it was on a rampage.

Finally, the neighbor's barn stood in the distance, which meant she had less than a mile to go. Even though the barn had faded from red to orange over the past few summers, it was still bright enough to see from a distance.

The wind howled like the old tabby cat that stayed in their barn. It was a mooch, but Mama liked to keep it around. It ate the mice, which wasn't a bad thing.

A rumble of thunder sounded in the distance, practically vibrating Petunia's chest. Her heart rate accelerated, and she stumbled over her own feet. Regaining her balance, she rushed down the road, clutching the small flour pouch as tight as possible.

Since her oldest brother Martin had been killed in the Warren tornado that past January, she got a little antsy when the wind blew. Mama told her to deal with it. Said she was too old to act like a baby over a bit of wind.

Now that she was sixteen and a half, she guessed Mama was right. She was a woman. Not that being sixteen mattered much. She'd been a woman since the second grade. That's when she'd quit school to chop cotton full-time and help with the other farm work. It seemed like yesterday she'd walked out of the school for the last time with tears pouring down her face.

No matter. Things couldn't change. Working to help support the family was her lot in life. Even more so after Martin passed. He'd been a hard worker, and now she had to help Mama and Lloyd pick up the slack.

Better to accept it. Life was easier that way.

Daddy sure wouldn't step up to support the family. He was never around long enough to do much of anything except get Mama pregnant and whoop

Petunia over something she hadn't done. Then, he would disappear for months on end.

It didn't matter that Mama had lost the last three babies. He kept coming.

If you asked Petunia, Daddy was nothing but a no-count, good-for-nothing, sorry excuse for a man—not that anybody ever did.

Her blood boiled just thinking about him. Would it hurt him to pretend he cared about Petunia as much as he loved the other kids? Instead of acting like she was a burden most of the time. If he wasn't treating her like she was a nuisance, he seemed happy pretending she didn't exist.

At least she hadn't gotten a whooping since she was thirteen. Now, he ignored her or barked orders worse than her last schoolteacher. He'd never love her like the other kids, so maybe she should find a way out of Arkansas.

She'd been born in Alabama. Maybe she should go back and find a good husband who would love her. She never would understand why they moved to Arkansas in the first place, especially since Daddy kept going back to Alabama anyway. It made no sense.

Who even had the money to go to Alabama? Unless she snuck into the back seat with Daddy. But

Mama would tan her hide, so that was out of the question.

She'd have to find a husband here, she reckoned. Her sisters, Teresa and Evelyn, had found good men, so why couldn't Petunia?

A picture of Lonnie Richey's green eyes filled Petunia's mind, and she inwardly growled. The time for regrets over Lonnie choosing Teresa instead of her had passed. They were married, and Petunia couldn't change it. Lonnie turned out to be a lot like Daddy, never giving her a second look. His green eyes had been for Teresa and Teresa only.

Petunia clamped her teeth together. Why'd she go and think about Lonnie and ruin a perfectly good day already?

Finally, the little shack she called home came into view. She shook thoughts of her pitiful life out of her mind and took off at a dead run. Tearing the door open, she bounced into the main room only to slow down when she reached the battered couch and ratty old recliner. An image of Martin hauling it out of an abandoned house in Hazen the summer before entered her mind. A small smile played across her lips, and she trailed her fingers down the rough fabric as she passed it by.

The aroma of sizzling bacon caused her head to cock sideways. "I thought we were saving the bacon for Sunday, Mama."

Mama glanced up from the frying pan as she moved bacon onto a plate. Dissatisfaction furrowed her thick brown brow. "Girl! What in tarnation took you so long? Get over here and bring me that flour."

Petunia's face fell as she handed Mama the flour. "What's happened?"

Mama snatched the flour from her hand and poured some into the hot grease, followed by water, quickly stirring it into a gravy. "Your daddy's here is what's happened. You'd know if you hadn't took so long getting home, child."

Petunia wrinkled her nose. She guessed she wouldn't be getting much of that bacon after all.

Chapter 2

L oud snores vibrated through the thin walls, waking Petunia up. She rolled over and hit a spring on her raggedy mattress. Visions of stuffing cotton down Lloyd's throat danced around her mind. Anything to cut his snores off. Where was Mama when he needed a good thumping? Probably asleep like most normal folks.

The back door slammed, and Petunia shot off the bed. It wasn't even four o'clock in the morning. Who would be up at this hour? She slipped on her only pair of boots and tiptoed to the bedroom door.

Voices drifted from the backyard. She eased the kitchen window up a notch and sat on the floor. She'd love to have a piece of cake to snack on. Or some pie. Her stomach complained by growling for what seemed like an entire minute. That's what she got for thinking of sweets when she knew they didn't have the stuff to make any of that right now.

Maybe she'd take on some laundry from town to make extra money.

The wind carried Mama's voice through the open window. "Oliver Dewitt Hollings, I swear if I find out you've cheated on me with that Marshall woman, I'll kill you both."

Daddy balked. "Calm yourself down, woman." His voice lowered, so Petunia leaned onto the screen. "Ain't nothing going on between me and Gail."

"Lies. She thinks she's better than me and our kids, but she looks at you like you're her man. Not mine."

Petunia clamped her hand over her mouth. Surely, Daddy wouldn't cheat on Mama with that woman.

"Your cockeyed notions are a pain in the neck, woman. I ain't tellin' you again. Nothing happened. Her legs broke anyways."

Things got quiet for a few minutes. Petunia would give anything to see what was happening. Or hear what they whispered.

Daddy spoke again, but his voice sounded different. "You ain't got a bit of room to talk about cheating. Not when one of the kids probably ain't even mine."

A crack sounded, and Mama spoke between sobs. The hurt in her voice made Petunia's heart lurch. "I told you my mama was a redheaded woman. Why do you keep accusing me of something?"

"You say she was a redhead, but how do I know that for sure since we never met?"

"Now you accuse me of lying about mama's hair color?"

"I don't know what to think. How did Carol Louise get that striking red hair?"

He only called Petunia by her given name of Carol Louise when he was mad over something.

Lloyd poked his head out of the little closet he called a bedroom. He slid down the wall, resting his hand on the floor beside Petunia's knee. "You shouldn't be listening to Mama and Daddy fight," he said.

Hot tears threatened to fall as her eyes searched Lloyd's. "Am I Daddy's kid?"

"Sure, you are. Don't let his rantings bother you none." He reached over and ruffled her hair. "Now go back to bed."

"But Daddy don't think I'm his kid." Her voice came out flat even to her own ears.

Lloyd's shoulder raised in a half-shrug. "Who cares what he thinks? I sure don't. And if you ask me, you're lucky if you ain't his kid."

Unable to hold the tears back, Petunia bolted off the floor and out the front door at a dead run. She ran until her legs were jelly, not caring she was in her slip of a nightgown. She had to get away from it all. And the bayou was the best place to do it.

When she reached her destination, the sun peeked beyond the trees above the water. A fish jumped out and back into the water. Bright pink, orange, and yellow waves softly skidded in the circles the fish left behind.

She rubbed the chill bumps that sprang onto her arms and breathed in the smell of early morning on the water. This right here was her happy place. It had been ever since Daddy got mad and cut down the swing Martin had set up in a tree for them to play on. That swing had been a piece of Martin after he passed away. Then Daddy took it away like everything else. All that had been left was ashes after he burned the swing in the woodpile.

She allowed her mind to drift back to a time of carefree laughter before working the fields fell mostly to Petunia and Lloyd.

She could almost feel the wind like the days her oldest sister Evelyn pushed her as high as she could go in their swing while Teresa pretended to have a tea party. Those days were few and had passed way too quickly. The memory shattered, and the people from those days seemed like colorful fragments of broken glass. Broken apart by too many days of mind-numbing work in the cotton fields.

She longed for a fishing pole to catch some good dinner and forget her worries. If her friend Opal was with her, she'd for sure be able to fish.

A branch cracked, and then someone cleared their throat behind Petunia. She spun around and met Verlon Marshall's questioning gaze. He raised his hands to display two cane fishing poles and a tackle box.

Verlon and his family lived in Chicago. During their childhood, he spent every summer in Arkansas with his aunt and uncle. He and Lloyd, being closer in age, spent a lot of time together back then. It had been three years since Petunia last saw him. The last time they met, he was a pudgy boy who seemed to take pleasure in pulling Petunia's hair.

Now, as he stood by the water, Petunia couldn't find an ounce of baby fat anywhere. The early morning sun cascaded down, casting a mesmerizing glow over his hair, transforming it from chocolate brown to a deep, almost lustrous black. As she observed him, she was taken aback by how much he'd changed. He'd grown into a striking man.

His eyebrows lifted as he set the tackle box at the water's edge. "Petunia? What in the world are you doing out here in your nightgown?"

Volcanic heat traveled from the soles of her feet to the top of her head. "None of your business is what."

He snickered and walked closer to where she stood. She bristled until he held his jacket out. "Put this on. You have to be cold."

Swallowing down the smart remark, she accepted the jacket. "Thanks."

He sat down on a log close to the water. "You didn't answer my question. Is everything all right?"

She raised her chin. "Maybe I wanted to catch some fish."

"Okay. Where's your equipment?" He craned his neck to look behind her.

She rested her right hand on her hip. "My what?"

"Tacklebox and fishing pole." He scanned the area. "I don't see it."

She stomped a foot, then instantly regretted it. "Because I didn't bring it."

He patted a space beside him on the log. "How about you join me then? Uncle Eddie was going to come, but Aunt Gail needed his help with something."

She glanced over his shoulder and shrugged. "I dunno."

"Come on." He pulled a fat worm out of a container. "You can keep whatever you catch."

A piece of fried Perch sounded too good to pass up. And she'd always had a good time fishing with Verlon when they were younger. "All right then.

But I ain't a baby. I can put the worm on my own hook."

He raised his left eyebrow before handing her a pole. "Never said you was."

Three hours later, she skipped home with a string of Perch, Crappy, and a Bass. She couldn't wait to show Lloyd. And Daddy would even be happy to see her if she brought home dinner.

She walked past the barn, and loud crying caught her attention. She stuck her head in and sighed. Mama lay curled up beside her raggedy cat, bawling like an abandoned baby. Petunia meandered over to her and sat down. Mama met Petunia's eyes and raised her arms. Petunia wasted no time slipping into Mama's embrace and holding her close.

"He left again, Petunia." Mama got out between sobs. "Don't ever marry a man who don't love you with all his heart."

Why would she say that? "Okay, Mama. I won't."

She should've known. Daddy was gone again. And it was all her fault.

Chapter 3

A balmy breeze skirted across Petunia's face, and she closed her eyes for a moment, a soft smile settling on her lips. She leaned her head back and watched a white cloud through the tree limbs as it completely covered the sun. She'd picked the perfect spot to put their blanket under the big oak tree. She loved church potluck days.

"Petunia. Hey." Lloyd elbowed her and nodded at the makeshift table holding the desserts at the church potluck. "Why don't you grab me a piece of Mama's banana cake before it's gone?"

Picking up a ladybug crawling across the blanket, Petunia let it crawl over her hand as she glanced at the folks scattered around the area. Little kids ran around screaming and playing games while the adults visited. Those not in line to make a plate sat in chairs or lounged on blankets. All except a group of men. They stood at the bottom of the church steps. Huddled up like they were figuring out a plan to save the world. Now that Daddy had come home, he was right in the middle of them.

Petunia let out a humph when Mildred Campbell and Judith Cooper strolled across the lawn decked out in fancy dresses and new boots. Petunia used to long to have light brown, curly hair like Judith's. If she was honest, she still did. Petunia figured Mildred wanted to look like Judith, too. While Judith had more of an older look, Mildred still had her baby fat. Not that Mildred was ugly, but she didn't seem to be as confident as Judith. Three of the boys she'd gone to school with flocked around them. You'd think they were going somewhere high society. Not a church potluck in the middle of Nowhere, Arkansas. Daddy always said they lived in the sticks, and she was beginning to think he was right.

Teresa and her new husband, Lonnie, joined the group of so-called high society snobs. Figures. Some days, Lonnie fit right in with that bunch. Especially the way his blonde hair always laid just right on his handsome face. Teresa was so lucky.

Lloyd pinched her arm. "Did you hear me?"

She balled up her fist and punched Lloyd on his shoulder. Her gaze landed on his messy hair, and for a moment, she considered jerking a plug from his head. If she'd been blessed with his hair, she'd keep it brushed all the time. "I ain't getting you no cake, Lloyd. Now leave me be. I'm trying to think."

"About what? Playing with dolls?" He cackled at his own stupid joke.

She shook her head and leaned her elbows on their blanket. "Shush. You know I don't play with dolls. I'm too old for that mess."

Verlon Marshall sauntered over and plopped down close to Petunia. He pushed a few strands of dark hair out of his blue eyes. "What y'all doing over here?"

Petunia ignored him. She was too busy keeping an eye on Teresa and Lonnie. Heat shot up her neck when Lonnie grabbed Teresa's hand and kissed it.

Lloyd and Verlon talked about somebody's new bull. A bunch of senseless rubbish just to talk about something.

Lonnie moved his hand from Teresa's and settled it in the crook of her back, close to her thigh. How could he? Showing such affection out in public. He oughta be talked to, and his ears thumped. Maybe she should go tell the preacher. Yeah, that's what she should do.

"Earth to Petunia." Lloyd followed her line of sight. "Who are you staring at?"

Butterflies flipped through her stomach, and she sucked in a breath. "Nobody!" She shot off the blanket. "I was just trying to figure out when I could get that cake."

A few minutes later, she marched up to Lloyd and Verlon with the last two chunks of banana cake. She handed Lloyd one and then bit her bottom lip. One piece left. Why'd Verlon come to their blanket, anyway? Shame caused her to blush. She shouldn't be thinking such hateful thoughts. Didn't Mama teach her better than that? Even though they didn't have much, it was good to share with others.

Petunia inwardly sighed before meeting Verlon's curious gaze. "Did you want this cake or not?"

Verlon grinned and held out his hand. "Why sure, Petunia. I'll take it." His arm muscles strained against his short-sleeved shirt, and Petunia inwardly balked. His mama needed to buy him bigger clothes that wouldn't show off his body like that.

The last piece of banana cake, and she wouldn't even get a bite. After a brief moment of imagining herself smearing the cake in his face, she smiled, curtsied, and handed it over.

She reclaimed her seat on the blanket and sighed. Maybe she could get something else. There was a fine-looking strawberry cake on the table. Didn't matter she broke out in hives every time she ate a strawberry. Maybe a whole piece of cake would do her in. At least she wouldn't have to watch Lonnie hang all over Teresa.

Verlon crawled across the blanket until he was directly in front of Petunia. He handed her the plate of cake. "I decided I don't want it after all. Would you eat it to keep it from going to waste?"

She eyed him a second before taking the plate. "I reckon I will."

He beamed at her, and a tiny flutter flew around in Petunia's tummy. She pushed it away as fast as it came. Absolutely no good would ever come from those feelings. His snooty Aunt Gail would never let her precious nephew look twice at a girl like Petunia. Not that she wanted him to.

He'd probably end up with a mean girl like Judith or Mildred. Judith kept smiling in their direction and fanning herself. She'd stop if she knew how silly she looked.

Verlon's smile deepened. "Good. Mama would wring my neck if I wasted something. Even though she's back home in Chicago, I have to keep her rules in mind, you know."

Petunia nodded before shoveling a piece of cake into her mouth. She rolled it around on her tongue and closed her eyes as the sweet and gooey sweetness slid down her throat. Now, this was living.

Lloyd set his empty plate on the blanket and turned to Verlon. "When you heading back to Chicago?"

Verlon glanced at Petunia before answering, "I'll be here a couple more months or so at least. Uncle Eddie needs my help since Aunt Gail broke her leg."

Petunia swallowed another bite of cake. "Is that why Mrs. Marshall hasn't been at church lately?"

Verlon stretched his arms above his head. "I suppose so." His hand brushed Petunia's ankle as his arms fell to his side.

Her eyes widened, and she jerked her leg out of his reach. He chuckled, his eyes sparkling with flecks of green. Now, weren't they blue a bit ago? How could they suddenly look green? Maybe Petunia's own eyes were playing tricks on her.

Teresa and Lonnie strolled up to their blanket. Teresa looked at Verlon through a hooded gaze before her eyes darted between Petunia and Lloyd. "Mama asked me to tell you two that Daddy's ready to go." She ended the sentence by upturning her pouty red lips into a smile Petunia could never pull off.

When Petunia was little, she'd walked into a nest of fire ants. A few of them crawled up her leg before she was able to get away. Their bite hurt like the dickens. She could still feel the sharp fire from their stingers. And right now, she felt just like a whole army of those suckers slammed into her chest.

"Fine by me." She scowled at Lonnie before grabbing her plate and sprinting to Daddy's car.

Chapter 4

Sweat dripped onto the barn floor as Petunia milked their new cow, Bessie. She was a beauty with her white and brown coat. Daddy had been gone three weeks, and they'd had her for two.

She sang Jesus Loves Me inside her head as she patted Bessie's side. The wind shifted and carried a pungent odor from Sampson's stall. Lloyd was late getting his chores done.

Petunia's friend, Opal, and her younger brother, Clyde Brown, walked into the barn carrying buckets. "Hi, Petunia. I can't believe you got a milk cow now." Opal attempted to run her hand down the cow's face. Bessie snorted, and Opal jerked her hand away, her dark eyes widening.

Clyde covered his mouth as a deep, hearty laugh echoed throughout the barn. His big laugh matched his bigger-boned frame. "Maybe the cow don't like black folks, Opal. You better step back."

Petunia shook her head and patted Bessie's side. "Nah, she's just ornery. Y'all are here early to use the well."

Opal shrugged but kept her leery gaze on Bessie, almost like she was ready to make a run for it. "Mama and Daddy made us come early so we can help Daddy in town later. And we better hurry before we get in trouble. See you later, Petunia."

"I wish I could go to town with y'all." Petunia rolled her eyes. No sense in wishing when she had too much to do around the house.

Opal moved her head up and down. "I can ask Daddy."

"Nah, it's okay. I got too much to do around here. See y'all later." She poked her head around Bessie. "Let's try to catch some fish this weekend."

"Okay. I'll try." Opal grabbed her bucket and headed out the door with Clyde trailing behind her.

She patted sweat from her brow when Lloyd ran into the barn. "Hurry up, Petunia. Mama made sausage and pancakes for breakfast."

Petunia jerked her neck to the side as her hand landed on her right hip. "Sausage and pancakes both? How in the world did she manage that?"

He screwed his face up. "Who cares? All that matters is we have a good breakfast waiting for us. Come on, already."

"Don't you need to muck Sampson's stall, knuck-lehead? I been having to milk Bessie while holding my nose."

He plopped his head back like he was waiting for something from the sky to fall into his mouth. "I'll do it after we eat. I swear. But I need you to come on."

She squirted the last bit of milk in the pail and raised herself off the stool. "I'm a coming. You sure are bossy this morning and worried about food instead of doing your chores."

He stuck his tongue out at her and hightailed it through the front door with Petunia close on his heels, lugging her pail of milk. The heavenly scent of sausage, pancakes, and sweet maple syrup surrounded her as soon as she walked inside. She pushed past Lloyd to get to the table first. Her jaw almost dropped to the floor. Verlon sat at the table with Mama. He landed a grin on Petunia.

Lloyd pushed her out of his way. "Move, squirt. I'm hungry. And we have a guest, so don't be rude."

Petunia smoothed her hair down, deposited the bucket on the other side of the stove, and then claimed her regular chair. She liked the one with a bit of blue on it. The others were plain brown or white. None of them matched, but they got the job done.

Verlon kicked Petunia's leg under the table, and she pressed her lips together to keep from laughing. A snicker escaped, and she slapped her hand over her mouth.

Verlon licked his lips and shoveled in a bite of pancake and sausage. "Mrs. Hollings, these are the best pancakes I've ever had. Thank you for having me over."

Mama beamed. "Anytime, Verlon. You're welcome at our home day or night."

An unfamiliar heat went up Petunia's stomach and didn't stop until it reached the top of her head. What could Mama mean by day or night? Older folks said the strangest things.

After breakfast, Lloyd took Verlon to look at his hunting dog, so Petunia helped clean the kitchen. Mama hummed a song and handed Petunia a freshly washed plate.

Petunia cocked her head as she rinsed the plate in her bucket of water. "Why you so happy, Mama? Is it because Daddy's gone? I thought that made you sad."

"Everything's gonna be just fine." She dropped a fork in the rinse water. "I didn't tell you, but your daddy sent the money for Bessie."

Petunia's lips lifted at the edge. "That's good. I'm happy Daddy did that for you."

"For us, child. He loves us, and that means a lot."
She continued her humming.

"Well, if that's all." Petunia dried a plate and picked
up another she'd rinsed.

Mama wrapped her hand around Petunia's wrist,
causing Petunia to have to hold the wet plate. "I have
to say something to you, and I need you to listen."

Petunia swallowed a lump down. Whatever she
had to say couldn't be good. "I can hear you, Mama."

Her gaze almost bore into Petunia's soul. "That
young man, Verlon, is in love with you, Petunia."

She was right. Mama may as well have hit her in
the forehead with a two-by-four.

Petunia gaped and stepped away from the sink.
"No, he ain't."

"Yes, he is. I know the look a man has when he's
in love. And he's got it." She let go of her wrist and
continued humming. But it wasn't a regular song
leaving her lips. No ma'am. It was the tune to Here
Comes the Bride.

That two by four she wished Mama had hit her
with somehow settled in the pit of Petunia's stomach.
"I don't give a hoot who he's in love with. It ain't
me. Or even if it is, that don't matter, not one bit."

Mama leaned so close to Petunia she could smell
the remnant of sausage and maple syrup on her
breath. "Don't you see? You need to encourage that

young man. He's a keeper. Handsome. Has a good job lined up at some hotel when he gets back to Chicago. And he loves you. What more could you ask for?"

She wouldn't even ask how she knew about his job. A vision of Lonnie touching Teresa's back swam around in her mind. What more could she ask for? She could ask for love. She could ask to feel the way she does about her sister's husband. But she couldn't say that to her. Not in a million years. How would Mama ever understand her feelings for Lonnie? How would anyone?

She kept her gaze fixated on drying the dishes. "I don't know."

A grin the size of the plate Petunia had just dried lit across Mama's face. "Then it's settled. You will encourage that boy and marry him before the summer's over."

Later that night, Petunia lay in bed staring at the ceiling. Even if she wanted to, how would she ever encourage Verlon Marshall to marry her? She didn't know how to flirt. If she did, she'd be the one married to Lonnie instead of Teresa.

On the other hand, maybe marrying Verlon wouldn't be the end of the world. It could be her ticket out of Arkansas. Never having to see Lonnie rub Teresa's back again.

Away from the cotton. From the heat. But most of all, away from Daddy. If she was gone, he'd be home more. And that's what Mama needed—daddy home.

Chapter 5

Minutes ticked by with Petunia staring a hole through the bobber sitting perfectly still on top of the water. Puffy white clouds floated across the silvery gray sky, threatening to spit out a few raindrops before the hour was out. Petunia covered her eyes and scanned the area, happy to see the clouds staying dry so far. They needed rain, but Petunia hoped it would hold off until they got done fishing.

Opal sighed and pulled her pole out of the water. "I don't think we gonna catch any fish this morning."

The lingering stench of rotten fish filled the air, and Petunia wrinkled her nose. "I bet the fish ain't biting because they can smell that." She said as she jerked her head toward the dead fish.

Opal stuck her tongue out and made a gagging sound. "You probably right."

Petunia stood and gathered her pole and container of worms. "Let's just go then. I need to get home in time for chores before breakfast anyway."

"Yeah, and it'll probably rain in a bit."

As they made their way down the dirt road, a low whining sound came from one of the deepest ditches in the area. It usually had water running through it, but the weather had been so dry that it held nothing but sticks and dirt.

"You hear that?" Petunia stopped and set her pole and worms on the ground.

Opal shook her head and pointed at the ditch. "It sounds like a cat."

Petunia took a deep breath and descended into the dry ditch, keeping an eye out for snakes. Opal had been right. A tiny orange kitten with a white patch on its side struggled to free one of its legs trapped beneath a log.

With determination in her movement, Petunia knelt beside the log and pulled it away from the kitten. The kitten stared at its leg for a second before looking at Petunia, its wide eyes filled with uncertainty. Letting out a scratchy meow, it slowly hobbled over to Opal.

Snubbed by a cat. It must be kin to Daddy.

"This poor thing will drown if it starts raining hard, and it looks starved. I gotta take it home and get it some milk," Opal said as she hugged the cat to her chest.

Petunia shrugged. "I think it likes you better than me anyway."

Opal clicked her tongue. "No, it don't. It's just scared, and it came to me because I was closer than you."

What a good friend. She always tried to make Petunia feel better no matter what.

"It came to you because it could sense that you're kind. But thanks for trying to make me feel better." Petunia climbed out of the ditch before and put her hand out for Opal. As she helped Opal and the cat, a sweet aroma like brown sugar filled the air. Opal always smelled so good.

After accepting help, Opal eyed the kitten. "I'm gonna call it Buford."

A blank look crossed Petunia's face. Buford? Clamping her mouth shut, Petunia didn't dare say anything mean about the name. Instead, she half-smiled before almost tripping over a rather large rock.

Opal maneuvered Buford and her fishing supplies to a comfortable position. "I heard Mama and Daddy talking about Verlon Marshall last night."

Petunia nearly choked on her own spit. "What about him?" She kicked a rock, and it landed at the bottom of the ditch.

Opal stroked the kitten across the head and grinned. "Daddy said Verlon stopped and helped change a flat on his car."

Petunia took Opal's fishing pole out of her arms before raising her brow. "Well? What else did they say about him?"

Opal's brows raised to match Petunia's, and a grin split her lips. "If I didn't know better, I'd think you was crushing on Verlon Marshall."

Rose-red splotches spread across Petunia's neck, and she quickly covered it with her free hand. "I ain't no khaki wacky, Opal. Now, what did they say about him?"

A fit of laughter overtook Opal. After she finished cackling, she wiped away a few tears and leveled her gaze on Petunia. "I never said you was boy crazy. I know you ain't like that."

"Nope," Petunia said, trying not to pressure Opal into answering her question.

"Mama said Verlon was nice and helpful. And I hope you do like Verlon. He's a good person," Opal fluttered her lashes, "and a dreamboat."

Petunia bit the side of her lip and settled her gaze on a cloud resembling a turtle as it floated around a few other shapeless clouds. "Mama thinks Verlon is in love with me."

As soon as the words came out of her mouth, she regretted them. Why'd she go and say something like that out loud?

Opal squealed, and the kitten jumped out of her arms. Petunia scooped it up and handed it back to Opal, and then she took off speed-walking down the road.

"I hope your mama's right. You deserve to have a good life." Opal said as she bounded up beside Petunia.

Petunia stopped and dropped the poles and worms before grasping Opal's wrist. "You deserve to have a good life, too. And one day, I just know we both will."

Opal's lip quivered as a half-smile appeared on her face. "Mama always says the Lord will take care of us. I trust He will."

"Your mama's a smart woman. I know the Lord will take care of us both." The corners of Petunia's mouth turned up, and she pointed at the sky. "Help me find some animals in the sky. I see a turtle over there."

Opal threw back her head and gasped. "I see it." She canvassed the sky for a few seconds before pointing to her right. "Look at that, Petunia. It's a heart in the sky. It's a sign that you and Verlon are meant to be."

As Opal said, Petunia's skin prickled when she saw a perfectly shaped heart. Could Opal be right? Could it be a sign?

Buford chose that moment to let out a screech of a meow. Petunia shook off the unwelcome feelings and skipped down the road, determined not to give Verlon Marshall another thought.

Chapter 6

Go after some flour, Petunia. Run to Teresa's and get some meal, Petunia. Did Lloyd not have legs? Why'd Mama always make Petunia go after stuff? It wasn't fair.

Daddy may have sent the money for Bessie, but that's all he'd sent. They couldn't even afford to buy a lousy bag of cornmeal from the store. This last time he showed up at the house for one day. He'd left that next morning without even speaking so much as a word to Petunia. So that left her walking in the heat to bum a little meal off Teresa. She couldn't even ride Sampson. Mama told her no. It was too hot for that horse to be out right now.

Too hot for the horse, her foot. If it was too hot for Sampson, wasn't it too hot for Petunia? She kicked a rock before plopping down under a partially naked tree. Taking a swig from her pouch of water at least soothed her dry throat and mouth. At least she'd remembered to bring it this time.

Thinking of something else was the only way to get her mind off the heat. Like what Mama had said about Verlon. Could he possibly want somebody like Petunia? She wasn't nothing special. Not like Teresa or even Evelyn.

And Verlon, well, he had a look in his eye that most boys around here didn't. A look that told Petunia he had plans, and nobody could stop him.

Too many times, Petunia had dreamed of making Daddy proud. Would marrying Verlon do that? Even though he was no Lonnie, maybe marrying Verlon wouldn't be that bad. She might not love him, but he sure was something special to look at.

Wouldn't that make for a good life? She'd have to ask Teresa if having a handsome husband could make her happy. No, that made no sense. Teresa loved Lonnie, so it wouldn't be the same.

A frog croaked, jolting Petunia out of her thoughts. She better get going, or she'd be sitting here at the same time tomorrow. Before she could move, Judith Cooper and Mildred Campbell paraded up to where she sat.

Judith put her arm up to Mildred and sneered down at Petunia. "Look who we have here. What you doing out here, runt?"

Mildred ogled Petunia, but she remained silent. She looked like she might pass out with her red face. Petunia almost felt compelled to offer Mildred a drink of her water. Almost.

Instead of offering to share her water, Petunia shot off the ground and attempted to walk past them without answering Judith. It was better to ignore the bully and her loyal followers.

Judith blocked Petunia and continued with her hateful banter. "I hear you have your eye on Verlon Marshall. You think you're good enough for that boy?" Her nose twitched, and she leaned closer to Petunia. "You smell like you ain't had a bath in weeks."

Petunia bristled but managed to keep her expression neutral. "You need to leave me alone, Judith. I ain't doing you no harm."

Judith's neck reddened, and she clenched her fists at her side. "You ain't doing me no harm? Is that the best you got?"

"I said leave me alone." Petunia's heart pounded in her chest. There's no way this would end well. Not with Judith's body shaking like it was.

"You need to leave Verlon alone, Petunia Hollings." Judith bared her teeth and stepped closer to Petunia.

Petunia attempted to walk in the other direction.

"Oh no, you don't," Judith said before grabbing Petunia's hair and jerking her to her knees.

That did it.

Before she thought twice, Petunia scrambled to her feet and tackled Judith. Her chest tightened as she shoved Judith's head into the dry leaves.

"Get her off me, Mildred." Judith howled.

Petunia's stomach sank, and she looked over her shoulder. Mildred's face seemed sad, but she pushed Petunia off Judith anyway. Time seemed to slow as Petunia fell sideways into the same leaves Judith had just been in.

When Petunia hit the ground, Judith landed on top of her with fists flying. Stickers pierced Petunia's back through her thin blouse. She raised her arms to block Judith. Mildred pinned Petunia's hands above her head. Her nose stung from the blows. Mildred gasped before scurrying away.

Ignoring the metallic, almost sweetness covering her tongue, Petunia sunk her nails into Judith's throat and threw her off.

Without missing a beat, Judith gained her feet and sank her teeth into Petunia's side.

A deep ache swirled through Petunia. She closed her eyes, crying out for help. But no help would come. It was up to Petunia to protect herself. She buried her hands in Judith's hair and jerked with all her might. Judith let go of Petunia's side and bared blood-covered teeth.

Veins bulged in Petunia's neck. She wrapped her hands around Judith's throat, squeezing with all her might. Judith stared at Petunia with a panicked gaze before snapping her mouth shut as her hands fell limp to her sides. Traces of blood lingered in the cracks of Judith's lips.

Petunia shuddered as she tried to control the desire to choke Judith until she passed out. Maybe she shouldn't even try to control herself. This was Judith's doing. Judith started the fight, but it would be Petunia who finished it.

Suddenly, Judith's body flew out of Petunia's arms. Petunia opened her eyes to find Opal blocking Mildred and Clyde standing directly in front of Judith.

Judith and Clyde whispered something Petunia couldn't make out. The seconds ticked by, and then suddenly, Judith let out a shriek that could've busted Petunia's eardrums if they weren't already ringing something fierce.

Tears streamed down Judith's dirty face, and her voice trembled. "How dare you touch me, Clyde Brown."

Clyde rubbed his temples and lowered his head. "I'm sorry, Misses Judith." There was an edge to Clyde's voice Petunia had never heard before.

Opal shook her fist. "You get on out of here, Judith Cooper. Devil!"

Judith wrapped her hand around her throat and coughed. For some reason, zeroed in on the pieces of brown leaves clinging to Judith's matted-up hair.

More than ten seconds couldn't have passed before Judith grabbed Mildred's arm, and they started to walk away. Suddenly, Judith stopped and narrowed her eyes. "Y'all just wait. My brother and daddy will make you stupid people pay for this."

Petunia had never been able to get along with those two girls. For some reason, they hated her. But what happened today would change things. It marked the beginning of war.

A fire lit Petunia's side, but also her heart. Judith and Mildred would pay for this. But Petunia was afraid they wouldn't be the only ones.

Chapter 7

What had Petunia been thinking when she agreed to go to the carnival with Verlon? She swallowed down the tingly sensation that had her nerves on edge.

She had no experience with dating. Was this how it was supposed to feel? Like you'd eaten a rotten barrel of hog slop? If that was the case, she didn't want any part. She'd go on this one date because she said she would, but that would be the end of it.

She stretched her leg out and slid a pair of stockings on. A sharp pain tickled her side, and Petunia sucked her breath in. The place Judith had bitten a chunk out of her had been bandaged but still hurt like the dickens.

Ignoring the sizzling hatred for Judith and even Mildred wasn't easy, but Petunia had to focus on looking her best. The black skirt and tan button-up top she'd picked out was one of her church outfits. It would have to do.

Mama pecked on her bedroom door before sticking her head in and handing Petunia a cream and black scarf. "Petunia, I thought you'd want to wear this scarf with your shirt. It belonged to your grandmama."

The scarf had a faint scent that reminded Petunia of a rose garden. She held the scarf to her chest and landed tear-filled eyes on Mama. "Oh, Mama. I sure would love to wear it!"

"Then it's settled." She stepped back and looked Petunia up and down. "You look like a grown-up. So pretty."

"Thank you." Petunia tied the scarf around her neck. She wrung her hands and cleared her throat. "Am I supposed to feel sick to my stomach?"

Petunia looked at Mama sideways when she laughed. "That just means you're nervous, child."

Why would a person want to be nervous? Made no sense to Petunia. She glanced at Mama with weary eyes. "And that's a good thing? Seems like an awful lot of trouble to me."

Lloyd hollered from the living room. "Lonnie and Teresa are here with Verlon."

Closing her eyes, Petunia inhaled a deep breath through her nose and let it seep out. She had no desire to ride with Lonnie and Teresa. None. But Mama thought it best she had a chaperone for her first date. She'd rather have ridden with Judith and Mildred.

Mama hugged her and walked away, humming a tune Petunia wasn't familiar with.

"You ready, slowpoke?" Lloyd stood at her door, steadily tapping his foot.

Petunia's right hand landed on her hip. "Why are you in such a hurry, brother? You got yourself a date, too?"

His ears turned pink, and he grinned. "MaryAnne said she'd meet me there since her daddy won't let her go on no date yet."

She'd almost made it to the door when Lloyd opened it. Verlon stood there with a few Black-Eyed Susans in his hand. His tan slacks and blue shirt made him look older than usual. More like a man than the boy she'd fished with.

He scratched the nape of his neck. "Hi, Petunia. I wanted to give you these since it's our first time out together."

Why was her stomach going on like a roller coaster? She didn't have no feelings for Verlon. He was handsome, but that was all she thought of him. Right?

Petunia took the flowers and mustered up a smile. "Thank you, Verlon, that was kind of you."

Mama brought a glass out of the kitchen cabinet. "Put them in here, and I'll run water on them for you. Y'all get on out of here and try to have fun."

"Bye, Mama." Petunia kissed her cheek before heading out for the date she didn't want to go on.

The sick feeling in Petunia's stomach turned to excitement when they arrived at the carnival. The usual empty lot lit up half the town. And the music blared loud like the last rodeo Petunia attended with Evelyn and James.

She hopped out of the car and grabbed Verlon's hand. "Come on, Verlon. I heard there are darts, and I want to try them."

Teresa stood in front of Petunia and nodded her head at Verlon. "I need to talk to Petunia."

Verlon joined Lonnie and Lloyd, who were standing by the car.

Teresa's face held a look Petunia hadn't seen in a long time. Rage. "I have a plan to make those sorry girls pay for what they did to you."

Petunia's brows raised, and she pulled her head back. "What kind of plan?"

Teresa's lips turned up, and her hand flew to her hip. "I've been saving back some of our hog slop in a bucket the past few days. And I want you to save droppings from Bessie and Sampson for the next week."

Petunia cocked her head and squinted her eyes. "What for?"

"Just do it and bring it to my barn when I say to." Teresa took a few steps toward their group before turning back to Petunia. "I'll tell you the rest later. We need to go before the boys get too antsy."

After they walked around for a few minutes, Petunia's heart dropped. Mildred Campbell and Judith Cooper stood hand in hand with a couple of the local boys Petunia couldn't stand. Mildred elbowed Judith and pointed at Petunia. They snickered before turning back to trying to pop balloons.

If only they knew what they had coming. Petunia wasn't sure, but whatever Teresa had planned would be good.

Petunia let go of Verlon's hand and turned in the other direction. "Can we get something to drink before we play some games?"

Verlon eyeballed the group, popping balloons, and then intertwined his hand with Petunia's. "Sounds good. Are you hungry? How about a hot dog?"

Her face lit up, and she squeezed his hand. "Okay. I could always eat."

After getting a hot dog and drink, they claimed an empty bench near the roller coaster. Ketchup and machine grease wafted through the air as Petunia took a bite of her hot dog.

Verlon chomped his hot dog down in three bites before washing it down with a few swigs of drink. He reached out his hand and tucked a lock of hair behind her ear.

She met his eyes when warmth spread across her cheek where his hand had touched. He studied Petunia for a minute before she unglued her eyes from his.

Verlon jiggled his eyebrows and eyed the Ferris Wheel. "Wanna ride with me?"

She sucked down the last of her drink and nodded. Remnants of a shiver clung to Petunia's skin as she climbed into the seat beside Verlon. He clutched her hand to his chest as the Ferris Wheel jolted.

Colorful lights allowed Petunia to see the town from a new perspective. The church she'd always wanted to visit looked spectacular with its shiny windows. Lloyd and MaryAnne walked in front of the dart game, hand in hand. She gasped and pointed at them. "Lloyd and MaryAnne are so cute together. I think she's the one for him."

She turned to find Verlon's eyes brimming with something she couldn't pinpoint. He brought her hand to his lips before putting her hand on his heart. "Mama always told me that when I find true love, I should hold onto it."

The look on his face made Petunia's stomach somersault. The Ferris Wheel stopped, saving her from saying something stupid.

After playing every game and riding every ride, they piled into the car and headed home. Once Lonnie pulled up at their house, Lloyd hopped out and went inside.

Verlon walked Petunia to the door, stopping a few feet away. "I sure had a good time with you tonight, Petunia. Would you be up to going fishing after I finish helping Uncle Eddie tomorrow?"

A zip of lightning passed through Petunia. "Why, sure, Verlon, I'd love to go fishing with you. I had a ton of fun. See you tomorrow."

Verlon's lips stretched into a smile before he turned toward the car. "Good night, Petunia."

Petunia closed the door and leaned against it. She guessed she'd have to eat those words from earlier since she'd just agreed to go fishing with Verlon. Maybe feeling like she'd eaten a bucket of hog slop wasn't the worst feeling in the world after all.

Chapter 8

Once again, Petunia couldn't sleep. Her sore body didn't blend well with a lumpy mattress that had runaway springs. After trying to force sleep to come for an hour, she threw her cover back and hopped out of bed.

Her brain was on fishing with Verlon. She pulled on a loose sundress and headed outside. Fresh-cut grass permeated the air. Petunia stopped on the porch and raised her face, reveling in the moment.

Mama had the cat in her lap in their swing. "Morning, child."

"Morning, Mama. Is it okay if I go see if Opal can come over and let me show her how to milk Bessie?"

"Why it sure is."

Thirty minutes later, Petunia got almost past the orange barn when the wind carried voices from the other side.

"I done told you I can't do this, Judith."

Petunia froze in place, and her eyes fixated on a brown spider relaxing on its web hanging from the roof. She had to be hearing things.

"I done told you I just want a little kiss. Just one little peck." Judith answered.

"Leave me be. Please." That voice sounded awfully familiar, but he was speaking too low for her to be sure.

"I can't. I love you, and I know you love me, too." Who was in the barn with Judith?

"Feelings don't matter. Me and you can never be, Judith. I know you gots other beaus. You need to be with one of them."

There were a few sobs, and then, "I don't want to live without you. I don't care about anything else. Just say the word, and I'll tell everybody I love you."

"No. We will never be together, and you better not say a word, or things will get ugly."

The sobbing stopped, and there was a distinct hopefulness in her tone. "As long as we've got breath, there's hope."

Petunia's body tingled as she listened to the private conversation. She wanted to leave, but her body wouldn't cooperate. The spider stared at her like she was invading its space—and maybe she was.

She had better make a move before she got caught. But she wanted to know who was in the barn. Petunia eyed a few bales of hay stacked up. Should she?

Before she could talk herself out of it, she slipped behind a hay bale and waited. Within minutes, Judith stomped around the barn and started walking down the road.

Taking a deep breath, Petunia poked her head around the hay bale and got the shock of her life.

Clyde Brown came around the barn and looked Petunia right in the face.

His eyes widened, and he stood there staring at Petunia without saying a word. He looked to be in shock. Petunia knew the feeling. Her body still had traces of tingles.

To make things worse, Judith came stomping back down the road and stopped when she saw Petunia. Without a word, she swiveled her body and took off at a dead run.

Clyde watched Judith before turning to Petunia with a look of dread. "It ain't what you think."

Petunia sucked in a stuttered breath and choked on her own spit. "Listen here, Clyde. Judith Cooper ain't nothing but trouble. You better steer clear of her."

Clyde broke eye contact with Petunia and bit his lip. "I been trying to stay away from that girl, but she's making it hard on me."

Petunia picked a piece of hay from the bale and stuck it inside. "Well, it's time she understands she needs to leave you be."

Clyde's forehead wrinkled, and a look of hope crossed his face. "But how?"

"I'll think about it and let you know."

Chapter 9

Petunia's heart pounded in her chest. Her probing gaze scanned the area underneath the barn where she and Teresa hid in the loft. Soft mists of rain fell from the sky and seemed to tell Petunia she needed to rethink their plan. Or maybe it was Petunia's conscience that was pricked.

A waft of air hit her nose, and she gagged. Hog slop mixed with poop and pee had to be one of the nastiest smells ever. She almost felt guilty for what Teresa had talked her into doing. But not quite. Petunia may not feel guilty, but her stomach clenched the same.

Even though Petunia picked at a loose thread on her shirt, she couldn't help but be filled with nervous anticipation. This had to be a bad idea. But didn't Judith and Mildred deserve what was coming?

"That stuff stinks to high heavens, Teresa." Petunia fanned her face and made a gagging sound. "I can't believe I let you talk me into this."

Teresa laughed so hard she held her stomach. "Oh, shush up. You know you want to do this."

Petunia opened her mouth to argue but didn't bother. She hated to admit it, but excitement buzzed in the air. After fifteen more minutes of breathing the bucket of death, their targets came around the corner. They were right on time to pick up the eggs they always bought from Teresa.

Judith shoved Mildred and let out a shrill laugh. "Sometimes you can be such a drip."

Mildred stopped in her tracks and wagged her finger in the air. "Just because I don't think the way you do don't mean nothing, Judith."

Judith started walking but turned around, facing Mildred. "Yeah, it does. It means you're a pain in the neck."

"Whatever." Mildred stomped past Judith.

Petunia elbowed Teresa when the two girls got close to the barn. Her brow puckered, and her heart palpitated. "Are you sure we need to do this, Teresa? It seems awful mean."

Teresa gawked at Petunia with her mouth half open. "Wasn't it awful mean for Judith to bite a plug out of you and Mildred to hold you down?"

Petunia sighed and rubbed the place where Judith had bitten her. "Yeah. It still hurts."

A firm look of resolve crossed Teresa's face. The look that had always let Petunia know there was no room for argument. "Then help me with this bucket. They're almost under the barn."

Without thinking about it, Petunia grasped the bucket and helped Teresa pour the contents on the unsuspecting girls below, with her aim purely on Judith.

Judith screeched and threw the bucket she'd been carrying onto the ground. She wiped her face. Another ear-splitting scream echoed throughout the air.

A small amount had hit Mildred on her arm. She yelled and took off running straight for the animal's water trough.

She glanced at Judith and yelled back at her. "Come to the water trough. You can at least get some of it off."

Teresa laughed so hard she cried the entire time the scene played out.

At least the misty rain had turned into a steady stream falling from the sky. However, it didn't help Judith much since the watery mixture had turned her hair into a wet, stinky mess.

All Petunia could do was watch as a piercing regret filled her body.

Early the next morning, Petunia had more regrets, especially when Mama woke her up way before sunrise with a switch in her hand.

Before Petunia could react, Mama jerked the cover off her and lit her legs with the switch. Usually, Petunia would try to run or at least cover her legs. But not this time. She deserved every red mark the switch left behind.

Loud voices drifted into her room before Lloyd stepped inside. "Mama! If you don't want me shooting one of these Cooper boys, you need to get in here. They're out for Petunia's blood."

Mama's trembling hand dropped to her side before she marched out the bedroom door.

Lloyd turned to Petunia before cocking the shotgun he carried in his hand. "Don't leave this room."

He didn't have to worry about that. Her legs would probably buckle underneath her before they would carry her weight. That switch hurt something fierce. She longed to run her legs under cool water, but that would have to wait.

When the sun began to rise, Mama opened Petunia's bedroom door. "You can come out now. Time to pay your dues, child."

She scrambled off the bed and headed straight to the sink. After sopping a washrag in cool water, she turned to Lloyd. "What's happening?"

His mouth set into a firm line, and Petunia could tell he was fighting mad. "You're gonna have to get a whooping in front of Cyrus Cooper and his yuck of a son."

The cool water streamed down Petunia's leg, and she cried, "Why? What else happened?"

Lloyd walked over to the window. He punched the wall before he answered. "Because of what you done! Now you come on outside, and don't make Mama come in and drag you out."

Nausea struck Petunia at her core, and she glanced at the back door. She probably wouldn't get far if she tried to run for it. "I don't want another whooping!"

Lloyd settled a stern gaze on Petunia. "Come on and take it, or they're gonna run us out of town. Or worse."

The flipping in her stomach got worse. She may as well leave town for good because she'd never live this one down, especially when Daddy got home.

Petunia swallowed her pride on top of vomit that knocked on the back of her throat and stepped outside for the dreaded spanking she deserved. Tears pooled in Mama's eyes. Tears that matched Petunia's.

When she met Judith's hard stare, shivers mingled with Petunia's rushing blood. Of course, she'd be here for the spectacle.

Petunia touched Mama's arm before turning to Judith. "I'm sorry for what I done, and now I'll take my punishment."

Cyrus Cooper thrust his fist in the air and pointed at Petunia. "You better believe you'll take it. Next time, it'll be worse 'cause it'll be me doing the beating, not your mama."

Mama tore into Petunia with a belt. After a few minutes, Petunia dropped to the dirt and cried.

Mama threw the belt down and walked over to Cyrus and his son, Trevor. "It's done, now leave us alone."

Judith snaked over to Petunia and leaned close enough to whisper. "Don't ever tell nobody about anything that's happened. Do you hear me?"

A shadow crossed Petunia's face, and she narrowed her eyes. "You're such a hypocrite, Judith Cooper. I know what you're up to."

Judith dug her nails into Petunia's arm and spoke through gritted teeth. "You need to come with me to the barn." She turned to their folks, and her tone changed to include a bit of syrup. "Me and Petunia gonna go to the barn and talk things through."

As soon as they got inside the barn, Judith glared at Petunia. "You better keep your stinking mouth shut. If you say a word, I'll make up a story about you and Clyde and ruin you."

Baffled by what Judith said on top of the whooping, Petunia shook her head. "What do you mean? Why'd you even tell your daddy anyway?"

"Mildred told her folks, and they told him. You just better keep your mouth shut, or I'll tell everybody you and Clyde are sneaking around to see each other." Venom poured from Judith's voice, and her eyes darkened.

A string of snot dripped from Petunia's nose, and she wiped it on her sleeve before meeting Judith's gaze. "You know that's a bunch of gibberish, but I won't say a word. For Clyde's sake."

A few hours later, Petunia lay on the couch while Lloyd stood at the window.

Mama sat beside her, rubbing a salve on her legs. "I hate this happened, child. But you know you brought it on yourself."

"I know I did, Mama." Petunia eyed the salve and shrugged before pulling herself off the couch to stand next to Lloyd. "You just did what you had to do. I thank you for doctoring me up."

She held Petunia's chin and looked into her eyes. "Why'd you do it? Did something happen you ain't tellin' me?"

Petunia studied a rip in the cushion like it was the most interesting thing ever. "I'd rather not say. Please don't make me."

After letting out a sigh, she closed the salve and put it in a kitchen cabinet.

Lloyd turned his gaze to look out the window before asking the question Petunia had been dreading. "Who put you up to that, Petunia? I know you didn't come up with something so cockeyed on your own."

Petunia swiveled her body and crossed her fingers behind her back. "Nobody."

He strode across the room until he stood directly in front of Petunia. "Don't lie. Now ain't the time."

Instead of answering, she shoved past Lloyd and ran out the front door.

She had to warn Opal and Clyde not to say nothing.

Chapter 10

A million stars danced across the deep navy sky as Petunia lay in bed, lost in thought. She yawned and rubbed the bridge of her nose as her gaze lingered out the window.

It seemed like Daddy had been gone forever. Not that Petunia was upset over him missing the big blow-up with the Coopers. At least everyone seemed to have moved past it.

She'd filled Verlon in on most of it, careful to leave out the part about her getting a whooping in front of the Cooper family. That was too embarrassing to share.

Amazingly, Teresa had been coming over and helping Petunia with her chores. But Petunia still hadn't told anyone it had been Teresa's idea. And she wouldn't. Petunia had done it of her own free will. She could've said no, but she hadn't.

Clyde and Opal had been sent to stay with their aunt close to DeValls Bluff, which made Petunia's heart hurt. She missed her friends and felt like it was her fault they'd been sent away.

Petunia had promised their parents she wouldn't say anything, and they seemed satisfied but said they couldn't take a chance with their kids' lives. Whatever that meant. From what Petunia understood, they planned to move with them as soon as possible.

What could Daddy possibly be doing for so long? Instead of going to sleep, Petunia's mind raced with possibilities.

Could it be he was working a big, important job? Maybe he saved lives on the side, and that's why he stayed so grouchy. Who wouldn't be grouchy if they spent most of their time doing dangerous things? That had to be it.

Satisfied she'd figured out Daddy's problem, Petunia curled into a ball and closed her eyes. Before succumbing to deep sleep, someone shook her shoulders. "Sis, you wanna go fishing?"

Fishing?

Petunia rolled over and put her hands over her ears. "Leave me alone, Lloyd. I'm trying to sleep."

"Okay then."

She raised her head and tried to make out where Lloyd stood in the dark room. "Who goes fishing at dark anyhow?"

"I reckon just me, MaryAnne, and Verlon."

That got her attention.

She sat up on the side of the bed, her mind racing with the idea of seeing Verlon. "What do you mean? Verlon's going fishing?"

Even though Lloyd whispered, his impatience came through to Petunia. "That's what I said, ain't it? Either come on or hush up before you wake Mama up."

"I'm a coming. But I want to ride Sampson. I ain't walking."

"Whatever you say. But you'll have to walk him a ways so Mama don't hear."

"I know that. I ain't stupid, Lloyd. Now go on so I can put on my pants."

"I sometimes wonder," Lloyd mumbled under his breath as he quietly closed her bedroom door.

She had slept in a t-shirt, so she slipped on her old work pants and boots. A month ago, Lloyd's remark would've made Petunia fighting mad. But not tonight. Her heart seemed to be floating in her chest and had no room for bad feelings.

Which was weird. Because Petunia used to always have room for bad feelings.

Two hours later, close to midnight, the foursome sat on a couple of logs, laughing about not being able to catch any fish.

Lloyd playfully pushed MaryAnne off the log. She landed on her bottom with a thud. She jumped off the moist ground and shoved Lloyd so hard he tipped off the log backward. To be such a small girl, MaryAnne didn't seem to have a problem holding her own against Lloyd's attempt at flirting.

After they both sat back down, MaryAnne rested her head on Lloyd's shoulder. Petunia shook her head. She'd never do something like that to Verlon. No way. Not without him asking her to.

The night sky seemed made for their enjoyment. Twinkling stars danced around the c-shaped moon and put on a show the Lord could charge admission for—but He never would. Petunia had to think about how much the Lord loved His people to give them such beauty to see.

Petunia's blood hummed with a feeling she'd never experienced. At least it made her feel good. Or maybe it was the fact her brain seemed out of whack, so she didn't know what she was feeling.

Verlon reached his hand out and brushed a lock of hair behind Petunia's ear, which made her forget what she was even thinking about. He did that a lot. Petunia guessed her hair must always be flying everywhere.

He sighed and dropped his hand to his lap. "Why don't you take me for a ride on Sampson?"

Lloyd's head whipped around, and he grunted. "Now, y'all can't be going off too far."

Petunia stood and tapped her foot. "We'll just go to those trees yonder and back, Mr. Bossy Pants."

A few minutes later, Petunia and Verlon soared through the air, or at least it felt that way with the way Sampson showcased his running.

They reached the edge of the tree line when Sampson abruptly stopped. His body appeared to shiver, and deep exhales came from his nostrils.

Petunia leaned her head close to his neck and spoke in her most soothing voice. "What is it, boy? It'll be okay."

Verlon tensed before wrapping his arms around her body. Her back went rigid, and she opened her mouth to ask him what he thought he was doing.

Before she spoke, Verlon clamped his hand over her mouth and leaned into her ear, speaking so low she barely heard him. "Don't even breathe loudly, Petunia. There's a panther in the tree above us."

She looked up only to find that Verlon was right. A black panther rested gracefully on a thick limb jutting out from the tree. Its glossy fur shimmered under the soft light of the moon and its piercing eyes glowed like lanterns. If not for the moon and stars shining so bright, the panther would've completely blended in with the night.

Verlon continued in his low voice. "Lean into Sampson's neck."

Petunia tried not to think about the butterflies trying to make a nest in her stomach. Instead, she immediately obeyed Verlon. He shielded her body with his and dug his heels into Sampson's sides.

Petunia took a deep breath, attempting to quiet the fluttering sensation in her stomach. She pushed the anxious thoughts aside, focusing instead on Verlon, whose presence offered a sense of calm. Without hesitating, she followed his lead, trusting his instincts. Verlon enveloped her with his sturdy frame, creating a protective barrier between her and the panther. With determination, he pressed his heels firmly into Sampson's flanks, urging the horse into action. The powerful animal responded instantly, its muscles tensing as it sprang forward, carrying them away from danger.

Petunia longed to look behind them but kept her head pressed to Sampson's neck instead. She held her breath until they cleared the trees. That's when it hit her. Verlon put his body over hers to protect her. Who did that?

The fear of getting killed by a panther left her as quickly as it had come, replaced by a deep feeling she couldn't quite describe.

Chapter 11

Daddy's stern expression swept back and forth from Lloyd to Verlon. His loud voice caused Petunia to jerk and focus on him instead of Verlon. "I'm gonna trust y'all to take care of my car tonight. You hear?"

Lloyd nodded. "Yes, sir."

Verlon followed suit. "We'll take good care of the car and Petunia."

Daddy waved his hand. "Petunia's tougher than most men I know. She can take care of herself." He pinned Verlon with a bloodshot wink. "She could probably whip you."

If Petunia could vanish into the earth beneath her feet, she would embrace the chance with open arms—even if that meant landing in a patch of horse manure.

Verlon shoved his hands inside the pockets of his jeans and winked at Petunia. "I'd never want to find out."

Petunia fanned her face and bit her tongue to keep from laughing at the look on Daddy's face. She'd never seen him speechless before.

A little later, Lloyd let out a whoop as he shifted gears to cross the wooden bridge. He grinned at MaryAnne, who sat in the front seat directly beside him. Her parents finally agreed to let her go to the picture show with Lloyd, Petunia, and Verlon. But they made Verlon promise not to let them out of his sight.

After giving the car a little too much gas, it screeched and kicked up a cloud of dust behind them. MaryAnne giggled and pressed her body closer to Lloyd, if that was even possible.

For once, the horrible odor of singed chicken feathers drifting in the wind didn't faze Petunia. She had Verlon beside her, and his shirt held the scent of woodsy aftershave, and that's all she focused on.

Verlon captured her hand in his and raised a brow towards the front seat. Petunia raised one shoulder and grimaced.

A broad laugh that encompassed Petunia's entire being left Verlon. Even though she was drawn to him, she couldn't gather the courage to press her body close like MaryAnne did with Lloyd.

Once at the picture show, Petunia rubbed her hands together and grinned. Finally, she was getting to watch Red River starring John Wayne. She'd been after Lloyd to bring her since the year before.

A sob escaped Petunia when John Wayne's character lost his fiancé, Fen, to an Indian attack. Fen reminded Petunia a bit of Opal. They had the same face shape. If only she could see Opal and talk to her about Verlon.

Verlon rubbed along her hand with his thumb. She cut her eyes at him, and his lips lifted at the corners. She smiled back and, for the first time in her life, had no doubt she could be herself without somebody making fun of her.

Is this how Teresa and Evelyn felt about Lonnie and James? Heat saturated her neck as she pondered moving closer to Verlon. Could she expect a proper kiss soon? Did that happen before the wedding or after? She'd need to ask Teresa how things worked.

By the time Petunia got home, she was as confused as ever. And Daddy was gone again.

Chapter 12

Petunia rubbed her lips with Vaseline and stared at her reflection in the small mirror. She couldn't stand anything else on them, but she wanted them to look better. She'd be happy if she could just get a little of Teresa's full pouty lips instead of the thin lips she had to live with. At least her bottom lip had a little shape.

When she'd asked Teresa about kissing the day before, she'd laughed and accused Petunia of having smooching on her mind. Then she told Petunia to be patient and follow Verlon's lead. He planned to leave for Chicago soon so maybe they'd never kiss.

Verlon's birthday was today, and he had invited her family to dinner with his Aunt Gail and Uncle Edward. A wave of nerves stirred within her. She couldn't believe they had been dating for over a month. Even though Verlon's Aunt Gail took every opportunity to express her disapproval of Petunia, the feeling was mutual. Petunia didn't want to have dinner at their house, but today was about celebrating Verlon turning twenty-one. He was a man now, old enough to make his own decisions.

Lloyd blasted into her bedroom. The one she thought she had to herself since both sisters married off. But somehow, Lloyd always barged in on her. "Verlon just pulled up in an automobile!"

"Petunia," Mama hollered from the front room.

Petunia clicked her tongue. "Guess I need to go before she drags me out the door."

Lloyd fiddled with the button on his shirt. "I want you to know I'm proud you're my sister. You deserve so much more than this town can offer. I think Verlon's a good man, and y'all are lucky to have each other."

After play-punching Lloyd in the shoulder, they walked out of her room. "Awe, thank you, brother." She said as she stepped outside with Mama and Lloyd right behind her.

Verlon leaned against a black Ford Tudor sedan in a white t-shirt, and a pair of loose tan khakis rolled up an inch above the top of his white Converse. The sky put on a show like none Petunia had ever seen with the way the sun turned orange as it dropped out of the bright pink and yellow sky. Or maybe Petunia had seen the sky look like this, and it was the way she saw things that had changed. Ever since Verlon, she looked at things through different eyes and she found that she spent more time seeing things. She looked for the good instead of the bad.

A grin split Verlon's face, and he let out a low whistle. "Is that a new dress?"

A blast of heat covered her face, and she nodded. "Mama made it for me. She calls it a wraparound dress."

Mama had insisted she have a new dress for Verlon's birthday celebration, so she took on extra laundry from town to pay for the fabric. Even though Petunia told her not to. But in the end, they worked on the laundry together.

His admiring gaze lingered on Petunia so long that she squirmed. "It sure is pretty. That color looks nice on you."

"Thank you, Verlon." She leaned against the car before kissing his cheek. "Happy birthday." The lingering trace of spicy leather caused Petunia's heart to flip.

He ran his fingers across the place she kissed. "That's the best birthday present I coulda got."

She lowered her eyes and leaned down to pick her purse up. Anything to keep Verlon from noticing the splotches lining her neck. "Whose car?"

He whirled around and took both Petunia's hands in his. "It's mine. I've been saving a year for it. Do you like it?"

She squeezed his hands and threw her head back to look the car over. "I love it. It's a beauty and a much better present than any old kiss from me."

"You're wrong about that." He raised her hand to his lips and held her arm close to his chest. "Y'all ready to head out?"

Mama shooed Lloyd into the back seat and climbed in behind him. "Well, come on, you two lovebirds."

Petunia freed her arm and stepped away from the car. Verlon opened the passenger door, and she smiled before climbing in. She couldn't believe she was in a fancy car with a good-looking man and not even seventeen yet.

After a few minutes of driving, Verlon pulled into his aunt's and uncle's place. He hopped out and opened the door for Petunia before helping Mama out of the back seat.

Petunia ran her palms across the front of her dress. Verlon picked her hand up and squeezed it. "Everything is gonna be fine. Don't be nervous."

Fifteen minutes later, Petunia took in her surroundings from the Marshall's dining room. How lucky they were to have an entire room just for eating. Swirls of cinnamon hit Petunia's nose and caused her mouth to water. She couldn't wait to sink her teeth into a piece of Verlon's cake.

Gail Marshall leaned both bony arms on the table and looked at Mama. "Well, Dorothy, I'm surprised Ollie's not back in town. What's he off doing this time?"

Petunia glanced at Mama, silently begging her to be nice.

Mama tossed her hair over her shoulder. "Oh, he's working to support his family. He sent me the money to buy a milk cow a month or so ago."

Gail smirked. "You don't say?"

She took a sip of iced tea. "How's your leg? Oliver told me you broke it."

Gail pursed her lips into a flat line.

Edward scratched his graying head and then answered before Gail had a chance. "Her leg seems to be healing nicely." He peered at Gail. "How'd Oliver know about your leg?"

She spooned in some beef stew before she met his gaze. "There's no telling, Eddie. You know how town gossip is."

Verlon stood up, his chair screeching across the floor. "I have something I want to say." His eyes landed on Petunia, and he bit his lower lip.

Petunia swallowed, and her heart thumped wildly. Surely this wasn't what she thought it was.

Gail stood up so abruptly her chair fell backward. "Let's cut the cake first, Verlon. I've just been on pins and needles waiting to eat a piece."

Verlon didn't even spare Gail a glance. He leaned down on one knee and opened a small brown box.

Petunia couldn't take her eyes off the ring nestled inside on red velvet. Verlon removed it and held it in his right hand. "Carol Louise Hollings, I love you so much. Please say you'll be my bride. My Petunia."

Her mouth dropped open, and she lost her voice. Was Gail crying? She couldn't focus on that right now. The oval-shaped Moonstone ring with tiny diamonds wrapped around it captured her attention. A ring like she'd never seen.

She looked up from the ring and clapped her gaze on Mama standing with her hands wrapped underneath her chin. She seemed to compel Petunia to say yes, and there was no reason not to.

She scooted to the edge of the chair and put her left hand out. She couldn't get her voice box to work, so she simply nodded repeatedly.

Verlon let out a yelp, slipped the ring on her finger, and spun her around. Mama cried and laughed at the same time. Lloyd beamed. Even Edward smiled at her. But not Gail. Tears streamed down her face like the time Old Man Brooks lost his hound dog. And those tears didn't look like happy ones.

Chapter 13

A warm buttery honey scent filled Petunia's senses. Petunia took a bite of fried sweet potatoes and savored the crispy goodness. She swallowed the bite and looked from Daddy to Mama.

Mama stabbed a piece of meat with her fork but didn't take the bite. Instead, she gaped across the table. "I told you Verlon will be good for Petunia. He loves her and will be taking her away from all this." She flipped her hand around the house.

Daddy laid his spoon on the plate full of fried sweet potatoes and neck bones she and Mama had worked hard to cook. "Who'll be helping you and Lloyd in the cotton fields next month? Have you thunk this through?"

"All I know is Petunia deserves a chance at happiness. And why can't you stay home and help?" She shifted in her seat and then took a swig of her buttermilk.

Petunia grimaced. Yuck. Who actually enjoyed drinking rotten milk? Nobody but Mama.

Daddy piled his spoon full of sweet potatoes and slowly chewed them. He closed his eyes before pinning Mama with his gaze. "How many times do you need to be told that I'm working? I can't make any money in this dead town, so I haveta go somewheres else."

Lloyd had no idea how lucky he was that he decided to eat supper with MaryAnne over at Teresa and Lonnie's. How could Mama and Daddy argue about her life right in front of her? Didn't she have a say in it?

After wiping her mouth, Mama scowled. "You don't seem to make much money no matter where you go."

Petunia had never seen Daddy's face turn so red. Mama was getting him told!

His weary voice raised an octave. "Now, listen here. Didn't I send you the money for the milk cow? Or was that somebody else?"

Mama's shoulders relaxed. "That was you, Ollie. And we appreciated it."

Daddy lightly slapped the table like he knew he'd won the argument. "Petunia needs to wait until she's eighteen to get hitched. And I told Cyrus Cooper he could ask for her hand."

Petunia's heart stopped in her chest, and she gawked at Daddy. "Cyrus Cooper? He's old enough to be my daddy. Can't I have a say in this?"

Daddy didn't even look at her. "You're a child, so no, you can't."

Mama reached across the table and squeezed Daddy's hand. "Let's talk about this later."

He pulled his hand away, then squared his shoulders. "I think we need to talk about it now. Teresa and Evelyn waited until they were eighteen, and she ain't no better than her sisters."

Mama flinched and followed Daddy's example by dodging Petunia's gaze. "I guess you've got a point."

Petunia slammed her fist on the table and raced around it until her face was close to Mama's. "You're the one who wanted this! You! Now you're siding with this sorry excuse for a man who can't even stand the sight of me."

Daddy stood up and whipped his belt out of the loop of his pants. Petunia spun around and tore off for the front door. Daddy snaked his arm out and grabbed her hand. She jerked, but his grip was too firm for her to escape.

The first lash on her bare legs set her knee on fire. She ground her teeth together so hard she thought they'd break. She'd rather eat possum soup than give him the satisfaction of hearing her cry.

The second lash caught her side and wrapped around her stomach. It was like someone sucker-punched her with a firebrand. The third one landed on her back as she fought to get away. Her eyes rolled back in her head. Amazingly, none of her teeth snapped.

"Ollie! Stop this!" Mama yelled in the background.

He didn't listen.

The fourth lash hit her arm, and another landed on her leg. Each stripe left a trail of fire behind. She lost strength in her legs, and her knees buckled. After curling up in a ball, Petunia covered her head and face with her arms, waiting for the next lash, but none came.

She glanced up through glossed-over eyes. Lloyd stood in Daddy's face, both fists balled up. "If you ever hit my sister like that again, I'll kill you dead as a doornail."

Daddy shoved Lloyd. "Boy, I'd like to see you try." He stepped over Petunia and walked out of the room. "I'm going to bed."

Mama leaned down beside Petunia and rubbed her hair. "I'll run you a cool bath. That'll make you feel better."

Petunia's body twitched as she glared at Mama. A cool bath? Really? A pang of regret hit her. What did she expect Mama to do? Fight Daddy? She wouldn't come out on top if she ever tried.

A few hours later, Petunia sat on her twin bed, cracking pecans. She'd almost filled up an entire bowl of hulls. She'd make Daddy think twice before hitting her like that again. She'd deserved a proper spanking for talking bad to him but not a beating. She had red whelps all over where the belt had burned her tender skin.

She tiptoed out of her room. Daddy snored so loud she figured Bessie and Sampson were awake, so the coast was clear. She eased the door open and crawled into the room. When she reached Daddy's side of the bed, she gently placed the entire bowl of pecan hulls sharp side up on the floor.

Once back in her room, she slipped her boots and a thin sweater on and stared out the window. Before she knew it, the good morning crow coming from the front yard jolted Petunia's eyes wide open. The rooster's timing couldn't have been more perfect.

She peeked around her parents' bedroom door just as Daddy sat up in bed. He rubbed the back of his neck, yawned, and stood, landing right on top of the pecan hulls. He fell to the floor and let out a scream. "You little CUSS!"

Petunia almost knocked Mama down, getting out the front door. "What's happening, Petunia?"

"Can't talk now, Mama!" Petunia got out between breaths. She ran to the barn, praying their only horse wasn't in a bad mood this morning.

A smile lit her face as she rounded the corner of the house. Lloyd stood there with Sampson, saddled and ready to go. He handed her the reins. "You better get somewhere he won't think to look."

"Thank you, brother." She grabbed the reins, jumped on Sampson, and left a trail of dust behind.

Chapter 14

Brother Otis wiped the sweat from his brow with his meaty hand as his voice boomed from the pulpit. "Let's follow the ways of a just, righteous, and Holy God. Let us be obedient to Him and ready to go when He calls us home."

Petunia scowled at the red welp on her arm and covered it with her shirt sleeve. Hopefully, nobody would notice the marks the belt had left behind. Especially Verlon.

This had to be the longest sermon in the history of man. Or maybe it just felt long when your bottom ached like it had been hit by a bull. Over and over. And the hard pew didn't help at all.

Almost as soon as Petunia focused her mind on the lesson, a fly buzzed around her head and landed in her hair. She swatted at it, and it finally flew off to bother someone else.

Verlon scratched behind his ear but kept his complete attention on Brother Otis. At least he was listening. Petunia would be if her body wasn't protesting. She usually loved hearing Brother Otis preach. Blocking her mind from the pain the best she could, she stared hard at the preacher.

He picked up his Bible, flipping through the pages. "Turn with me to the second book of Timothy, chapter four, and let us read verses six through eight together."

"For I am already being poured out as a drink offering, and the time of my departure is at hand. I have fought the good fight, I have finished the race, I have kept the faith. Finally, there is laid up for me the crown of righteousness, which the Lord, the righteous Judge, will give to me on that Day, and not to me only but also to all who have loved His appearing."

Brother Otis stepped back from the pulpit and briefly studied each section of the pews. "Now listen here, good people. Are you trying your best to live like Paul? Are you fighting the good fight? Or are you going through the motions like a foolish hypocrite? Are you ready to go when He calls?"

Petunia squirmed in her seat. Did she try her best to be like Paul? Or not? Boy, oh boy. She'd have to talk to Brother Otis sometime soon.

The song leader started their closing song, which snapped her back to attention. She couldn't allow herself to get lost in her own mind like that at church. She'd pray for more control and to focus on God, not her own pain, next time.

Verlon's back went rigid, and she turned to find him staring at her arm. When he met her eyes, Petunia gulped. His body remained stiff, but he put his attention back to the song leader.

When the service ended, he took a deep breath and closed his eyes a moment before turning to Petunia. "Who did that to you?"

Her face burned worse than the marks left behind by the belt. She'd let her sleeve rise up. Now she was gonna have to tell him she got whooped like a kid. But she couldn't.

She needed to get out of the church building. To run away and cry like the kid she was. Anything to keep from telling Verlon what Daddy did to her. If only her legs would move. Laughter came from outside, and Petunia wished she could be out there with whoever was having a good time.

"Petunia?" Verlon's tone was low and even as he leaned closer to her.

She took inventory of the one-room church house. They were the last two people in the building besides Brother Otis who stood just inside the door.

"It was my fault for getting smart with him." Petunia's voice broke, and she couldn't stop the blasted tears from falling.

Now, he'd back out of everything and leave her behind in Arkansas. Why couldn't she act like a woman? Who'd want to marry a snotty brat who cried over the littlest of things?

He shifted in the pew, turned his body sideways, and looked at Petunia. "So, it was your daddy? Why'd he hit your arm?"

She fixed her vision on the wooden floor, focusing on a nail raised slightly higher than the rest. May as well lay it on the line. Better Verlon knew it all. "He hit me everywhere he could, Verlon. He was mad and didn't care where the belt landed."

Verlon sprung to his feet and marched past Brother Otis.

Every muscle in Petunia's body screamed as she raced after him. "Verlon!"

By the time she got down the steps, Verlon had almost reached where Daddy stood talking to Eddie and Gail. Her insides surged like a tornado when Verlon stormed up to the group and punched Daddy in the nose. He fell backward, and Verlon continued to pummel him. Daddy got a punch in, but Verlon kept going at him. Mama screeched and ran toward the fight.

Petunia could've sworn she heard Sister Edna laugh, but she had to be wrong.

A weight seemed to cover Petunia's entire body, making her heart work overtime. She dragged in a breath as Eddie broke up the fight.

What had she done?

Chapter 15

August 1949

There was no way Petunia could make it across the yard to the outhouse, so she put her hands on her knees and lost her breakfast right then and there by the fencepost.

Mama sidled over and rubbed her back. "You're gonna have to toughen up, child. Can't be letting your nerves cause you to get sick."

Petunia spit until her mouth tasted like a wad of the cotton she'd gotten so good at picking. "I can't help it, Mama. It's not ever day I get married, you know."

Mama gritted her teeth. "I know it, and that blasted daddy of yours ain't even here yet."

Petunia narrowed her eyes. "It don't matter to me. He ain't my daddy no how."

Mama's face flushed as she extended her hand and slapped Petunia's jaw. "Carol Louise, I better not ever hear that come out of your mouth again." She leaned in so close that the strong odor of onions wafted into Petunia's nose. "Do you hear me?"

"I hear you, Mama." Petunia rubbed her cheek. "You didn't have to go and slap me. My goodness."

Mama lowered her eyes. "You're right, and I'm sorry. But you need-ed it after what you said. Oliver is your daddy, and don't you forget it. He's doing right by you, letting you and Verlon get married, you know."

"I won't forget, Mama." Petunia hugged her. "I'm sorry, too."

A smile crossed her face and then she hugged Petunia back. "All is forgiven. Now, let's go get you married off."

Three hours later, everyone in Petunia's family other than Daddy sat in the church building. Even Verlon's parents and great-aunt Helen had made the trip from Chicago. His Uncle Edward and Aunt Gail were also in attendance, surprisingly.

Petunia stood on the church steps, peeling a piece of white paint off the railing. Trying to build up the courage to walk down the aisle without an escort. She should've known that the louse Mama called her daddy wouldn't darken the door of the building. Not for her wedding. Her hair wasn't brown enough for him.

She glanced down at her borrowed dress and smiled. At least Eve-lyn's ankle-length simple white wedding gown had fit her. Just the way Petunia liked things. Simple. Mama had fixed her hair in a bun, and Teresa tied it all together by bringing a bouquet of pink Perennials.

Lloyd moseyed down the steps and leaned on the railing across from Petunia. He looked so grown up in his pressed suit and brown tie. "Would it be all right if I stood by you today, sister?"

Tears burned the back of her throat, and her lips trembled. "What are you doing just standing there? Let's get me down the aisle."

He gave her a cockeyed smile before poking his head inside the door. He gave a thumbs up to Evelyn, and she started singing *"Have I Told You Lately That I Love You"* by Gene Autry since they didn't have an organ.

Brother Otis held his Bible in front of him as he read from Mark, chapter ten: "But from the beginning of creation, God made them male and female. For this reason, a man shall leave his father and mother and be joined to his wife, and the two shall become one flesh. Therefore, they are no longer two, but one flesh. What God has joined together, let not man separate."

After agreeing to love and obey Verlon and him agreeing to love and cherish her, Brother Otis looked from her to Verlon and smiled. "Verlon, you may now kiss your bride."

How long could two seconds feel like? Petunia would've sworn she stared at Verlon for ten minutes of gut-churning, nausea-inducing waiting before his lips met hers.

How long could two seconds stretch out in a moment of unbearable anticipation? Petunia felt as if she had been locked in an unending gaze with Verlon for what seemed like ten agonizing minutes. He anchored his gaze to hers until finally, his lips met hers.

The cool scent of mint lingered on Verlon's breath, invading her senses. His soft lips caused Petunia's knees to shake as she leaned on her tippy toes, pressing her lips to his.

Someone coughed, and Verlon backed away from Petunia. Heat scorched her neck so bad she was surprised her goozle wasn't boiling. And her face? Well, it was even hotter.

Chapter 16

A few ants crawled off the tree and onto Petunia's foot. She glanced down and slapped them onto the ground.

The sun had disappeared behind a group of clouds and stayed there the past hour, giving everyone outside a bit of a break from the heat. Especially with the breeze that had somehow turned cool.

She looked around the churchyard and took a deep breath. Three tables with white tablecloths were filled with meats and vegetables. A yellow tablecloth covered the dessert table. Sister Edna did a great job organizing the food. Mama made a banana cake for the wedding, and her sisters each made sweet bread. So many people showed up that it seemed like the whole town was there.

Tingles fell from her heart to her fingertips. She was a married woman. How she ever got Verlon to marry her was a mystery to Petunia. But here she stood, watching people mull around, eating and laughing. They seemed to be happy and celebrating. Happy for her. Someone who wasn't worth a nickel.

"Why're you over here hiding? Still can't believe you tricked Verlon into marrying you?" Spittle flew out of Gail's mouth and landed on Petunia's cheek. "I know I can't believe it."

Petunia wiped the spit off with the back of her hand. "I didn't trick nobody."

"Aunt Gail, I'd suggest you watch how you speak to my wife." Verlon walked up and put his arm around Petunia's waist.

Gail's full lips pressed into a thin line. "Just speaking my mind."

Verlon used a handkerchief to wipe the sweat off his forehead, then met Gail's eyes. "Today is not the day for that. It's the happiest day of my life."

"Whatever you say, nephew." She shot daggers at Petunia as she stomped around the tree.

Verlon kissed the top of Petunia's head. "I'm sorry for that."

Petunia's heart drummed out of her chest. "No call for you to be sorry. You didn't do nothing."

Verlon smiled and tugged Petunia's hand. "Let's go talk to Mama and Daddy."

She held her ground behind the tree. "I promise I'll treat you good all my days, Verlon."

He leaned toward Petunia until his lips almost met hers. "And I promise the same to you, my Petunia."

A fizzy sensation erupted inside Petunia as her husband kissed her lips for the second time that day. Not only were her cotton-picking days over, but she was also gonna get to kiss this man for the rest of her life. How'd she ever think Lonnie was the one for her?

Judith and Mildred skipped up to them, arm in arm. Judith let out a bitter laugh. "My my, I guess you two are in love after all."

Mildred crossed her arms and glared at Petunia. "Y'all are married now. You don't have to sneak around, you know."

Petunia gave both girls a sideways glance. "I'd suggest you both mind your own affairs and stay out of ours."

Judith's mouth hung open as Petunia walked away from the two girls who had always seemed pleased with her discomfort. They'd spent many years doing their best to make Petunia miserable. Especially Judith. Thankfully those days were over. Things were looking up for Petunia. Everything would be perfect if only she could take Mama and Lloyd with her to Chicago.

Hazel Marshall wrapped Petunia in a sweaty hug. "You made such a pretty bride. My Verlon's a lucky man."

Verlon's great aunt Helen pulled Petunia close and kissed her cheek. Petunia rubbed the place she'd kissed and grinned.

Ralph Marshall clapped Verlon on the back. "I'm proud of you, son." He pulled Petunia close for a hug when Hazel let her go. "Welcome to our family, Petunia."

Petunia's brain buzzed with elaborate plans. Could this really be happening? She would be leaving Arkansas and starting a life in a whole new state. It was unbelievable.

Brother Otis and Sister Edna walked up with a man holding a camera. Petunia had never seen one up close. Her hands itched to take it away from the man.

Edna clapped her hands together. "This is Robert Warrington, and he's gonna take some photographs for you, Petunia."

The man took off his hat, revealing a bald head with a mole above his left ear. "Apologies for being late. I couldn't get my blasted car to start."

Mr. Warrington spent the next hour snapping pictures of Verlon, Petunia and their family. Afterwards, the reception ended way too soon for Petunia's liking. Even so, she smiled within herself at the memories she had made. Verlon stood near the passenger door of his car, ready to help Petunia inside.

She glanced at Verlon before wrapping her arms around Mama. A pinch of nerves hit her stomach. "I'm gonna miss you."

Mama's lips edged up at the corners. "I'll miss you, too. But the Lord's gonna put you where He wants you, Petunia. Remember that and always trust Him."

Petunia nodded, swallowed her tears down and then spent the next few minutes saying her goodbyes to the rest of her family.

After she settled in the front seat, she rolled the window down and waved at everyone standing in the churchyard. She poked her head out the window and hollered, "I'll see y'all soon!"

People yelled their goodbyes and waved as Verlon pulled onto the road to start the trek to their new life in Chicago.

Chapter 17

Petunia opened her eyes, yawned, and then snuggled into the fluffy pillow that Verlon had brought for the drive. After a few minutes, she lifted her head and squinted out of the car window. A faint white glow across the darkened sky caught her attention.

She glanced at Verlon. "Where are we, and what in the world is in the sky?"

Verlon kept his left hand on the wheel as he rubbed her neck with his right hand. "Hi, there, my sleeping beauty. That glow is the great city of Chicago."

Scrunching her face up, she leaned closer to the window and cocked her head. "Chicago glows?"

He shook his head. "The glow is from all the city lights."

Petunia wrinkled her nose. "Oh. Okay."

Verlon chuckled. "You'll see what I'm talking about when we get closer to town. Are you excited about living in an apartment, Petunia?"

She loved the idea of living there with Verlon. "I sure am."

"I'm thankful Mama knows a woman with the perfect location. Close to downtown, so we can go see shows and eat out. I picked it out before coming to Arkansas." His eyes crinkled into a smile. "It was gonna be my place, but I sure am happy it'll be our place now."

At the sight of his smile, Petunia's insides flipped. "Me, too. It all sounds so nice, Verlon."

Verlon tapped his thumb along to the beat that wafted from the radio. A tune Petunia had never heard played. "I can't wait to show you around. I think you're gonna love Chicago."

They continued making small talk until they crossed the city limits of Chicago. Petunia's eyes grew wide as she took in the city. The stores stood taller than she'd ever seen and lit up fancy-like. Standing lights lined the roads, and cars buzzed around everywhere. Petunia gasped and worked to roll her window down. She just had to see the lights up close.

A giddy laugh escaped her lips. "Now I know what you meant, Verlon. There are lights everywhere."

Verlon laughed along with her. "I knew you'd like it."

Petunia scanned the buildings, and her hands gripped the door. "I do. I wonder how they got those buildings up in the sky like that."

Verlon stopped for a few people crossing the road. The people waved, and he waved back before turning to Petunia. "Architects design them, and the builders use heavy steel beams to hold them together."

Petunia raised her eyebrows. "Can we go inside one?"

"We sure can." Verlon answered as he clicked the blinker to turn right.

Within a few minutes, they stopped behind a line of cars. People were lined up underneath the most fantastic building with the word "CHICAGO," all lit up with a few names Petunia didn't recognize underneath.

The people didn't seem to be going anywhere. They just stood there laughing and talking. "What are they waiting for?"

Verlon followed her line of sight. "Oh, they're waiting to see the show."

She craned her neck, looking back at the people as the car started moving. "Wow. I wanna see the show, too."

"And you will, my dear." The corners of Verlon's mouth turned upward. "The Chicago Theatre will be our first stop tomorrow night."

Petunia's grin split her face, and she scooted her bottom over beside Verlon. "I can't wait." She couldn't remember ever smiling so much that her cheeks ached.

The cars started moving, and Verlon followed behind them. After several minutes, they finally pulled the car into a parking spot in front of another building.

Petunia swiveled in her seat to get a better look at the red brick building. She'd never lived in a place made of brick.

Verlon hopped out and sprinted around the car to open her door. After helping Petunia, he grabbed a suitcase and headed up the walkway.

A man with a buzz cut meandered down the sidewalk and stopped directly in front of Verlon. Compared to Verlon's muscular frame, the man seemed tiny, almost feminine. "Hello there. You must be the new tenants."

They shook hands, and Verlon nodded. "I'm Verlon, and this here is my wife, Petunia."

A warm breeze caused Petunia's hair to tickle her neck, and she giggled. Verlon and the man watched her rub her neck. She cleared her throat and let her hands drop to her sides.

The man turned to Verlon. "I'm Charlie Gray. My mother, Florence, owns this building, and I'd like to welcome you both on her behalf."

They exchanged a few pleasantries before Verlon excused himself and Petunia. Charlie continued down the sidewalk, waving as he walked.

Petunia stepped inside and took a deep breath at the sight before her. She gaped at the shiny black and white floor and, for a brief moment, longed to play hopscotch. As she walked past a table and two high-backed chairs, she raised her feet one at a time to see if she was leaving marks on the floor.

Verlon pulled on a handle and then opened a door made of bars that led to a box. Surely this wasn't their place. She followed him inside, and he pushed a button on the wall.

The box started moving, and Petunia grasped Verlon's arm. He wrapped his hand around her waist. "You're okay. The elevator is taking us to our floor."

She screwed her lips up. "I'm really on an elevator? Well, ain't that something. How'd you know which button to push?"

"You're really on an elevator, Petunia." He pointed to the buttons. "See the numbers on them?"

Leaning closer, she stared hard at the buttons. "Yeah."

Verlon ran his finger over button number two. "We live on the second floor, so I pushed the one with a two on it."

"Oh." Steadily working on peeling a piece of thumbnail off, she glanced at Verlon. "So, there's ten buttons. Does that mean there's ten floors?"

A grin jotted across his face. "Yes. That's right, Petunia."

After stepping off the elevator, Verlon unlocked the second door on the right. Once inside, Petunia's head spun in every direction.

Petunia stepped into the vast kitchen, her eyes widening as she tried to absorb every detail in a single glance. The room took her breath away with marble countertops that gleamed under the warm glow of crystal pendant lights. She couldn't help but recall the only other kitchen she had ever seen that came close to this one—the one belonging to Miss Irene Mink, the wealthiest woman in Des Arc.

Years ago, Petunia had been one of the first-grade students able to take a tour of Miss Mink's grand Civil War-era home. She vividly remembered the awe she felt as she stepped into that magnificent kitchen, with its polished wooden cabinets filled with fine china and an impressive array of cooking utensils hanging from gleaming racks. In that moment, she'd grasped how different her life was compared to the luxurious existence of others.

Miss Mink had been kind, chatting with the children and offering them cookies from an ornate tin. Petunia could still taste the sweetness on her tongue. It was with a pang of sadness that she remembered the news of Miss Mink's passing recently. The memory of the woman's elegance and generosity lingered in Petunia's mind as she glanced around her new home.

When Petunia followed Verlon into the living area, she brushed her fingers over the velvet on the lime green sofa. She swallowed as she made her way to the window. Her eyes grew wide as she took in the view of a vibrant garden filled with colorful blooms, a playground, and more buildings standing tall against the sky. "Oh, Verlon, I don't know what to say."

He joined her at the window and pulled her hand to his mouth. "So, you like it?"

The curve of her neck moved as she swallowed the lump in her throat. "Like? No. I love it."

Chapter 18

September 1949

Petunia scanned their kitchen and mentally pinched herself for what could've been the hundredth time. She hummed a tune as she sliced sausage to go with their eggs for breakfast.

After putting the sausage on, she sipped her coffee and settled into a light-yellow dining room chair. She glanced at the other three matching chairs and bit her bottom lip.

The grease popped inside the skillet and landed on the stove as the sausage sizzled. A gurgle came from her stomach. Verlon better hurry, or she'd be tempted to start breakfast without him.

Like he could read her thoughts, Verlon came out of the bathroom in a white button-up and gray slacks. He kissed her lips. "Good morning, dear. Thank you for pressing my shirt. It looks nice."

The smile on her face seemed permanent. "You're welcome." She tied a blue apron on and used a spatula to get the sausage out of the skillet. She'd hate for her new Fruit of the Loom checkered dress to get ruined by grease!.

Police sirens blasted from outside their apartment. Verlon stepped to the window as the sound grew faint. It seemed like police sirens went off daily around here. Nothing like the country she was used to.

Verlon moved to the table before glancing at his watch. "Father said they would be here at nine to get us."

"That's plenty of time." She sat two plates of fried eggs, toast, and sausage on the table before topping Verlon's coffee off. "What do you think's gonna happen at the lawyer's office?"

Verlon blew on his coffee and then took a sip. "I figure Auntie Helen left Mama everything she had."

She tipped her head to the side. "Did she have much?"

He nodded. "She was quite wealthy."

Petunia's eyes grew wide. "She always seemed so down to earth and friendly. Nothing like the rich folks I know."

He speared a piece of sausage and plopped it into his mouth. "Auntie's husband started a business after the last World War. It ended up being quite successful."

"Oh." She took a bite of toast with grape jelly. She closed her eyes. Would she ever get used to such food? "I can't believe they never had children."

A sigh fell from his lips. "They had a boy who died when he was a baby."

Petunia gripped the table, and her lips turned downward. "That's so sad, Verlon. So, she spent her time alone after her husband died?"

"She spent most of her time with her sister." He took a sip of coffee, "and then with me and Mama after Grandma passed."

A short horn blast interrupted their conversation. Petunia shoveled the last bite of egg in before looking out the window. "It's your parents."

Later that afternoon, Petunia sat on the sofa across from Verlon in their living room. She pursed her lips as she read a letter from Evelyn. A lot had happened since she'd been gone.

She laid the letter down on the sofa and glanced at Verlon. He seemed to be deep in thought. "Well, are you still shocked?"

He scratched his neck directly beneath his hairline. "I was not expecting Auntie to leave me everything like that."

Petunia crossed her legs and let her black heels drop to the floor. "Your mama didn't seem to be surprised."

Blowing a breath out, Verlon nodded. "She told me they'd talked about it, and that's how they both wanted it."

She scooted forward and met his gaze. "So, now what? You gonna quit your job?"

A smile quirked across his mouth. "Not yet. I like working at the Cass Hotel. But we can plan for our future. Figure out how we can make a difference in people's lives. I want to send your mama some money every month. And there's another thing I've been meaning to talk to you about."

Petunia raised an eyebrow and then settled back into the sofa. "Oh? What is that?"

"I've been thinking about joining the military." He leaned his elbows on his knees in the recliner. "And before you say anything, just think about it. We could travel the world helping people."

"Really?" Traveling the world sounded good, but she wasn't quite so sure about having a military husband. She looked at the letter, purposely avoiding his eager gaze.

"Yes. I want to do it." Verlon's legs jumped up and down like he was ready to take off at a run.

"I'd already talked to a recruiter before coming to Arkansas."

Her breath tangled in her throat. She picked the letter up and quickly reread it. "Evelyn said that MaryAnne's folks been letting Lloyd court her and they're going steady now. And Teresa is expecting a little one. She's already five months in."

"That's wonderful news." He sprung out of the chair. "Say, why don't we go to town tonight? Get some dinner and see a show? We can figure out the rest later."

A mischievous look crossed her face. "That sounds good. I'm starving, like always."

Verlon laughed and picked her up off the sofa, twirling her around the room. She cackled, and he abruptly stood still. She watched his eyes as emotion flitted across his brow. "What's wrong, Verlon?"

He pressed his forehead to hers. "Nothing at all, my Petunia. Life couldn't be better. I love you so much."

Her lower lip trembled. "I love you, too. More than I can say."

His lips met hers, and she sighed from deep within. His kiss would forever be her favorite place, no matter where they were. It was even better than the bayou.

Maybe joining the military wouldn't be too bad. She had always wanted to see the world. And who better to do it with than the love of her life?

Chapter 19

Petunia would never get used to using the elevator without Verlon's help. Still, she held the grocery sack in one hand and pushed the button to go up with the other one.

Charlie Gray entered the lobby and rushed over to Petunia. "Here, let me help you with that."

A smile crossed Petunia's face. "Thank you, Charlie."

His gaze lingered on her face before ogling her legs as she stepped inside the elevator. "You're welcome, Mrs. Marshall."

The elevator jostled as it started moving. A shiver passed over Petunia, and she scooted closer to the wall. This had to be the most uncomfortable ride she'd ever had in the elevator. At least her dress fell way past her knees.

She swallowed and raised her lips in a half smile. "How's your mother doing?"

"Oh, she's just fine." He licked his lips, and Petunia could've sworn he smirked. Maybe it was a smile. "How's Verlon enjoying his job?"

"Just fine, I reckon." The elevator stopped with a thud. She quickly stepped out and turned to say goodbye.

Charlie held his hand up. "Will you do me a favor?"

She swirled around and shook her head. "I'll try."

He stuck his hands in his jeans pockets. "Ask Verlon to introduce me to the blonde lady he was having lunch with today?"

The elevator kicked into gear as Charlie pushed the button to take him to the top floor. Petunia stood there with her mouth wide open.

What blonde woman? And why did Charlie look so pleased with himself?

By the time Verlon came in from work, Petunia's chest had tightened so hard she could explode. A thousand scenarios played through her mind. Was he cheating? Now that he had more money, would he be divorcing her? Her mind worked so hard she couldn't even focus on her favorite television show, The Lone Ranger.

He hung his car keys on the holder and leaned down for a kiss. Before his lips met hers, Petunia bolted out of the kitchen chair. "Who did you have lunch with today?"

His face screwed up, and he cocked his head. "I had lunch at my desk. Why?"

Her stomach churned. "Who's the blonde lady, then? Did she eat with you at your desk? Or was she there to discuss your military training?"

His jaw twitched, and his right hand went to his hip. "What blonde lady?"

Shots sounded from the television. Tonto had been taken hostage. Petunia jumped, stomped across the room, and turned it off.

Petunia gritted her teeth, and heat inched its way up her neck. "I was told you ate lunch with a blonde lady today."

His face flushed a stained pink that matched Petunia's skirt. "That most certainly did not happen. I ate lunch in my office at the hotel. Alone. Who told you this?"

She bit her bottom lip, and her eyes darted to the door. "Charlie Gray."

"He's a liar." Without another word, Verlon stomped through the door and let it slam behind him.

A few minutes later, he returned with Charlie in tow. Sweat beaded across Charlie's forehead. He wiped it with a napkin before speaking. "Mrs. Marshall, please accept my apology. Your husband has informed me that I was mistaken."

She closed her eyes and took a breath. "Did he now?"

His lips pressed into a thin line. "Yes, ma'am."

"Were you?" Petunia twisted her wedding ring around her finger before pinning Charlie with her gaze. "Mistaken, that is?"

He shrugged. "He says I was, so I had to be."

Verlon glared at Charlie. "I would never take another woman to lunch alone. I'd appreciate you not spreading gossip to my wife."

Charlie's face twisted, and Petunia took a step closer to Verlon. A smile flashed across his lips. One that Petunia had no doubt was forced. "It won't happen again."

Verlon closed the space between himself and Petunia before meeting Charlie's brown gaze. "See that it doesn't."

Charlie's jaw trembled, and he walked toward the door. "If that's all, I'll bid you both a good night."

The door slammed behind Charlie, causing Petunia's bones to turn cold. She opened her mouth, but no words would form. How did you say you're a ridiculous person without sounding, well, ridiculous?

Verlon pulled her close. "That man is just jealous. He's interested in you, Petunia. I want you to stay away from him."

She nodded. "I will."

He caressed her cheek in such a way that Petunia's knees went weak. "Don't ever think I'd be with another woman. You hear me? You're my life. My whole life."

Her pulse quickened, and she licked her lips. Waiting for the kiss she'd so stubbornly missed earlier. And Verlon did not disappoint.

Chapter 20

Petunia leaned over the rim of the pristine white toilet, her throat constricting as waves of nausea surged through her. She'd come a long way from the dilapidated outhouse she'd grown up using.

After getting rid of the sickness, she rinsed her mouth and headed to the kitchen to start breakfast. As she stirred a bowl of batter for pancakes, she played the past month over in her head. She'd gotten sick several times. It was almost a daily thing at this point. What could be wrong? Was she dying? Should she say something to Verlon?

She paused. She'd missed a monthly cycle. Could she possibly be expecting? Mama had her first babe at fifteen, and Petunia was well past that age.

If that was the case, she didn't need to get rid of the sickness after all. A bubbly sensation replaced the earlier sick one, and she bounced on her toes.

Verlon came into the kitchen, sporting a clean-shaven face. "Morning, beautiful."

"I think I need to see a doctor." She handed him a cup of coffee and moved to the skillet.

He set the coffee down and grasped her hands, pulling her away from the stove. "Are you ill?"

She shook her head and then looked at her belly. "Not ill."

Following her gaze, he let out a whoop. "Are you saying what I think you're saying?"

Her cheeks reddened, and she nodded. "I may be expecting our first babe."

He pulled her into an embrace and danced around the table.

Three days later, they drove away from the doctor's office with the good news. Petunia caressed her belly and turned to Verlon. "I can't believe we're gonna have a baby."

Keeping his eyes on the road, Verlon laughed. The laugh caused Petunia's insides to turn to mush. How could a laugh do that to somebody? Getting married had caused her to get all sappy. Maybe the song by Ella Fitzgerald that played on the radio did it.

He thumped his thumb along to the music on the steering wheel. "I'm taking you out tonight. Do you want to see a show?"

Her head bounced up and down. Yep, she definitely had to be spoiled. "Sure. I heard Jack Carson has been at the Theatre for a while. Maybe he's still there."

"It's a date." His face lit up, and he held his hand out, motioning for her to come closer.

A spark zapped her heart as she scooted across the seat. "Verlon? What if I have the baby while you're in training?"

After pulling Petunia close, Verlon screwed his lips up. "Dr. Alverson said you were due in May, right? I'll be done with training by then. I'll talk to my Commander to see what I need to do if something happens while I'm there."

She lowered her head. "I guess I'll need to stay here for at least a month or two after the baby is born. Then I'll join you on our traveling adventure."

He kissed her cheek and pulled her as close as he could get her.

Later that evening, after the show, Verlon and Petunia strolled down the sidewalk. She looped her arm through his as the lights danced across the buildings.

She still couldn't believe she was in Chicago, married to the finest man she'd ever known, and now she was expecting. And Verlon didn't care about her hair color, like Daddy. She guessed she'd never understand why Daddy didn't love her, but at least she had love now. How'd she ever get so lucky?

Police sirens wailed from all around them. Verlon eyeballed a police car, and he picked up his speed. "Seems to be a lot going on tonight. Let's get on home."

The tallest man Petunia had ever seen raced toward them. He gasped for air and collapsed on the ground.

Verlon moved Petunia to his back. "Hey, buddy. What's wrong with you?"

The man took a few more breaths and then met Verlon's eyes. "There's a riot in Englewood."

Petunia stepped around Verlon, a deep frown furrowing her brow. "What kind of riot?"

"People are everywhere. My college roommate got beat up and arrested." The man hung his head in his hands. "And I don't know what happened to his girlfriend. Last I saw, she was inside a police car, too."

"What for? Why is there a riot?" Verlon's calm tone seemed to help the man focus.

The man wiped under his nose with his shirt sleeve. "Some Jewish fellas had some black folks inside their house, and now people are in an uproar. Most of their neighbors are trying to get at them."

Petunia blanched right before Verlon stepped between her and the man. "For what?"

"I guess to kill 'em." His face flushed, and he started talking so fast that Petunia had to concentrate on understanding him. "Somebody was yelling they ain't taking over their neighborhood. They've knocked their windows out with rocks. I mean, they're everywhere."

"What can we do to help you? Do you need to go to a hospital?" Verlon leaned near the man while keeping one arm in front of Petunia.

The man bolted off the ground and grasped Verlon's arm. "Get your wife out of here. They don't care if you're a woman or a man. These people are out for blood. And the cops are helping them." He let go before disappearing down the sidewalk.

Petunia's eyes followed the man until he was out of sight. "How could people do this over skin color? I don't understand." She put her face in her hands and wept.

Verlon scanned the sidewalks around them and across the street before grabbing hold of Petunia. "Let's get you home. I don't understand it myself, but we can talk more about it when we get somewhere safe."

Petunia stared into the distance with a heavy heart as they drove away with sirens blaring all around them.

Chapter 21

Early 1950

With a groan, Petunia admitted her mother-in-law's meatloaf tasted better than anything she'd ever eaten. Verlon insisting that she not stay overnight at the apartment alone hadn't been such a bad idea. At least she didn't have to cook.

She drained her glass of milk and patted her growing belly. "You sure know how to make good meatloaf, Hazel."

Hazel's eyes lit up. "I'm glad you enjoyed the meal, dear."

Glancing at her stomach, she grinned. "I think we both did."

After dinner, they settled in the living room to watch an episode of The Lone Ranger.

Ralph handed Petunia a letter from Teresa. "You have mail. Still nothing from Verlon, though."

A letter from Teresa was an odd occurrence. She usually only got mail from Mama or Evelyn.

Hazel clucked her tongue. "I wish he'd send something already."

Lighting a cigar, Ralph leaned his recliner back. "That boy is probably so busy he can't even think with all the training."

Petunia focused on the letter.

Dear Carol Louise,

I'm writing to let you know that daddy hasn't come home since before you got married. Mama and Lloyd have been taking care of everything themselves since you're not there to help.

Lloyd and MaryAnne are getting married next month, so mama will be moving in with me and Lonnie. The wedding will take place on March 18 at the church building. I told Lloyd you may not be able to come, being pregnant and all. But he still hopes to see you there. Lloyd got offered a job at the sawmill in town. He wants to take it since there's nobody to help around the house. MaryAnne works at the shirt factory, so she won't be helping at all around the farm.

Little Jonathan is doing well. He's growing like a weed! Well, I don't have much else to say, so I'll close out.

Love,
Teresa

Petunia stuck the page back inside the envelope. "I need to go home next month for my brother's wedding."

A swirl of smoke left Ralph's mouth. "But you're expecting. How do you plan to make that journey so close to delivery?" Ralph's hand stopped midair with his cigar and his mouth hung open.

Hazel turned in her seat and stared at Ralph, almost like she wanted to argue with him. Instead, she kept her mouth shut.

Petunia lifted her eyes to meet Ralph's. "I'll take an airplane if I have to. I can't miss Lloyd's wedding."

Hazel found her voice and turned toward Petunia. "You won't be going alone. Ralph and I will go with you."

Petunia fanned her face. That smoke smelled worse than a skunk on a bad day. "Y'all are already doing so much for me. You've given me a place to stay while Verlon's away, and you treat me like a queen. I can't ask you to travel that far with me."

Ralph thumped his cigar into the ashtray. "Hazel's right. We will be going with you, and that's that." He turned his attention to the television. "Now, let's see what kind of trouble Tonto gets into this time."

So that was that. End of subject. Now Petunia knew where Verlon got the look that let her know there would be no argument.

Chapter 22

For one riveting moment, Petunia imagined what it would be like if the airplane crashed into the ground as the clouds passed by the window. She squeezed her eyes shut and held onto the armrests.

A sharp pain traveled through her abdomen, and she grimaced. That's what she got for thinking such foolishness. The baby was letting her know to stop that mess. This would be the first and last time she'd be sitting by the window. If it wouldn't be too much trouble, she'd ask Hazel to swap seats with her.

Hazel bunched her eyebrows together. "You all right, dear?"

"I'm fine." Petunia placed Hazel's hand on her stomach. "Baby was moving around and kicked my ribs."

Hazel leaned close to Petunia's belly. "Grandma can't wait to meet you, baby boy."

Baby boy? Petunia had always hoped for her first child to be a girl. What would she do with a boy? Thump his ears like her mama thumped Lloyd's?

"Hmmm." Petunia pressed her side. "What if she's a girl?"

Hazel sat back in her seat and chuckled. "Oh, he's a boy, that's for sure. Take my word for it."

Petunia dropped her brows and looked back out the window. A shrill of excitement hit her with the thought of staying at the hotel in town. She'd always stared at it and wondered about the people who stayed there. She would never have dreamed she'd be one of them staying three whole days.

She pulled at the tie around her maternity dress and blew out a breath. At least the dress fit her well, and no one would know she was pregnant unless they looked twice. She traced the sewn-in twirls in the fabric with her fingers.

Hazel put her hand over Petunia's. "You look wonderful. No need to be nervous."

Petunia laid her head on Hazel's shoulder and smiled. She opened her mouth to thank Hazel but inhaled a lung full of smoke from Ralph's cigar. She coughed until they landed at the airport in Little Rock.

Petunia's heart quickened as she walked up to Evelyn's car. They embraced, and Evelyn greeted the Marshalls. Ralph and Hazel loaded their luggage into the trunk while Petunia and Evelyn caught up.

Evelyn leaned against the side of the car and grinned. "You don't even look like the same person, little sister. You look all put together like a grown-up."

Petunia twisted the bow on her dress. "Thank you, sister." She looked inside the car to find it empty. "Where's James?"

Evelyn held her arms out for a hug before answering. "He sprained his ankle. I was hoping to stay in your room at the hotel with you tonight. Would that be all right?"

Petunia stepped out of Evelyn's embrace and then clasped her hands together. "That'll be more than all right. I'd love it."

"James' ma drove up from Savannah, so he'll be taken care of. Teresa's invited everybody for supper." Evelyn raised a brow and looked at Petunia. "You fine with that?"

Petunia cocked her head and landed a look of confusion on Evelyn. "Why, sure. What would make you ask that? I'm excited to see everybody."

Evelyn moved close to Petunia and lowered her voice to a whisper. "You ain't still hung up on Lonnie, are you?"

Of course, her old crush on Lonnie would get brought up. Petunia glanced at the back of the car. Ralph and Hazel talked amongst themselves and paid Petunia and Evelyn no attention. Luckily. Or Petunia would have to wallop Evelyn.

She grunted. "Not at all. I'm happily married, Evelyn. Verlon is a great man who treats me like a queen."

Evelyn looked Petunia up and down. "He dresses you like one, too. I bet those shoes cost a fortune."

Petunia bit her bottom lip and held her foot out. The kitten heel pumps with four straps that started at her toes and ended with another strap around her ankle seemed to shine proudly. "These are a pair of the newest Mi Lady's shoes, Evelyn. I got them for $24.95."

Evelyn's head bobbed up and down and she whistled. "I saw them shoes in the Brinkley Argus paper a while back. Those are mighty fine."

Ralph closed the trunk and got in the car with Hazel piling in behind him. That meant he was ready to hit the road.

Chapter 23

Even though Petunia felt like a soulless piece of clay, she kept a smile plastered on her face for Lloyd and his bride, MaryAnne.

Her eyes focused on Brother Otis, but her mind drifted to Verlon, playing her time back home on a loop. Wondering if he was getting enough to eat. Was he able to lay his head down for rest? Was he doing good? Exactly what was he doing?

Two of the last three days in Arkansas had been the best ever. But for some reason, Petunia couldn't shake the dread that settled in her stomach.

On the first day there, Mama kissed Petunia and told her how proud she was of her new life. She'd clicked her tongue and whispered, "Aren't you happy I told you to marry Verlon, child?"

Petunia could still feel the heat that traveled up her neck. "I sure am, Mama."

She'd met little Jonathan, and he captured a piece of her heart. It was good to be home, but she wouldn't change her life with Verlon for any-thing. She just wished he would come home al-ready. That training he signed up for was just too long. How long could a wife be expected to go without her husband anyways?

And then Daddy showed his ugly face before the wedding. Of course, he'd show up at Lloyd's wedding. His hair was nice and brown.

After the wedding, Lloyd and MaryAnne both looked so happy. Petunia almost felt bad that she'd been too busy worrying about Verlon to enjoy the ceremony. At least nobody had to know that her mind was a million miles away.

Ralph and Hazel sat at a table with Petunia's family. Her heart warmed as she watched them interact. Thank goodness Daddy disappeared after the ceremony was over.

The dessert table seemed to call her name, so she ambled across the room. They had a nice spread of cakes and bread. MaryAnne's mama must've recruited the whole church to help fix food for the wedding.

After a few seconds of scanning her options, Petunia decided on a piece of chocolate cake. She took a generous slice and inhaled the cocoa good-ness. A door slamming caught Petunia's attention.

Daddy beelined toward Petunia. He stopped, staring at her outfit, and his bottom lip flopped down before spitting a string of tobacco on the floor.

Sneering, his mouth twisted into what Petunia would call disgust. "Well, look at you all dressed up like yer somebody. With yer hair all gussied up and clothes so 'spensive they could feed yer mama for a month."

Turning on her heel, Petunia took a couple of steps away from him, but he grabbed her arm. "You think you're too good for us country folks now, don't ye?"

"I never said that." Petunia closed her eyes, willing herself to be patient and kind. "I'm expecting a baby, you know. Hazel thinks it's a boy, but I ain't so sure."

He ignored the comment and kept on talking ugly to her. "I hear you flew here in one of them airplanes and then refused to stay with Teresa."

The cake that smelled so good mere seconds ago made her want to gag. She set the saucer on the table and pinned Oliver with her eyes. "That's not how that happened."

He talked over her. "You're one of them stuck-up folks staying in the hotel instead of the family now that you're married, ain't ye?"

Her hands dropped to her sides, and she bunched them into fists. Anything to keep her calm. "No."

He slapped his knee and chortled like he'd heard the funniest joke. "Let me guess, the Marshalls are too good to stay at Teresa's? Was that it?"

Petunia glanced at their table. Ralph met her eyes and stood up, before Hazel grabbed his arm and shook her head.

She forced a smile on her face. For Ralph's sake. "No. They're fine people. You'd know that if you'd shown your face at my wedding."

It's like she'd never said a word. He talked so low that nobody knew what he was saying, how he let her know he hated her. "I had somewheres more important to be."

"Yeah, I guess you did." She looked up and met Lloyd's concerned gaze.

Thankfully he walked over. "You okay, Sis?"

A pain shot through her groin, and she winced. She needed to find a seat before her legs gave out. "Just fine, brother. Thanks for checking."

Oliver barked out a laugh and walked away. She could no longer bring herself to think of him as Daddy. He was Oliver now.

Chapter 24

June 1950

"Hazel?" Petunia used the arms on the recliner to push herself out of the chair. "When do you think Ralph will be home with Verlon?"

Ralph had left to pick Verlon up from the airport over an hour ago. Petunia wanted to go, but Ralph had insisted she stay behind with Hazel.

Hazel came into the room, drying her hands on a towel. "It depends on traffic, honey."

Petunia took a step from the recliner when a popping near her pelvis caused her to stop. Warm moisture traveled down her thighs, and she glanced at Hazel. "What just happened? I'm wet down there and it's still coming a little." She lowered herself into the chair.

Hazel dropped the towel and ran to the phone. Before she picked it up, Ralph and Verlon walked through the front door. Hazel went into protective mode. "Petunia is in labor. Let's get her to the hospital."

The color drained from Verlon's face, and he dropped his bag and scooted over to Petunia. He kissed her lips and let out a whoop as he helped her to her feet. "I'm gonna be a daddy."

Once at the hospital, nurse Gayla Elmore took charge and had Petunia in a room ready to deliver. Petunia's legs quaked as shivers took over. How did women do this and live?

Dr. Alverson calmly instructed Petunia to remain calm and then ordered something for her pain. Verlon rubbed her forehead with a wet rag as he whispered how much he loved her in her ear.

Many hours later, they welcomed Martin Allen Marshall into the world. She'd lived through it and had a beautiful baby boy to show for it. She handed Martin to Verlon and pressed her hand to her mouth, trying to keep from crying. A deep sense of family crept into her bones. How lucky Martin would be to have Verlon.

A snore came from Verlon's side of the bed. Petunia clamped her hand over her mouth to keep a laugh from slipping out. He looked so peaceful she couldn't bear the thought of waking him.

He'd been home on leave for a few short days that she didn't want to end. She'd never understood how Mama went months without seeing Oliver. Well, on second thought, if Verlon was like Oliver, she'd probably enjoy time without him, too.

"Good morning, my lovely," Verlon whispered.

Petunia scratched her ear, where his breath tickled. Between giggles, she said, "Morning. "

Verlon trailed his fingers down her cheek. "Penny for your thoughts?"

She couldn't tell him she was thinking ugly thoughts about Oliver. Instead, she laid her head on his shoulder to hide her flushed cheeks. "I've missed you."

He kissed her head. "I've missed you, too."

She popped her neck and rubbed the ball of muscles that had formed a knot beside her spine. "I don't want to be away from you, Verlon."

Verlon moved Petunia's hand and rubbed her neck. "I feel the same way. I'm just thankful we won't have to be apart much longer."

While Verlon rubbed her neck, she closed her eyes. Sleep sounded so good. Her sleep schedule had gotten out of whack since the baby was born.

She cracked one eye open and grinned. "Yeah, I wish I could go with you to get our new house ready in California."

"At least it'll be ready by the first of July." He planted a kiss on her shoulder. "I'll be back to get y'all before you know it."

Martin Allen chose that time to let out a screech. She rolled out of bed and leaned into the bassinet, cuddling Martin in her arms.

After finishing his breakfast, Martin let out a small burp, and she continued lightly tapping his back. "He stays hungry."

Verlon chuckled as he pulled his robe on. "How about mama? You hungry?"

"You know I stay hungry." She looked into Martin's eyes, and her heart skipped a beat. "This little fella drinks all my food up."

He took the baby and spun him around before handing him back to Petunia. "Why don't you relax while I make breakfast?"

Seeing Verlon with Martin caused her heart to kick into high gear. And the offer to cook breakfast? Oliver had never offered to cook for Mama. He'd be mad if she even mentioned it.

Petunia bit her bottom lip. "Really? You're gonna make breakfast?"

"I sure am. That's something I learned about myself while in training." He jiggled his eyebrows and then skipped out of the bedroom. "I can make a decent fried egg."

She lowered herself and the baby to the bed. "Okay then."

Later that evening, they enjoyed dinner with his parents. Afterward, they turned on the news station. Ralph and Verlon huddled up with their cigars. At the same time, Petunia and Hazel discussed Martin's sleep and eating patterns. Hazel held him close to her bosom, rocking him in the new chair they got just for him.

Ralph exploded out of his chair. "You've got to be kidding me!"

Martin started crying, and Hazel took him to the kitchen, mumbling something about getting him a bottle.

Petunia watched her leave the room before turning to Verlon. He stood there, stock still and white as a sheet. She grasped his hand. "What is it?"

He never took his eyes off the television screen. "President Truman has ordered the ground troops to Korea."

"What does that have to do with you?" She clamped her hand across her mouth as soon as the words came out. "You're a ground troop, then?"

"I am." He pulled her close to his side. "It looks like moving to California will have to wait, Petunia."

She took a step back and probed his eyes. "Will have to wait? For how long?"

"Until after the war."

That good breakfast Verlon made threatened to come back up.

Chapter 25

October 1950

Another three months had passed without her husband. This is not what Petunia signed up for. Spending time in her apartment during the day and the nights with her in-laws was not the marriage she had in mind.

Verlon frequently reminded her she promised not to stay alone at night. It was 1950, not the seventeenth century. She should be able to stay alone. Even though she wanted to stay in her own home, she still gave thanks for her life. It was more than she would've thought two years ago. Life would be everything she could want if only Verlon was home.

Picking up an ink pen, she sat at the desk and started writing Mama a letter. Her stomach fluttered, and she ran to the toilet. A few minutes later, she returned to the desk.

Dear Mama,

Well, I've been alone for months now since Verlon is off fighting in the stupid war. I wish I knew what to do.

How do you deal with Oliver being gone all the time? I never knew it would be so hard. I miss him so much, Mama.

Martin Allen is the most handsome baby boy. I can't wait for you to meet him. You'll just love him! And guess what? I'm expecting another. It's soon after Martin, but I can't help it. God's will must be done, and I sure do love being a mama. I just wish I had my Verlon here to help me.

How are things with you? I miss seeing you. I want to come home soon, but I'm afraid I'll miss Verlon if he comes back.

Please borrow a phone and call me. I long to hear your voice. You're about the only one who can talk sense into me. Haha

I love you,
Your daughter, Petunia

After she finished writing her letter, she opened one from Evelyn. The letter opener fell under the desk, and she sighed. She'd pick it up later. She was still too nauseous to bend over that far.

Evelyn sent news that she and her husband were moving to Tyronza, a small town between Memphis, Tennessee, and Jonesboro, Arkansas, and opening a bed and breakfast.

Good for them. She hoped they did well with it.

She strolled to the window and looked at the park below. Things had changed since the first time she saw this view. She reflected on the past few months and shivered. A slice of longing cracked into her ribcage, and she snapped the curtains shut.

Stupid Korea. Stupid President Truman. Stupid. Just stupid.

A knock on the door interrupted her melancholy. The door swung open, and her neighbor, Molly Inman, bounced inside. "Hey! You ready to go mingle?"

Petunia inwardly groaned. The answer was no. She did not want to mingle with their landlord and the other tenants. Hazel and Ralph had forced her into coming. They told her she had to leave the house for a bit or she'd go crazy. Ha. The joke was on them. She was already crazy. Crazy without her husband. Crazy missing his face. His smile. His laugh. Him.

Molly's lips turned downward, and she put a chubby hand on her waist. "You don't have to go if you don't feel well. I can go alone, you know."

Petunia grabbed her jacket. "No, it's fine. Martin's being spoiled rotten by his grandparents, and I'm already here. No sense in backing out." Petunia grinned and wiped her forehead like she'd gotten away with something sneaky. "I'm just thankful it's not a costume party this time."

Molly's face brightened, changing to one of beauty. Petunia had overheard Charlie Gray and another man talking about Molly being a plain woman and too big to find a husband soon after Molly's family moved into the building. Petunia had not so politely taken them to task. What they didn't know was Petunia would've given anything to have Molly's brown hair and happy attitude. It didn't matter that Molly had extra weight on her, not to Petunia.

Molly cleared her throat and moved closer to Petunia. "Did you hear what I said? I said I love dressing up for Halloween."

"You would," Petunia mumbled, instantly regretting being hateful.

Molly put her hand on her hip and wagged her finger at Petunia. "I heard that. What's eating at you, Petunia?"

Petunia massaged her temples before meeting Molly's inquisitive gaze. "Oh, it's nothing, I just found out I'm expecting another baby."

Squealing, Molly jumped up and down. "I knew it. You'll have a girl this time. I just know you will."

That comment caused a grin to crack on Petunia's face. "I hope so."

Molly stopped jumping, and a serious expression crossed her face. "You're sad because you miss Verlon? Is that why you don't want to go to the party?"

Petunia nodded. "I hate that Verlon's gone to Korea. Especially now, but my in-laws will kill me if I don't get out some. They think I'm depressed or something."

Molly looped her arm through Petunia's. "Then it's settled. Let's go have a good time."

"Sound good." A grin tugged at Petunia's mouth. "I heard there's pie."

Molly giggled all the way to the top floor.

When she left the party a couple of hours later, Petunia grudgingly admitted she had enjoyed herself. Maybe Hazel was right. She needed to quit moping around the house and get out more often.

Once inside her apartment, she clicked the lock into place and walked over to the refrigerator. She stuck a piece of cake inside and boxed up another two pieces for Ralph and Hazel. She'd have that for a snack tomorrow or the next day when she stopped by to water her plants.

She groaned as the box slipped from her hands and tumbled to the floor. As she pushed herself upright, she held onto the table to steady herself. With a determined sigh, she bent down to retrieve it. As she straightened up, she gripped the edge of the table, using it for balance. The faint glow of a distant streetlight spilled through the window and cast shadows around the room. She paused. Her heart raced as she locked eyes with Charlie Gray, who sat silently in the darkness of the living room, his presence shrouded in the dim light.

Chapter 26

Charlie raised himself out of the chair and stepped toward Petunia. "My dear, I've been waiting an hour for you to get here. What's taken you so long?"

The blood drained from her face. "What are you doing in my apartment, Charlie Gray?"

He cocked his head, and the gleam in his eye said he was up to no good. "We have unfinished business."

Petunia turned on her heel, running as fast as possible to the door. Her hands trembled as she grasped the doorknob. As she reached for it, something cracked her skull, and she was thrust into the door.

Her forehead throbbed worse than anything she'd ever experienced. What had she been hit with? A sledgehammer? Hot iron filled her mouth as she fell backward into Charlie's arms. Her eyes fluttered open as weightlessness encompassed her. Her feet skidded on the carpet as Charlie drug her into the living room.

He lowered her onto the sofa, covering her mouth tightly as he sat beside her. The remnants of blueberry cheesecake stuck to her lips from his hand, causing her to gag. Her throat tightened, and she couldn't make a sound even if she hadn't had his hand cutting off her oxygen.

To be such a small man, he had a grip like Petunia figured a bull would, if it had hands. His tongue darted across his lips, and he grinned. "I'm going to remove my hand from your mouth. Do not scream. If you do, I will stab you."

Hard, quick jabs skipped through her heart as Charlie brought his face closer to hers. This is why Verlon didn't want her here at night. He was trying to keep her safe. Her mind pulsated with regret for not listening. She had to get out of this mess. Where was his knife?

Charlie pulled her close and stared into her eyes. She gripped the back of his head in her hand and smiled. "Wait a minute. It don't have to be like this, Charlie."

He paused, a smug look crossing his features. As he leaned close, she scurried backward and kicked the side of his face. He touched his jaw and narrowed his eyes before landing on Petunia, wrapping his hands around her throat.

She pressed against his chest with all her might. His nostrils flared as he stood. He pulled a pocketknife out of his pocket. She almost laughed. She'd used bigger knives to skin the fish she caught as a kid.

He raised his hand and backhanded her. "You will not act like you don't want to be with me. Do you understand?"

Knocking came from the front door right before Molly's voice came through the opening at the bottom. "Petunia? Are you still here?"

Petunia's stomach hitched. Molly!

Charlie clamped his hand over Petunia's mouth and leaned close to her ear. "Try to get her attention, and I'll make sure she regrets it."

A few more knocks came before Molly's footsteps echoed down the hall. Along with the bit of hope Petunia had.

Another slap rang loudly in her already pounding ears. Heat from her throbbing cheek exploded into her eardrum. That sorry piece of trash hit her. Again.

She leveled stormy green eyes on his face. "You need to get out of my apartment."

He laid the knife down and picked her up, planting her on her feet in front of him. "I'm not going anywhere. I own this building, remember? You better cooperate."

She couldn't allow this to happen. Thinking back to when she put Lloyd out, she had to do the same thing to Charlie. She forced her lips into a pleasant smile and raised her face.

He grinned and let out a surprised gasp. "This is more like it. You better not be tricking me again."

As soon as he relaxed his stance, Petunia stepped back and kicked him in the same place she'd kicked Lloyd. His grin turned into an expression of agony as he dropped to his knees.

Petunia wasted no time stepping around him. Her heart pounded as she made it to the kitchen. She opened the door.

The door slammed shut. Charlie buried his right hand in her hair as he closed the door with his foot.

She cried out and jerked away from Charlie. She swung her fist, connecting with his cheekbone. He backhanded her, and she lost her balance. Her knee cracked, and she landed on all fours in front of Verlon's desk.

The thought of Verlon caused a fire to light in her belly. She had to stop this man no matter what it took. For Verlon and their babies.

"You shouldn't have done that." His voice came out calm and low.

While Charlie continued berating her, she turned her face toward the wall. Her glistening gaze landed on the letter opener she'd dropped earlier, and a lightness settled in her heart. She'd never been so thankful to see anything in her life. Stretching, she touched it with the tip of her finger and inched it closer until it was close enough to pick up.

Once he stopped talking, he turned her over onto her back. The look on his face caused a jolt to replace the lightness in her heart. She pushed it away as he leaned close to her.

"Shall we finish what we started, my…"

Before he got the words out, Petunia shoved the letter opener into his left eye. He jerked it out with a howl. "I'm going to enjoy this," Charlie said as he raised the bloody letter opener above his head.

As Charlie looked at Petunia with his one good eye, Petunia had no doubt he would enjoy hurting her.

The door burst open. Ralph rushed into the apartment, followed by a policeman.

"I told you something had to be wrong," Ralph yelled at the policeman.

Petunia trembled with relief as the policeman handcuffed Charlie. He tried to jerk away from the cop, but the handcuffs proved to be stronger than him.

Ralph shoved Charlie before scooping Petunia off the floor and heading out the door. "I'm getting you to the hospital. Thanks to Molly, you're gonna be just fine."

The only thing on Petunia's mind was her unborn baby. Would the baby be just fine?

Chapter 27

Petunia opened her eyes to Hazel hovering above her. The machine by the bed beeped loudly as it pumped fluids into the IV.

Hazel gasped and swiveled her body around. "Ralph. She's awake."

Ralph appeared on Hazel's other side. He met Petunia's gaze. "How are you doing?"

Sunlight poured in the window behind Hazel. Petunia squeezed her eyes shut and attempted to lick her lips. It was no use. The darkest, driest spot in the Sahara Desert probably held more moisture than Petunia's mouth did.

Hazel poured a glass of water and held it to Petunia's lips. "Here you go, honey. Take a few small sips."

Running her hand across her stomach caused a smile in Petunia's heart. The baby was still there! "My baby's okay."

"Yes, he's just fine." Ralph patted her hand. "And so is his mama."

She scanned the room, furrowing her brow when she didn't see her son. "Where's Martin?"

Hazel wiped a few drops of water off Petunia's chin before dabbing at her puffy and bloodshot eyes. "Molly's keeping an eye on him for us. He was playing when I left this morning."

A groan escaped Petunia's lips, and she scrunched her eyes shut. "How did you know to come to my apartment?"

"Molly called the house after thinking she heard a scream from your apartment."

Petunia made a mental note to hug Molly's neck when she got out of there. "I've been here all night?"

Hazel pulled a small chair close and leaned on the side of the bed. "Yes, Dr. Schumann wanted to keep you overnight for observation. Ralph slept in this chair so you wouldn't wake up and be alone."

Petunia smiled at Ralph. So, this is what it's like to have a father figure who cared. Even though she'd been through a terrible ordeal, Petunia couldn't stop the warmth that spread through her chest. Oliver would've dropped her off and gone home to his bed.

Ralph's face seemed haggard, and Hazel kept sniffling. What could've happened? "Hazel? Why have you been crying? Because of me, or is it something else?"

Tears flowed down Hazel's face. "We have something to tell you. We're not sure how to say it."

Ralph cleared his throat. "Petunia, a soldier came by the house this morning and talked to Hazel." His voice caught on the last word.

He may as well have stabbed Petunia in the heart with a butter knife than keep talking. She covered her ears and shook her head. "I don't wanna know."

Hazel's sobs pulsated through Petunia's body, leaving a trail of ice behind. Ralph clasped her hands in his. "I'm sorry, but you have to hear this. Verlon's group took heavy fire. There were no survivors."

Petunia's eyes burned as she kept her tears at bay. Something was not right. "Did they find his body?"

His shoulders slumped. "There are bodies, but they're all unrecognizable."

"Then it's not him." Petunia ran her hands through her hair. "I'll believe it when I see his body and not a minute before."

Petunia's gaze fell to her feet as her eyes welled up with tears. She struggled to get words out as she fought the urge to lose control. "Can I have some time by myself?"

Hazel stood firm by Petunia's side. "I don't think that's such a good-"

"Of course." Ralph cut Hazel off. He walked around the bed and led Hazel out the door.

Outside the room, Ralph's words drifted through the open door. "Hazel, I don't think Petunia will accept that Verlon's gone. We need to treat her as our own daughter and love her through this."

"I agree with you…"

Chapter 28

The nauseating stench of stale bread and sweat filled the police station. Petunia wiped her nose and struggled against the urge to cover her ears. A man being arrested shouted that someone was setting him up, and the arresting officer yelled just as loudly in response.

The only bright spot in the experience was the snow pattering against the front window, leaving a delicate trail of snowflakes behind.

She glanced at Ralph for clarification. "Did this cop just say I musta done something wrong?" Her lips drew into a hard line.

Even with his ruddy complexion, Petunia could tell Detective Redfield's face blanched. "It's my job to ask questions to find out what happened, Miss Marshall."

She squeezed her leg underneath the desk. If she didn't keep her hands busy, she'd be tempted to deck the smug cop. "It's Mrs. Marshall."

When a phone rang a few times, he looked at a thin woman in her mid-thirties. "Penny, can you get the phone?" He turned eyes of steel on Petunia. "Mr. Gray swears you invited him over to your apartment."

The urge to jerk a knot in his head almost overtook Petunia's senses. Instead, she took a breath and squeezed her leg even harder. "Why would I do that? I'm a married woman."

Detective Redfield tapped a pencil on the desk for a minute before answering. "Hadn't your husband been away in the military? Maybe you wanted some company."

Petunia shot out of the chair and leaned over the desk. "I ain't no loose woman, Detective."

Ralph stood up and gently tugged Petunia back into the seat. "Petunia, keep your cool. Detective Redfield is only asking because this is what the lawyers will try to say happened."

A muscle twitched in Detective Redfield's cheek. "Exactly. And if you act like that in court, Charlie will walk away scot-free."

"After what he did?" Petunia should've known the cops would be on the rich boy's side.

"Yes. It's your word against his." He shrugged before leaning his elbows on the desk. "And the Gray family has a lot of old money and are well-known. I think this is a waste of your time."

Petunia shook her head and fought back the angry tears that threatened to fall. "So, he'll just get away with it? I swear if I was back home, Charlie would've already been in a world of trouble."

A nervous flicker passed over Detective Redfield's features, and he avoided Petunia's stare. "That's not all we need to talk about."

Petunia shifted in the hard chair and grunted when the baby kicked her ribs. "What else could there be to talk about?"

Detective Redfield's voice came out brutal and uncaring. "Mr. Gray has indicated the desire to press charges against you."

Petunia raised an eyebrow, and laughter sprang from her chest. "You've got to be kidding me. That sorry piece of rubbish has a lot of nerve."

She glanced at Ralph, who met Detective Redfield's gaze with a cutting glare that had Petunia squirming in her seat. "This conversation is over, Detective. If you need to speak to Mrs. Marshall again, contact our lawyer."

"Hold on, now." Detective Redfield shoved upright. "I want to make a deal before you leave."

Petunia wanted to ask what kind of deal, but the look on Ralph's face kept her quiet. She'd never seen him look so scary.

"Then I suggest you contact our lawyer." Ralph's tone came out hard and left no room for argument.

Detective Redfield clamped his mouth shut and gave a quick nod.

Ralph stared at him for another second before turning his attention to Petunia. "Let's go, Petunia."

Ralph dropped Petunia off at home before speeding away. When he returned hours later, he went straight to the bedroom he and Hazel shared. But not before Petunia saw bloody stains on his white shirt.

A few minutes later, he returned to the living room in fresh clothes. Petunia gasped when she noticed a cut on his cheek and scratched-up knuckles.

Hazel pursed her lips. "What happened to you?"

Leaning back in the recliner, he lit a cigar and breathed in the smoke. "All you need to know is Charlie has decided to leave town and not press charges against Petunia."

Chapter 29

The colder it got, the quicker the days passed by. It was so much colder in Chicago than Arkansas ever was. It made her miss home, at least a little.

Ralph and Hazel wanted to have a funeral for Verlon, but Petunia fought them tooth and nail. How could they even think about that? In the end, they agreed on a small service honoring his life. Petunia didn't like it, but at least that helped Hazel stop crying all the time.

After the service, Petunia spent her days caring for Martin and waiting for Verlon to come home and tell them the funny story about how he lived through the Korean War.

But right now, she straightened her skirt and smiled at Molly. "Thank you for coming over today. I'm happy for the company."

Molly settled on the other end of the sofa before pushing her new black-rimmed glasses up her nose.

If only Molly would go fishing with her like Opal used to. For a moment, Petunia's mind drifted to her days in Arkansas on the wet banks of the Wattensaw Bayou, playing hide and seek with her brothers and sisters or fishing with Opal and Clyde.

Molly's voice jolted Petunia back to the present. "I'm happy to be here. After everything that's been happening with these racial riots, Daddy doesn't want me getting too far from the apartment, but he's fine with me coming here."

Petunia's eyebrows raised. "I can't say I blame him. Why do people care if black people live nearby? They ain't gonna hurt nobody."

Molly shrugged. "Beats me. Daddy won't get involved, seeing we're Jewish. He's afraid we'll be targeted ourselves."

Hazel flitted out of the kitchen with a tray full of tea and cookies and then headed back to the kitchen.

Petunia poured tea into three cups and handed one to Molly. "Please help yourself to a snack."

Molly reached for a lemon cookie as Martin teetered up to her. She smiled and ruffled his brown hair. "Hi, there, little fella. You're one lucky boy to have such a strong mama."

"I second that," Hazel added as she walked into the living room carrying napkins and silverware. "My son picked a good one."

Molly's lips formed a thin line. "That weasel, Charlie, picked the wrong woman to attack, that's for sure."

Petunia grimaced. "Thanks to you, Ralph. The police got there when they did. After everything, I'm convinced the police are in Florence's pocket."

Hazel handed Martin a toy truck. "Yes, I can't believe he tried to say you invited him over."

Molly raised her voice. "I can't believe the police tried to charge you for what you did! You were trying to protect yourself."

"He's a bad man." Petunia rubbed her stomach. "I was so scared he was gonna hurt the baby."

A cloud passed over Hazel's eyes. "If Verlon were around, he'd make that slimy snake pay for what he did to you. Instead, he's getting off without so much as a mark on his record."

Petunia dropped her eyes to the floor. "Verlon sure would make him pay, Hazel."

Hazel sighed. "I'm sorry, Petunia. I shouldn't have brought Verlon up like that."

As heat traveled up her neck, Petunia shook her head. "We can't live our lives without ever talking about Verlon."

Hazel squeezed Petunia's hand before sitting across from Molly and Petunia. "And we have Martin and a little one on the way. They're a part of my boy, and I thank you for sharing them with us."

Petunia nodded. "No matter where we end up, you and Ralph will always be a part of their lives. I promise." She bit off a chunk of a chocolate chip cookie. "And I'm sure Ralph didn't let that weasel get off without at least a little hurt."

"That's all we ask, to be a part of their lives." Hazel's eyes teared up before a half-smile appeared. "To be a part of your life. And you're right about Ralph. He doctored his hands for a week after he visited Charlie."

Petunia's eyes formed circles. "I bet he did."

Molly cocked her head and screwed up her mouth. "I'm not even going to ask about that one. I'm just glad he's gone."

Hazel sipped her tea and met Molly's gaze. "Say, have you had a chance to watch the new show called I Love Lucy?"

Molly's face brightened, and she clapped her hands together. "Yes, ma'am. Daddy and I haven't missed an episode since it started."

A wave of relief passed over Petunia at the subject change. She added a lump of sugar to her tea and breathed in the sweet scent. This and a few cookies were just what the doctor ordered.

Chapter 30

May 1952

Too often over the past year and a half, Petunia had relived her last moments with Verlon in her mind. How many more times could she do it without going mad? A hundred? Two hundred? A thousand?

Little William Ralph squealed when Ralph tickled his belly. Martin tugged on Ralph's shirt, wanting some attention. Ralph scooped him up and gave him a good tickling. She closed her eyes, reveling in the sweet laughter. Without these moments, she'd already be mad. She scolded herself. There wouldn't be any going mad anytime soon because the boys needed her.

The phone ringing interrupted her line of thought. They shared a party line with the neighbors, so Petunia never got too excited when it rang.

Hazel answered it and motioned for Petunia. "It's Evelyn."

Scurrying over, Petunia sat on the bench before speaking into the receiver. "Hello, Evelyn. It's Petunia."

"Petunia, we need you home. It's Mama." Evelyn's words seemed to come out rushed.

Petunia shot up off the bench. "What do you mean? Is she…"

"Mama's alive, but the neighbor's horse trampled her good."

"What?" Petunia massaged her forehead and lowered herself onto the bench.

"Just listen. It's mainly her leg. Petunia, they think she's gonna lose it. She's running a bad fever and has been asking for you."

A hitch clicked in Petunia's stomach. "Oh no. Is Mama still with Teresa?"

"Here's another problem. Teresa is sick with them measles. Mama is with Lloyd and MaryAnn."

"Who's taking care of them?"

"MaryAnn done had to take off work to care for Mama, and Lonnie was taking care of Teresa until the doc put her in the hospital at Searcy. I've got Jonathan with me in Tyronza."

Petunia closed her eyes. How would she deal with this so far away? "Where's Oliver?"

"You mean Daddy? Sounds like you done got too big for your britches, sister. Show some respect."

Resisting the urge to let Evelyn have it, Petunia swallowed angry bile. "Well, where is he?"

The line fell silent for a few seconds before Evelyn continued. "We don't know. That's another reason we need you home. MaryAnn can't stay off work too much longer."

Maybe Evelyn wanted money. That must be it. "Listen, I send Mama money ever month. I'll send more so y'all can hire somebody to help."

"Well, ain't you something. Did you hear me say Mama is asking for you?"

Okay, maybe she had been wrong about the money. "I heard. But you have to realize I have a family here in Chicago."

"I never thought the day would come when I agreed with Daddy. But you have turned into somebody else. Too good to leave your fancy house in Chicago to help your own mama. It's a shame."

Petunia stood up as her voice rose an octave. "Wait a minute, that's not fair."

"Sounds fair to me. I'm gonna let you go."

Petunia closed her eyes as a pinch of regret pitched inside her stomach. "Evelyn, please listen to me. I'll try to come."

"Whatever. I'll borrow the money to take care of her. Don't worry about us Arkansas folks. We'll be fine."

"What in the world's wrong with you, Evelyn? You're acting like I've done something wrong."

"I'm just tired, Petunia." A long sigh came from the end of the line. "Just come home if you can. If not, we'll figure something out."

Hazel and Petunia took the boys for a walk after breakfast the next day. The rising sun peeked over the apartment building as they strolled down the sidewalk. A warm breeze sent a few loose strands of hair dancing around Petunia's ears.

Hazel waved at a man across the street before turning to Petunia. "Ralph and I talked last night. We think you should leave the boys with us and go take care of your Mama."

Petunia knitted her eyebrows and met Hazel's gaze. She considered saying yes but didn't want to be away from the boys. That and put Hazel out. "I can't possibly do that to y'all."

The stroller came to a stop as Hazel slowed her pace. "Yes, you can. We're your family now, too, and will help in any way we can."

Shifting Martin to her other hip, Petunia scrunched her lips together. "Maybe I do need to fly down for a week or two."

Martin wiggled his way out of Petunia's arms when the park came into view. Jumping up and down, he pointed at the merry-go-round. "Play, Mama!"

After crossing the street, Petunia helped Martin on the merry-go-round and glanced at Hazel. "The boys won't know what to think if I'm gone."

Two women Petunia didn't recognize meandered over with two little girls about Martin's size. The girls jumped on the merry-go-round with Martin and let out a squeal.

After greeting the women, Hazel laid her hand on Petunia's wrist. "Fly down, and let's see what happens. We'll bring the boys to Arkansas if Dorothy needs you longer than a couple of weeks."

A car door slammed across the street, and a man wearing a suit jogged into an apartment building. Petunia's eyes followed him as he disappeared through the front door, and she imagined it was Verlon coming home for lunch.

Her life should be so different right now. She should be a happy homemaker, wife, and mother. Not a teenage widow dreaming of what should've been.

Snapping out of the fog she found herself in, her words came out firm even to her own ears. "I don't want to be away from the boys longer than two weeks. That's the limit for me. I don't even want to be gone two weeks."

Hazel's head bobbed. "We will bring the boys there after two weeks and rent a hotel room for a while if you see that you're needed longer. Ralph said he'd ask Edward to pick you up from the airport."

Laughter rang from Martin as he shuffled off the merry-go-round. Hazel picked him up and twirled him in the air. His laughter doubled as he reached for Hazel's face.

Petunia's heart expanded in her chest. The boys would be well taken care of for two weeks, but Mama may not. Who knows what could happen if she lost her leg?

Petunia nodded. "Thank you so much, Hazel. You don't know how much this means to me. It does sound like Mama needs me."

Hazel set Martin down and met Petunia's gaze. "No need to thank me, we're family, and we help each other. That's what family does."

Petunia hugged Hazel as if she were her own flesh and blood. "I'll leave on the next flight out."

Chapter 31

The airport bustled with travelers as Petunia stepped down the sidewalk. A horn blasted when a pudgy man walked in front of a car. She picked up her pace as soon as she laid eyes on Verlon's Uncle Edward.

He waved and popped open the trunk. She'd opted to keep her luggage light. She didn't plan on being away from Chicago too long.

He loaded the suitcase and small bag before wrapping Petunia in a hug. "How ya doing, sweetheart?"

Petunia laid her head on his shoulder before taking a step back. Verlon had Edward's eye color. How had she never noticed that?

She offered the biggest smile she could muster, considering her heart flipped with the thought of Verlon. "Hello, Mr. Marshall. I'm doing as well as can be expected."

He put his hand on his hip. "What's with this Mr. Marshall talk? I'm Uncle Eddie to you now."

She dropped her eyes to her nails. "Sorry, Uncle Eddie. Did Aunt Gail not feel like coming with you?"

Waving a dismissive hand, he rolled his eyes as he opened the trunk. "Nah, she's been in a tizzy over something somebody said in town earlier. Told me she had a headache and would be in bed the rest of the day."

Petunia opened the passenger door and leaned on the doorframe just as a few raindrops hit her head. "That's awful."

"Don't you worry about her. She'll snap out of her mood in a day or so." Ignoring the rain, he closed the trunk and walked to the driver's door. "Let's get you home to see about your poor mama and sister."

They made small talk on the drive home. The rain had stopped, but clouds rolled in the sky, threatening to start back up at any moment. Finally, Edward pulled the car over and helped Petunia unload her things before heading back down the winding road. She ran her hands through her hair as she took inventory of her surroundings. The gray clouds rolled away, and white puffy ones took their place in the light blue sky. The weather had always changed without much notice, and this time Petunia was glad about it.

When a ribbon of excitement twirled inside, Petunia hoofed it across the yard. A dry, gentle breeze seemed to push her forward as she approached the porch.

The square house Lloyd and MaryAnne called home boasted black shutters, a dark gray roof, and a tiny front porch. Petunia itched to peel off the piece of black wood that had splintered apart by the front door. Instead, she held her hands firmly at her sides until Lloyd opened the door.

No matter how hard she tried to stop them, the tears came anyway. Lloyd held his arms out, and she grasped him for dear life as the tears she'd kept at bay came like a flowing river.

She stepped away and blew her nose on a handkerchief Lloyd handed her. "I miss you something awful, brother."

"I miss you, too." He walked through a small living room with sparse furniture and a deep brown wooden floor. "Have you seen Teresa yet?"

She slipped the used handkerchief into her pocket and frowned. "No, Uncle Eddie dropped me off here first."

He rested on his heels. "The doc had to take Mama's leg."

Petunia sucked in a stuttered breath. "Oh no. She's already home? That seems way too soon."

Darkness crossed his features, and he lowered his voice. "I agree, but she refused to stay at the hospital. And I promise MaryAnne's taking good care of her."

A grandfather clock chimed, and Petunia's heart faltered. She put her hand over her chest and quickly bit back the yelp from her scare. "Mama's always hated hospitals, hasn't she?"

"Yes, she has. That's why she's already here instead of there like she belongs." He elbowed Petunia. "She's about as hard-headed as you are."

Petunia eyeballed the clock. It stood tall and grand. No telling where Lloyd had picked that up. "Ha ha, brother. Mama's got me beat."

Lloyd gripped her hand. "Evelyn said you've been sending money to help out. Thank you."

"Don't mention it." Her eyebrows rose, and she pointed at the clock. "Where'd you get that?"

He glanced at the clock, and a slight smile crossed his face. "It belonged to MaryAnne's grandma. Pretty, ain't it?"

"It sure is." She said as their eyes linked. "How's Teresa?"

A worried expression slid across his face. "She's not doing well at all. But why don't you visit with Mama, and then we can talk about Teresa?"

She nodded before following Lloyd into the bedroom. Her stomach sank with dread as she considered what he said about Teresa. How could she not be doing well?

MaryAnne lifted herself out of the chair she sat in and embraced Petunia. "I'm so thankful to see you here."

"I'm glad I was able to come, MaryAnne." Petunia glanced at the bed and then back at MaryAnne. "I should be the one thanking you for taking care of Mama."

MaryAnne cut her eyes at Petunia. "You don't have to thank me. She's my Ma, too, now."

Mama lay on her back with a stack of pillows beneath the stump where her leg used to be. It was wrapped in white bandages and appeared to have been amputated a few inches below the knee.

Her eyes cracked open, and she winced before turning her head toward Petunia. A toothless grin greeted Petunia, and her mama's eyes lit up. "Petunia? Are you really here, or am I dreaming, child?"

Grasping Mama's hand, Petunia smiled. "I'm really here, Mama."

"Look at you with your pretty white dress and your hair all curled up." A laugh left her lips, and she tapped her cheek. "Lean down here and give Mama a kiss."

Petunia's heart filled with memories of her childhood, of sitting in Mama's lap and hugging her tight.

She knelt close to Mama and kissed her cheek. "I love you."

Mama patted her face. "I love you, too, Petunia."

The door creaked open, and Lloyd stood there. "Sis, Daddy's pulled up yelling something about you and Lonnie. I've never seen him like this. He's fit to be tied."

Chapter 32

Petunia squared her shoulders. "Ain't nothing going on with me and Lonnie, and I am not in the mood for this."

Lloyd grabbed her hand and shook his head. "I think you better slip out the back door while MaryAnne distracts him. Take my truck to the hospital."

Petunia rubbed the corner of her eye to keep it from twitching. "I'm not running from that man."

Mama sniffled. "Child, please don't challenge him."

Petunia hit her bottom lip until she tasted blood. "I'm not scared of him."

Mama's lips twitched downward as her gaze stuck to Petunia. "Would you go out the back for me?"

Struggling not to run out the door and confront him energized Petunia's veins, but one look at Mama's stump and trembling lips deflated her. "For you."

After sneaking out the back door and waiting for Oliver to enter through the front, Petunia made the trek to the hospital. She glanced at her watch as she made a straight line to the entrance.

Lonnie stood outside the building smoking a cigarette. Petunia stopped in her tracks. "Lonnie?"

He ran his hand through his long greasy hair, and a wave of relief crossed his face when he met her eyes. "I'm so happy to see you."

Petunia's green eyes met his bloodshot eyes that appeared almost lifeless. "Lonnie, you look exhausted."

He ground the cigarette out on the side of the building. "I'm all right. I think it's just worry that's got me."

Petunia walked inside, with Lonnie walking closely behind her. She glanced at him. "Is Teresa not doing better?"

"Not really." His eyes darted past Petunia and around the entranceway. "Petunia, she's got pneumonia."

"Pneumonia?" Petunia swallowed down a thousand questions she wanted to ask. Instead, she closed her eyes and breathed a few deep breaths.

He shrugged. "Just act normal when you see her. I don't want her scared or nothing."

A nurse walked by, leaving a trail of disinfectant clogging Petunia's nasal passage. "What do you mean by that?"

Lonnie pressed the up button on the elevator and then stepped inside. "You'll see. Just act normal."

After making it to Teresa's room, Petunia tiptoed inside behind Lonnie, her heart stuck in her throat. How else but normal could she act? She knew what measles looked like since she'd been the only one in their family to have them as a kid. That's the only time Oliver stepped up to take care of her. He'd also had measles as a kid, so to be on the safe side, he made Mama, and all the kids leave the house until she was well.

Leaning over the bed, Lonnie whispered, "Darling? Are you up to visiting with Petunia?"

Teresa turned over, and Petunia dug her fingernails into the palm of her hands. She was not prepared to see Teresa after all. Her face and arms had red welts everywhere like she'd fallen into a bed of chiggers.

A half smile crossed Teresa's face. "Well, if it's not the family outlaw," she said as she coughed out a laugh.

Squelching the sob that fought to get out, Petunia stood by Lonnie and threw on a smile. "Yep, that's me."

Teresa gave Petunia a sideways glance before her lips curled into a full smile. "I can't believe you stabbed that man in the eye."

Petunia shrugged before pushing her hand underneath her nose to suppress a sneeze. "Me either."

Lonnie chuckled and scrubbed Petunia's head with his knuckle. "I can believe it. You've always been a knucklehead."

"Haha." Petunia knocked Lonnie's hand away and then elbowed him in the side. "Have you had many visitors?"

"Just Daddy and Lonnie so far. They gotta wait until I'm not likely to get them sick, you know."

A sour taste like lime stuck to the roof of Petunia's mouth. "So, Oliver's been here then?"

Teresa nodded. "Yes, Daddy has been here. He just left an hour or so ago. Why you calling him Oliver now?"

"Didn't you hear Lonnie say I'm a knucklehead?"

"He's not wrong." Teresa stared into Petunia's eyes but spoke to Lonnie. "Lonnie, can I talk to my sister alone?"

He tapped his fingers on his thigh, almost like he had a song playing in his head. "Sure thing. I'll be outside if you need me."

"Go on down to the dining room and get something to eat." Teresa watched Lonnie leave the room before turning to Petunia. "First of all, I'm so sorry about Verlon."

Petunia scooted the only chair in the room next to Teresa's bed. "I appreciate that."

Teresa motioned for Petunia's hand and then pulled her close. "I'm dying, Petunia."

Petunia shook her head. "No, you're not."

"Yes, I am. It's getting harder and harder to breathe every day."

Petunia's insides fell to the ground. Like the one time she rode a roller coaster at the amusement park with Verlon. "You just have the measles. You'll be fine."

"A person knows when they're dying." She blinked a few times and then set her lips into a firm line. "And I need you to promise me you'll marry Lonnie after I'm gone. I talked to Daddy about it when he was here."

Petunia gasped, and both hands flew up to cover her gaping mouth. Now she understood what Oliver was yelling about.

Chapter 33

"Mommy!" Martin yelled from the other end of the phone.

Gail stood to Petunia's right with her hands on her hips, watching Petunia like a hawk. She hated using Gail's phone, but theirs was the closest one.

Petunia held her nose together tightly. There's no way she wanted Martin to hear her cry. "Hi, my darling. Mommy misses you."

Hazel took the phone, laughing. "Oh, Petunia, he's done ran off to get his tractor."

Squeezing her nose even tighter, Petunia swallowed down the tears. "Oh, okay. How are they doing?"

"Just fine. They do miss their mommy, though."

"I miss them too. I miss all y'all."

"We can book the hotel any day now. Ralph's putting his assistant in charge of the hotel while he's away."

"That's why I'm calling, Hazel. Teresa has the measles something bad, and I don't want the boys anywhere near here until she's well."

"Oh, no. I'm sorry, but you're right about keeping the boys away. A young girl from the next town over recently died from the measles. Is Teresa going to be okay?"

The thought caused Petunia's head to pound like it was getting hit by a hammer. "I don't know the answer to that. She's got pneumonia and told me she's dying."

"Can we do anything for you?"

"Y'all are already doing it by keeping the boys away from this mess. I sure do appreciate it." Petunia rubbed the side of her head where the hammer kept hitting and cringed. "I want the boys here with me, Hazel. So bad I can hardly stand it."

"I know you do, honey. We love you and promise to bring them as soon as it's safe for them to be there."

"I love y'all. Will you please kiss the boys for me and not let them forget me?"

"I sure will. Don't you worry."

"Gail wants to talk to you before we hang up."

"All right, put her on."

As soon as Petunia made it outside of Gail's, she melted to the ground, and the tears came.

A few minutes later, Gail strolled outside and towered over Petunia. "You seem to mess up everything you touch."

Petunia's mouth fell open as her scalp blazed with fire. "What do you mean by that?"

Gail looked down her nose at Petunia. "You married my sweet nephew against my wishes and look what happened to him. He's dead. You come home and left your boys behind and now look what's happened. Teresa's near death, and your mama's a cripple."

Springing to her feet, Petunia met Gail's gaze. "This ain't my fault."

A rooster came at Gail, and she kicked him out of the way. Squawking, he spread his wings and came back at her. Gail kicked at him again. Petunia couldn't stop the laugh that escaped.

Gail's eyes widened, and she glowered at Petunia. "How dare you laugh at me, you piece of trash."

Petunia's nostrils flared, and she stepped closer to Gail. "You call me trash? I'm not the one who messes around with married men."

Gail raised her eyebrows. "I don't know what in the world you're talking about. You making up stories now?"

The only thing keeping her anger down happened to be coming at Gail again. No telling what she'd done to the poor rooster to make him dislike her so much.

Petunia spoke through gritted teeth. "I heard Mama and Daddy arguing a few years ago. Mama accused Daddy of cheating on her with you. So, who's the trash?"

Gail's jaw worked overtime, twitching like a dying bug. "There ain't never been nothing between me and your daddy. Quit spreading lies."

The rooster changed its target to Petunia. She kicked its backside, and it hightailed it to the backyard.

She took a deep breath but couldn't keep the hateful tone from slipping out. "I ain't spreading nothing. Just telling you what I heard."

Gail's neck flushed, and she waved her hands. "Get on out of here. Eddie may look at you as his niece, but I sure don't."

Petunia balled her fists but kept them firmly pressed to her side. If this woman wasn't Verlon's aunt, she'd stomp a mudhole in her backside and walk it dry. "I don't look at you as my aunt, either. You see me as trash? I see you as a low-down, lying, cheating piece of dirt."

Gail backed away from Petunia and ran into the house. But not before Petunia saw the tears flowing down her cheeks.

Chapter 34

The small nurse's station in the ICU was almost empty for once. Petunia laid her leather bag on the counter and waved at her favorite nurse, Jennifer Higgins. She always had a smile on her face, which was a nice change from the other nurse Petunia had met, who must spend her time practicing mean faces in the mirror.

Jennifer kept her flaxen hair in a tight bun, but it didn't take away from her delicate features. Even so, she carried herself with an air of authority that could've been intimidating if not for her friendly demeanor.

Jennifer closed the filing cabinet and walked over to Petunia. "Hey there, Petunia."

"Good morning, Jennifer." Petunia's eyes darted in the direction of Teresa's room. "How's she doing today?"

Jennifer's face remained neutral as she spoke. She tugged on the stethoscope that hung around her neck. "She's awake, but the medicine has been working overtime. You better get in there and see her before she goes back out."

"Okay." Petunia would love to be able to see through the curtain over the window. "Is Lonnie in there?"

"He left a few minutes ago to get some breakfast." The desk phone rang, and Jennifer picked the receiver up, politely asking the caller on the other end to hold. "You must've missed him in the elevator."

Petunia nodded her thanks and padded into Teresa's room. Monitors beeping made Petunia's head slightly pulsate, but she ignored the feeling.

The medicine must not have kicked in yet. Teresa lay in bed wringing her hands.

Teresa eyeballed her. "I've been waiting for you."

Petunia smiled and moved a piece of Teresa's hair out of her face. "Well, here I am."

Teresa took a raspy breath and clutched the sheet close to her chest. "Please tell me you've thought about marrying Lonnie."

Blowing out a breath, Petunia stared into Teresa's eyes. "Come on, now let's not get into that again."

Closing her eyes, Teresa lay still for a few seconds before her eyes blinked open. "I'm begging you, Petunia. I know you had a crush on him when you were little. Please, for me, marry him after I'm gone."

Petunia cocked her head and brought her shoulders up. "I was a lot younger, then. And who's to say Lonnie will want to marry me?"

A glimmer of hope crossed Teresa's features. "I've told him that's my wish. You and him marrying and raising Jonathan with your boys."

Petunia's face sagged. "Why are you doing this to me? I can't bear you talking about your death like…."

Desperation like Petunia had never encountered replaced the previous glimmer of hope on Teresa's face. "Can't you see? I can't change my outcome, but I can do something to make sure my son and husband are loved and taken care of."

A sob escaped Petunia's lips, and she stuttered. "I'm not the same person, Teresa. They may be better off without me. Everything I touch turns to mud."

The hope returned, and Teresa offered a small smile before she grimaced. "You ain't no bad person, Petunia. I trust you with my family."

The room seemed to spin around Petunia as she took in what Teresa asked. The thought of living with a man other than Verlon made her stomach clench in knots.

Teresa broke into a coughing fit, and Petunia gave her water. Jennifer marched into the room and checked Teresa's temperature. She pressed her lips together before leaving.

Petunia waited until Jennifer was out of earshot. "Can I think about it some more?"

"I don't have much time for that, Petunia. Will you tell Mama and Daddy I love 'em?"

Goosebumps prickled across Petunia's skin. She rubbed her hands down her arms and nodded. "You know I will. What about Evelyn and Lloyd?"

"Yes, please tell them, too. Just make sure Mama knows I understand why she ain't been to the hospital."

A surge of hurt welled up inside Petunia. Hurt, she had to hide from Teresa. "I'll do that."

Teresa scratched the side of her face. "Promise me you'll marry Lonnie. I need to hear the words, sister."

Petunia's internal organs turned to lava as she stared at Teresa. The pure love she had for Lonnie and Jonathan was apparent to Petunia. And who was she to let her down? Plus, what if Teresa lived? Then she wouldn't be marrying nobody.

Petunia straightened her back and made a promise she wished she didn't have to make. But for once in her life, she'd do something for somebody else, even if it meant her own unhappiness.

"I promise I'll take care of your boy." Petunia twirled her finger around the sheet at the foot of

Teresa's bed. Teresa looked at Petunia, expecting more. Petunia sighed. "And I'll offer to marry Lonnie."

Teresa's lower lip trembled as she nodded. "Thank you, sister. Now I can die in peace."

Teresa's last words echoed in Petunia's ears the entire way back to Lloyd's and kept her awake most of the night.

Chapter 35

In the end, Teresa had been right. The night Petunia made the promise, Teresa passed in her sleep. Why did she have to go after telling Petunia she could die in peace?

Would Teresa still be alive if Petunia hadn't made that promise? Could it somehow be Petunia's fault? She stared at the wooden coffin as Brother Otis stood beside it, allowing herself a moment of blame. Guilt was easier to deal with than loss.

Brother Otis cleared his throat and held his Bible close to his chest. "Today, we come to mourn the passing of our sister, Teresa Anne Richey."

His eyes dropped to the podium. "Teresa passed from this life Monday, June 9, 1952, at the Searcy Hospital. Teresa is survived by her husband, Lonnie Richey, and their son, Jonathan, father and mother, Oliver and Dorothy Hollings, sister Evelyn and her husband, James Hill, sister Petunia Marshall, brother Lloyd, and his wife, MaryAnne. Along with a host of friends and other family members. Teresa was greatly loved and will be missed by all who knew her."

"Will you bow with me for a word of prayer?" He bowed. "Our most righteous Father and God in heaven, we come to You with heavy hearts. On behalf of the family of Teresa Richey, we pray You would be with them in their time of loss. That You would be with them and mend their broken hearts, be with them in their trials and tribulations. For this is our prayer in Christ's name, Amen."

Otis wiped his forehead with a white handkerchief and let his eyes rest on their family. "Good people, I feel so inept as a gospel preacher at times like this. I wish I could take away your sorrow and the emptiness you feel and dry the tears from your cheeks, but I can't. This is not within my power. But know if I could, I certainly would. At a time such as this, the only true comfort we can find is in the word of God. So please, allow me this moment to read from that Word."

Otis flipped through his Bible. "Turn with me to John 14: 1-6."

"Let not your heart be troubled; you believe in God, believe also in Me. In My Father's house are many mansions; if it were not so, I would have told you. I go to

prepare a place for you. And if I go and prepare a place for you, I will come again and receive you to Myself; that where I am, there you may be also. And where I go you know, and the way you know."

Petunia's sight traveled behind Brother Otis and settled on the casket. The purple, yellow, and white spray of flowers Petunia had ordered seemed to accuse Petunia of doing something wrong by the way they flapped in the wind. Tears fogged her eyes, and her line of sight fell to her hands.

Brother Otis paused and took a breath. "Teresa would tell us time is precious, redeem the time God has so graciously given us. She would urge you to serve God with all your heart, mind, and soul."

"Would you bow with me for a word of closing prayer? Father, we ask that You comfort this family as only You can and teach us to look unto Thee for strength, counsel, wisdom, and understanding. Be with each one here today. Help us to understand that eternity is before us all and that without You, we are not complete and whole. Be with every family member, loved one, and friend, and heal their broken hearts. Help us, dear Father, to help the family in any way that we can and help us to walk the lives of men in such a way that we can be with You and Your Son and all the redeemed of all the ages in that beautiful place called heaven. For this is our prayer in Christ's name, Amen."

After the funeral, the town baker, Jacob Liverton, slid up to Petunia. "Howdy, gal. I hear you done run into a bundle of money."

Casting a dumbfounded expression on him, Petunia's voice came out sharp. "Do you really think this is the time to bring that up?"

He raised his hands and backed away. "No, you're right. Please accept my apology. I was just making small talk. I'm sorry, Petunia. Forgive me."

Petunia nodded. "I forgive you." Mama leaned into her hands, sobbing. Petunia's heart ached for her. "I think Mama needs my help."

Mama had come in a wheelchair she borrowed from Uncle Eddie and his wife. Petunia still couldn't bring herself to think of her as Aunt Gail.

Oliver left off talking to the preacher and put his hand on the back of Mama's wheelchair. Regret for telling Jacob Liverton she needed her slammed into her chest. She hadn't spoken to Oliver since Lloyd's wedding. Well, may as well get it over with.

Once she reached them, Petunia leaned close to Mama. "How you doing? Can I do anything for you?"

She looked at Petunia with puffy, red eyes. "No, child. I'm as good as I can be under these terrible circumstances."

"I can take care of yer mama." Oliver spat.

"Whatever you say." Petunia stared at them with glossy eyes. "I'm gonna speak to brother Otis."

Petunia took a bill from her wallet and placed it in Otis's hand. "Thank you for those kind words about Teresa, brother Otis. We appreciate you."

Otis glanced at the money, and his eyes grew round. He tried to hand the bill back to Petunia. "I can't take this money, Petunia. I did this funeral because I'm the preacher and loved Teresa, too."

Petunia folded her arms over her chest. "I'm not taking that money back. I want you to have it. Please."

He faltered but nodded. "I thank you, Petunia. So much."

A few minutes later, Lloyd loaded Mama in his truck before staring at the fresh mound of dirt.

Oliver slinked up beside her. "What you over here doing? Trying to figure out a way to hurt somebody else?"

Fire sliced through Petunia's insides. "Leave me alone, Oliver."

"It's Oliver now, is it? That's fine by me. I knowed I only had two daughters, and now I'm down to one."

She turned to leave as heat sizzled up her neck, but his voice followed her. "The way I see it, it shoulda been you put in that cold ground instead of Teresa. We'd all be better off."

He spit a stream of tobacco onto the ground and walked off. Turmoil swirled inside as Oliver marched up to Lloyd's truck. He pointed at Petunia before hopping in the back. Lloyd waved as they drove away. No telling what the liar said to Lloyd.

Now that she was alone, Petunia doubled over and sank to the dirt as her stomach twisted into a thousand knots.

Oliver wished she was the one that died. Hateful words from a nasty man. She shouldn't have expected anything else. He'd always been like that.

She scooped up a handful of dirt and let it slide down her arm. Her face went slack as a sudden bark of laughter exploded from her. Her stern stare penetrated the loose dirt as an ache filled Petunia's heart.

A whisper escaped her lips as she spoke aloud. "Me, too, Oliver. Me, too."

Chapter 36

The following week, Lloyd parked his truck at the back of the two-story Civil War home and turned to Petunia. "You sure you wanna look at this house?"

She grinned and grabbed the door handle. "This is exactly what I want to do. I want this house no matter what it takes. Come on, Lloyd."

Her realtor, Woodruff Blevins, greeted them and ushered them inside. Even though he had an easy job, Woodruff had the look of a man who worked hard. The wrinkles that lined his eyes and lips told Petunia he smiled a lot, so he must be happy with his life.

A rush of nerves tingled her stomach as she walked around the massive home.

Could a home like this really be hers? She couldn't believe it, but this could be where she raised the boys. The Mahogany staircase alone had to be worth a fortune. Not to mention the furniture it came with.

Mr. Blevins glanced at Lloyd and smiled. "I hear your lovely wife's expecting. Congratulations."

A grin split Lloyd's face. "Thank you, Mr. Blevins. We're sure excited."

Petunia rubbed her hand down her skirt and nodded at Lloyd.

Lloyd turned to the realtor and held his hand out. "She'll take it. What does she need to do to get moved in?"

The look on his face caused Petunia to laugh. "What's wrong, Mr. Blevins? Were you not expecting me to buy the home? We'd be neighbors. You do live next door, don't ya?"

His already red face turned a shade redder, and he stuttered. "Well, yes, but I, um didn't think you'd want the biggest house in town, Mrs. Marshall."

Lloyd clapped the realtor on the back. "Looks like she does. Let's get it going so she can bring her boys home. The sooner she can move in, the better."

Mr. Blevins tilted his head and frowned. "I only showed you because you requested to see it. Are you, um, sure you wouldn't like to see the nice three-bedroom home a few streets away? I don't want you to get in over your head."

Petunia peeked out the curtain and grinned. "Don't you worry about that. This home will do just fine. I think Mrs. Mink would've wanted me to have it."

Lloyd spoke up. "We'll have the lawyer contact you next week to get everything in order."

Mr. Blevins rubbed his forehead, and then a smile lit his face. Almost like he'd just realized he would be making a bunch of commission off the sale. "Yes, sir, I'll be happy to help."

A few days later, Petunia twirled around her living room and sprawled on the sofa. This really was happening. She had a home she'd often walked by in awe of as a girl.

Thankfully, the current owners let her move in before the closing date since she was paying cash for the house and furnishings. The attorney Uncle Eddie recommended had taken good care of her and kept things private and confidential.

She placed a few wedding pictures and one of her and the boys on the fireplace and smiled. Soon, they'd be home. Ralph and Hazel had booked a plane for Saturday.

Now, to move Mama in and live up to the promise she'd made Teresa. A knock on the door filled Petunia with dread. It had to be Lonnie.

She opened the heavy door and waved for him to come in. He'd have to marry her after seeing what kind of home he'd have as her husband.

Even so, her stomach churned, trying to find the right words. "Hi, Lonnie. How are you doing?"

"Not the best. But I have to keep going for Jonathan's sake." He looked around and let out a low whistle. "Look at you, Petunia. You've done really well for yourself. Verlon and Teresa would both be proud."

The lines of her throat tightened when Lonnie mentioned Verlon. But she had to live up to her promise. "Do you like the house?"

He gave a lopsided grin. The one that had always melted her heart as a kid. "Who wouldn't? It's a beautiful home."

Too bad that smile didn't even cause her heart to twitch these days. If it did, that would make what she had to do so much easier. "I need to talk to you about something."

He leaned against the wall by the fireplace and cocked his head. "What's that?"

She rubbed her hair with shaking hands. Why'd she have to go and make that promise? "Teresa and I talked, and I'd like you to move in here with me."

His eyes widened as he walked toward the front door. "Oh no, I don't think that would be appropriate, Petunia."

"Wait, that didn't come out right." Petunia's head seemed to be full of fog. "I'd like you to be my husband."

He stopped in his tracks. "No. I can't even think about something like that right now. Teresa hasn't even been gone a month."

"Why? We've both lost the love of our lives, so why not?" She had to swallow down the sour anger threatening to overflow. "We could try to help one another."

Lonnie's eyes darkened, and he stared hard at Petunia before speaking. "I guess you bought into what Teresa tried to do, huh? Did she make you promise to marry me?"

Petunia scratched the back of her neck. "We'll, yeah, she did. But it's okay. I'll do it."

"Well, I won't. Petunia, you had no right to make such a promise." He punched the air before gripping the front door. "None."

She folded her arms and spoke through gritted teeth. "Are you mad?"

He laid his head against the door. "I'm disappointed. We're not getting married. I'm mourning the loss of my wife, and I bet you're still mourning the loss of your husband."

She squeezed her eyes shut to keep the tears at bay. "Don't you think we could help each other deal with that loss?"

"I don't love you like that. I love you as my little sister." He stomped through the front door and turned to meet her wide-eyed gaze. "Please don't bring this up again. It's too painful."

Somehow, Lonnie managed to slam the heavy door behind him. Leaving Petunia standing in the middle of the room with her mouth gaping.

So much for her happy mood.

Chapter 37

Petunia kicked the back door of the small barn behind the house closed. She scanned the place for a hammer or knife. Anything to cause some damage. Nothing.

She really must be ugly. Undesirable. Maybe even disgusting. Unlovable. Who'd want someone who had a daddy that didn't even want them?

Nobody, that's who.

Who had lost her husband because he joined the military? Maybe he did it just to get away from her. That had to be it. It was her fault.

She spun around and slammed her fist into the side of the building. Pain shot down her hand, traveling to her arm. Pain that made her stop thinking about the life she should've had with Verlon. She slammed it again. And again.

Blood trickled in between her fingers as she continued to pummel the side of the building. It got to the point it hurt so bad it felt good.

She slammed the building again and let out a hysterical laugh. Someone walked up behind Petunia, and she swung at them. She missed as she opened her eyes.

Her old friends Opal and Clyde Brown stood there. Opal's hands flew to her hips. "Oh, my goodness, what you trying to do to yourself?"

"I don't know." Petunia's words came out slurred. A throb settled in the crook of Petunia's arm. At least a numbness covered her hand.

Opal let out a humph right before recognition flashed across her face. "Petunia? I thought that was you, but I wasn't sure when I saw them fancy duds you got on."

"Yep, it's me." Petunia stared at her hand with wide eyes. What made her do that?

Opal raised her arms for a second and then let them drop to her sides, almost like she wanted to hug Petunia but thought better of it. "What you doing in this person's backyard? Have you been drinking?"

Petunia shook her head. She'd have no problem hugging Opal if only she could move her arm. But right now, it wouldn't cooperate. "You mean my backyard? And of course not, I'm just in pain."

Opal cocked her head and looked at Clyde with wide eyes. "If you say so. Do you work here? Do you think we can use the washroom to see to your hand?"

Petunia's stomach pitched, and bacon and eggs from breakfast threatened to come up. She breathed in and swallowed. "What are y'all doing here?"

Clyde tugged on his earlobe and met Opal's gaze. "We lost Mama and Daddy and was told there was work here in Des Arc."

Petunia pointed at the back door. "Follow me." She made it two steps before collapsing in Clyde's arms.

Clyde's voice shook when he spoke. "Opal, I sure hope nobody sees me holding this white woman. I don't want no trouble."

The apparent fear in Clyde's deep voice caused Petunia to stir. She hopped out of his arms and held on to Opal to steady herself. "It's fine. Let's get inside."

"Are you sure about this?" Opal's eyes bounced around the yard before landing on Petunia.

Still muddled by the pain, Petunia tripped over the first step. "Just help me up these steps."

Glancing around the yard, Opal nodded. "All right, but I hope we don't get in no trouble for this."

Petunia attempted to squeeze Opal's arm. "I'd never do anything to get you in trouble. I promise."

Once inside, Petunia stepped into the kitchen and wrapped her hand in a towel. She made her way to the fireplace and motioned for Opal to join her. Picking up one of the pictures, she showed it to Opal. "See this picture? It's one of my wedding photos. And this other one is me and my two boys, Martin and William. This is my house, Opal."

Opal scanned the room before meeting Petunia's gaze. "But how in the world you done managed this?"

"It's a long story. If I can get you to help make some coffee and bandage my hand better, I'll be happy to tell you all about it."

Chapter 38

Watching Mama's face intently was all Petunia wanted to do as she gave her a tour of the downstairs. She pushed the new wheelchair to the bedroom she'd picked out for Mama, careful not to push too hard with her injured hand.

"Mama, do you think you'd want to live here with the boys and me?"

Moisture pooled in Mama's eyes. "Do I think I'd want to live here? Petunia, I never thought I'd have a place like this."

No matter how hard she tried, Petunia couldn't keep the grin from splitting her face. "This is the room I picked out for you."

Mama looked over her shoulder at Petunia. Her mouth moved a few seconds before words came out. "Say what?"

A childlike joy seemed to permeate Petunia's heart. "See the cream wallpaper? It has little navy flowers and matches the comforter. I thought you'd like the colors."

"Wheel me to the bed, child." Once by the bed, she ran her wrinkled hand across the fabric. "This is too nice for the likes of me."

Petunia dropped to her knees and grasped her hands. "Mama, nothing's too nice for you. I ain't never met a kinder soul than you. You deserve the world. I can't give that to you, but I can give you a home."

She gripped Petunia's hand. "You can't care for me and the boys. I'm gonna need a lot of help for a while."

Petunia rested an elbow on Mama's wheelchair. "Remember my friend Opal Brown?"

Mama's head moved up and down. "I sure do."

Contentment was within her grasp. She could help Mama, after all. If only Verlon could be here, but Petunia couldn't perform miracles. If she could, he'd be here with her and the boys. "I've asked her to move in with us, and her brother Clyde's gonna turn the barn into living quarters that he'll stay in."

Mama cut her eyes at Petunia. "You don't say? When did they get back in town?"

"They lost Mrs. Brown a couple of years ago, and Mr. Brown passed away last week. Now they don't have nowhere to go. They're gonna be working for me."

Mama's shoulders hunched over, and there was something of a sadness in her smile. "Them was good people. This world has no idea we lost some of the best when they passed."

Petunia nodded and planted a kiss on Mama's cheek. "I hope I have a heart like yours when I'm older."

As she drummed her fingers on her leg, Mama raised a brow. "You already do, child. Look what you doing for Opal and Clyde. That Verlon musta left you a fortune."

Petunia raised up and walked over to the window, working the pins and needles out of her leg. She pulled the curtain back. "I'm gonna make him proud by making sure our boys have something, Mama. I want to open up a business."

"What kind of business?"

Bouncing on her toes, Petunia let the curtain drop. "I want to open up a bakery. Make breakfast cakes and breads to start off before turning it into something big. I got plans."

Mama wheeled close to Petunia and cleared her throat. "What about your daddy?"

Petunia bristled but somehow managed to keep a straight face when she answered. "He's welcome out back with Clyde."

Mama stared at Petunia so long she almost had a trickle of shame invade her resentment. Almost. "Child, you need to make peace with that man. He ain't gettin' any younger, you know."

The breath in Petunia's lungs swirled around like a whirlwind as she sat on the side of the bed. "I need to ask you something, and I want you to be absolutely honest with me."

She narrowed her eyes, and the look in her eyes told Petunia she would be open to the one question Petunia longed to ask. "Go on, child."

It's now or never. Perspiration covered Petunia's armpits as she flung out her question. "Who's my real daddy?"

Seconds that seemed like minutes ticked by as she stared out the bedroom window. Petunia followed her gaze to find a dog dragging its leg as it tried to walk.

She guessed Mama's silence was the only answer she needed. She didn't belong to Oliver. "I think that dog needs help, Mama. I'm gonna go check on it."

"Okay. Be careful that it ain't rabid."

Even under the circumstances, the audible relief in Mama's tone didn't escape Petunia's attention.

Wary, Petunia looked back at Mama as she stepped out the door. "I'll be careful."

"Petunia." Mama barked the one word out.

Her heart jittered as she stood in the doorway. "Yes?"

Squaring her shoulders, Mama met Petunia's anxious eyes. "You're a Hollings through and through. Oliver's blood runs through your veins just as well as the rest. I ain't never cheated on that man. Even when I had a reason."

Squeezing her eyes shut, Petunia nodded her acceptance. Guess she needed to start thinking of the man as her daddy again.

Nah. He'd have to earn that title.

Chapter 39

Attending church service in town had always seemed unrealistic to Petunia. That's where the people she always thought were "somebody" attended. Her stomach quivered as she made her way through the double doors after service.

Even in her new Percale floral print dress, people probably thought she wasn't good enough to be there. And maybe they were right. Would she ever be good enough? Daddy would never think so. So why bother trying? It was time to forget about what that man thought. Once and for all.

The hot August sun beat down on her face, and she regretted wearing the jacket over the dress. She'd only done it because it was stylish. Stupid girl. One of these days, she'd learn to stop caring about what people thought.

Straightening her spine, she took a breath and smiled at one of the ladies passing her by. The woman smiled back, and a weight lifted from Petunia's shoulders.

She glanced at her in-laws with a grateful heart. She would've never gathered the courage to attend here if they hadn't been with her. Ralph carried William while Martin held Hazel's finger as he walked beside her.

After the service, a few people gathered around Mayor George Tomlinson and his wife, Cornela. Sheriff Keach waved Petunia over, so she fell back to say hello. The sheriff, with his movie star looks and smile that, never quite reached his eyes.

There Petunia went, judging people again. She didn't want people to judge her, right? So, why'd she always have something to say about other folks? Sheriff Keach could be the nicest person ever if she gave him the chance.

The preacher called for Sheriff Keach to come over, so Petunia made her way back to Ralph and Hazel. Cornela Tomlinson looked down her nose at Petunia as she walked by.

Cornela loudly whispered to the group of people she stood with. "I think it's funny how some people think a little bit of money makes them somebody, don't you?"

A woman Petunia recognized as the banker's wife glanced at Petunia and snickered. "Yes, it is rather amusing."

Ralph turned to Petunia and almost yelled. "Petunia, you should tell Mr. Mayor's wife about meeting John Wayne." He tapped his chin before shaking his head. "On second thought, don't waste your time."

Petunia clamped her hand over her mouth to keep from giggling at how Ralph stepped past the mayor and the group of snobs like he owned the place. The laugh that escaped when the mayor's wife got all red-faced couldn't have been stopped by a court order.

As Ralph pulled out of the parking lot, Hazel squeezed his hand. "Thank you for taking up for Petunia like that."

"I couldn't stand by without doing something. And before you get onto me, Petunia has met a man named John Wayne."

Hazel rolled her window down a notch. "I know, your cousin John Wayne Marshall."

Petunia hugged Ralph from behind. "I'll never get over the look on her face. Now I know why Mama wants to keep going to our old church once she's feeling well enough to get out."

Martin bounced up and down in the back seat. "I'm hungry."

Petunia smiled at her son. "Me, too, son. Opal put on a roast for lunch before she left this morning."

"I like Opal and her brother. They seem like good folk." Hazel commented.

Petunia tinkered with the window handle. "We were good friends growing up."

Ralph slowed down before turning into Petunia's driveway. "I'm thankful you have someone here to help you."

Her stomach clenched, and she leaned over the back seat. "I sure do wish y'all would move."

Hazel dipped her head. "Maybe we'll do just that when Ralph retires."

"You never know." Ralph turned the ignition off and glanced at Petunia. "What did that sheriff want?"

Hazel cut her eyes at Ralph. "I think he wanted to flirt with Petunia."

An ache rang deep in Petunia's bones, and she raised her eyebrows. "I don't think so. He knows I'm married."

Ralph and Hazel looked at one another before Ralph hopped out and got the boys out of the back seat.

Hazel placed her hand over Petunias. "Sweetheart, Verlon's been gone over a year now. He would want you to be happy."

Petunia scurried out of the back seat without saying a word.

Hazel jumped out of the front seat and yelled out. "Petunia! Don't be mad at me. I'm just trying to help."

Petunia swirled around. "I'm not mad. I just don't wanna talk about it, Hazel. I can't think of that right now."

"Fair enough." Hazel picked up her speed. "We better get in the house before the boys eat all that roast up!"

As Petunia turned back toward the house, she almost ran into Lonnie.

He took off his cap and squeezed it in his hand. "Petunia, we need to talk."

A hard cough fell from Petunia as a sheen of sweat broke across her brow.

Chapter 40

After the coughing fit was over, Petunia's heart hit her stomach like a bag of rocks. Could he have changed his mind about marrying her? If he did, how would she ever explain that to Hazel after what she just said about Verlon?

She glanced at Hazel and then nodded in Lonnie's direction. "What is it, Lonnie?"

His eyes darted from Hazel back to Petunia, and he took his baseball cap off. "Can we talk by ourselves?"

Hazel raised her left eyebrow and paused like she wanted to object. In the end, she walked toward the door. "I'll be right inside if you need me."

Petunia leaned against the side of the house. "Okay, we're by ourselves. What do you have to say to me?"

He looked at the ground as his thumb ran back and forth over the cap bill. "I'm just gonna say it."

A couple of cats flew past Petunia, and Lonnie anchored his gaze on them until they were out of sight.

Tapping her foot, Petunia threw her hands up. "Well? Go on already. Say whatever you need to."

He briefly met her curious yet impatient gaze before shifting his eyes to something behind her. "I asked Mildred Campbell to be my wife."

She flew off the side of the house, nearly shrieking. "You did what?"

He raised his voice to match Petunia's. "Jonathan needs a mama. Surely you understand."

She took a faltering step closer to Lonnie, putting on the brakes before she reached him. "Surely I understand?"

"Don't tell me you're still thinking about what you promised Teresa?" He rubbed his brow before bringing red-rimmed eyes to meet hers. "I think of you as my sister, Petunia. Love you like you are."

The door swung open, and Ralph stuck his head out. "Everything all right out here?"

The cackle that left Petunia's lips sounded bitter even to her ears. "Everything's just swell, Ralph. Teresa ain't even cold in the ground, but Lonnie here's done snagged his self another bride."

A red stain splotched down Lonnie's neck. "Now you hold on a minute, that there ain't fair, Petunia, and you know it."

Her pulse thumped in her neck as she jerked the back door open. Pausing, she narrowed her eyes at Lonnie. "I don't know nothing of the sort."

Sheriff Keach pulled into the driveway and rolled his window down. "Howdy, folks."

Petunia turned around and plastered on the most believable smile she could muster. Which probably made her look like a nut. Rejected by Lonnie again. Between Oliver and Lonnie, she must've set the record for the most rejections by one person.

"Sheriff." Lonnie nodded and then stomped to his truck. He stopped and turned toward Petunia before getting in. "I'll make sure you get invited to the wedding. For Jonathan."

Ralph reached the Sheriff's car and stuck his hand out. "Didn't we just see you?"

The sheriff shook Ralph's hand and smiled at Petunia. "Yes, sir. I'm making my rounds before I try to rustle up some dinner."

"We were just about to sit down to a mighty fine pot roast." Ralph raised his eyes at Petunia.

She wanted to growl, but maybe it's better to stay on the sheriff's good side. "You're welcome to join us, Sheriff."

His eyes lit up, and he opened the car door. "You said pot roast? That's an offer of vittles I don't believe I can refuse."

Lonnie stuck his hand out his window and motioned for the Sheriff to move his car. Sheriff Keach waved as he closed the door. "Let me get out of this fella's way, and I'll be right in."

As soon as the sheriff moved, Lonnie started to back out. The sheriff blocked Lonnie's path before saying something to him through the window.

Petunia squinted her eyes, doing her best to read their lips, but couldn't make out what he said.

The sheriff backed away from the truck, and Lonnie gunned the engine, squealing tires as he slid sideways out of the driveway.

Interesting. No telling what the sheriff said. But it sure made Lonnie mad.

For some reason, getting to know the sheriff sounded much better than it had earlier.

Chapter 41

Verlon walked through the front door and picked Petunia up. She squealed and wrapped her arms around his neck. She kissed his face over and over until there was nothing there. He'd disappeared and left Petunia alone yet again. Trying to focus on sleep, she breathed in and out. Praying she could catch at least one more glimpse of Verlon. She wouldn't even try to touch him if only she could hear his voice.

Wiping her nose on her gown sleeve wasn't the proper thing to do, but she couldn't help it. She just wanted her husband.

That afternoon found Petunia working to get her mind off Verlon. Rays of sun shone across Petunia's face as she pulled patches of weeds from the flower bed in front of her house. She needed physical labor to get her head on straight. On top of being a widow and losing her sister, too much had happened since she'd moved back to Arkansas. So much so that she couldn't get a grip on it.

Reflecting on the last week's events caused a scowl to cross her features. What could Mildred have that she didn't? Beauty? Grace? What was it?

Lonnie claimed to love her like a sister. Hogwash. That couldn't be it. He just didn't want to be with her. He didn't want her before he married Teresa, so why would he want her now? Maybe he was embarrassed by her.

Some of the weeds had deep roots, causing Petunia to wince when she met resistance. Grabbing the shears from the bucket, she whacked the weeds as close to the ground as possible.

William and Martin shrieked and ran across the yard, with Lloyd teetering along behind them, yelling something about cops and robbers.

Petunia wiped her forehead and grinned as she watched the boys having fun. "Y'all better run before Uncle Lloyd gets ya!"

"We won't let him get us, Mama!" Martin announced as he stepped out of Lloyd's reach.

Would marrying Lonnie really make Petunia happy? Not at all. A brick may as well have hit Petunia in the head as the thought struck her. Marrying that man was the last thing she wanted to do. The idea wouldn't have ever crossed her mind if she hadn't promised Teresa.

And she'd done her part to live up to that promise. Who was she to try to force herself on Lonnie? As far as she was concerned, that promise to Teresa was no longer possible. Lonnie could marry Mildred and live happily ever after.

Petunia would focus on opening a bakery and raising the boys. Or maybe just raising the boys. Thanks to Verlon and his Aunt Helen, she had enough money to live the rest of her life and then some.

Sheriff Keach cruised by going really slow. He threw his arm out the window and waved. She waved back and turned back to her weeding. What was that man up to? Was he interested in her like Hazel thought?

Now that Ralph and Hazel were back in Chicago, she had an empty space in her heart. While they visited, she'd kept busy enough that she didn't constantly think of Verlon. Of what her life should be.

The sheriff spun his car around and pulled into the drive. "Miss Marshall, I was wondering if you'd join me for dinner tonight at the fish house?"

Well, guess that answered her questions about his intentions.

Petunia cocked her head as she contemplated her answer. Dinner wasn't a marriage proposal, so what harm could it do?

She wiped her brow with her forearm. "I'm not ready to date anyone, but I would agree to go as friends, Sheriff Keach."

His lips turned up. "That sounds good. Friends, it is." His police car started moving backward but stopped. "Friends call each other by their given names. You can call me Stanley, you hear?"

Her stomach went a little queasy, and she almost backed out of going. When she opened her mouth, she found herself unable to tell him no. "All right. Um, Stanley. I'll see you tonight."

A smile bigger than the shears she'd just used to clip the weeds crossed his face, and he reminded Petunia of a fairer Ricky Ricardo from I Love Lucy. "I'll pick you up at seven." With that, he backed out of the driveway.

Petunia went back to cleaning up her flower garden, trying to decide if she'd made the best decision in agreeing to dinner. Too late to change her mind, so it didn't matter anyhow.

"Petunia!" Opal ran from the back of the house, waving her hands.

Raising herself off the ground, Petunia wiped her hands and met Opal's frantic gaze. "What's going on?"

Opal wrung her hands as tears streamed down her face. "Clyde's done got his self hurt. He needs a doctor!"

Lloyd sat up from his place on the ground, where the boys had him pinned. "What happened, Opal?"

Opal started walking around the house and motioned for them to come. When she spoke, her words came out rushed and breathless. "He said a bunch of men with sheets on their heads come in on him in the night and worked him over. He can't even get out the bed."

Petunia met Lloyd's gaze before following Opal. "Lloyd, you stay with the boys. I'll call the doctor and check on Clyde."

The door to Clyde's bedroom in the barn stood open. Petunia walked inside and found Mama sitting beside Clyde, cleaning his face. Dried blood caked beneath his left ear, and both eyes were swollen shut.

Doing her best to hold tears back, Petunia croaked out a few words. "Mama? How is he?"

Mama's voice trembled when she answered. "Someone wanted to hurt him, Petunia, and they done a good job. You better call the doctor, not that I think it'll do much good."

Petunia backed out of the barn and rushed into the house. After talking to Nurse Fleming, Petunia wanted to scream. How could a doctor be too busy to come to see about a patient?

Two hours later, after helping Opal and Mama doctor Clyde up the best she could, Petunia pulled into a parking spot at the only clinic in town. Slamming the car door didn't help her state. Her hands shook, and her stomach clenched in knots of fury like she hadn't felt in a long time.

Dr. Thompson paused in the hallway when Petunia marched through the door. He turned on his heel and headed in the other direction.

She caught up to him, grabbing his elbow. "Why did you refuse to come to my house to see about Clyde Brown?"

He shrugged her hand off his elbow. "Like Nurse Fleming said on the phone, I had more pressing patients to tend to."

Her fists clenched into tight balls, and she struggled to keep them at her side. "Like who? Where are these other patients?"

His upper lip curled, and he took a step back. "Miss Marshall, I'm unable to discuss my patients with you. Now, run along. I don't have time to waste talking to you about a colored man's medical problems."

Before she could stop, her hand snaked out and cracked the doctor across the face. She spoke through teeth she ground together as she met his shocked expression. "You oughta be ashamed of yourself, you snake."

A nurse high-stepped it down the hallway with a red face. "Ma'am. You can't put your hands on Dr. Thompson."

"Looks like I just did." Petunia narrowed her eyes before stomping out of the office.

Chapter 42

Despite the scene at the clinic, Petunia managed to get ready for dinner an hour before time. Pacing the floor did her no good. If Mama found out, she'd scold her good.

Sheriff Keach showed up at seven sharp in a pair of slacks and a white button-up shirt. He perused Petunia's blue dress and matching cap. "You look mighty fine this evening, Petunia."

A tinge of red colored her cheeks, shocking Petunia that she reacted to the compliment. "Thank you, Stanley."

A vivid image of Verlon's face clouded her vision, but she shook it off. He wouldn't mind if she had dinner with the sheriff. Or would he? Doubt inched inside Petunia. Maybe she should back out of the dinner. But that would be hateful.

The sheriff's mild voice interrupted her inner argument. "I sure hate to bring this up, but Dr. Thompson stopped by my office."

Petunia chuckled and shrugged. "I bet he did."

He sucked on his teeth and tipped his head to the right. "He was mighty upset wanting to press charges against you, but I talked him out of it."

Petunia held her tongue. Now was not the time to be ugly about the doctor. "I appreciate you for doing that."

He pulled his shoulders back and wagged his finger. "You can't go around slapping folks, Petunia. I promised him it won't happen again."

She pursed her lips and said what the sheriff wanted to hear. "It won't. I just lost my cool."

"The good doctor seems to think you've got a soft spot for Clyde." He rubbed his jaw and glanced through the doorway. "The coloreds live out back, don't they? Surely you ain't living under the same roof as colored folks."

Petunia bristled. "Clyde stays out back, but I need Opal in the house to help me with Mama and the boys."

"We can talk about it more later on." His lips broke into a wide grin when Mama rolled into the room. "It's good to see you, Mrs. Hollings. I'm glad you're getting around better after that unfortunate accident."

She let out a humph and spit a string of brown spit into her snuff jar. "I ain't getting around that good.

I need to make sure you know to take Petunia to the fish house and straight back here after y'all eat."

The sheriff's smile faltered. "Well, would I not be able to take her to a picture show?"

Leaning forward in her chair, Mama shook her finger at the sheriff. "No, you will not. Fish house and home, you hear me?"

He threw his head back and laughed. "Yes, ma'am, boss lady. I'll bring her straight home after eating."

Petunia breathed a sigh of relief Mama hadn't heard about her slapping the doctor.

They arrived at the restaurant a few minutes before it got busy, so they were seated right away. Crispy fish fried in cornmeal batter permeated the air, accompanied by hints of ketchup and onion.

Petunia sucked her stomach in when a slight growl settled in her belly. How embarrassing. The waitress lumbered over to their table and sat a plate of fish, a plate of hushpuppies, and fries in the middle of the table.

Blonde curls stuck to her head like she'd been dunked in a horse trough. She waved a hand in the air and looked at them with no trace of a smile. "All we serve is fish and the fixings. What'll you have to drink? We got fresh sweet tea or water."

They ordered sweet tea before putting fish on their plates. Stanley dug in without offering to say a prayer, so she said her own.

The night seemed to be going well. Stanley's company wasn't terrible, and they made small talk about nothing of great importance.

At least until Judith Cooper walked into the restaurant like she owned it. Not far behind came her rat of a daddy, Cyrus, and his son, Trevor. They looked so similar with their long beards that they could be mistaken for brothers. Petunia met Judith's scowl from across the room before dropping her gaze to her plate.

Oh no. Why did she have to be here the one night Petunia was?

Judith made her way to their table and landed eyes of fury on Stanley and then Petunia. "What are you doing here with this woman?"

Stanley swallowed his bite of food and turned to Judith. "We're on a proper date, Judith."

Judith bared her teeth at Petunia. Her words came out slow and hard. "Stanley is my man. Not yours, you low-down colored lover."

Stanley wiped his mouth and threw his napkin on the table. "Listen here, Judith. We only went out a few times. Now, I'm courting Petunia. And just because she has colored folks working for her don't mean she likes 'em."

Petunia's fingers clutched her napkin, and her voice raised high enough that people in the restaurant stopped eating. "We are not on a date. We're here as friends. Remember?"

Judith skewered Stanley and then Petunia with a look of fury that made chills crawl over Petunia's arms. "Oh, Petunia likes 'em, you fool. Don't you know she's been best friends with her maid since they were kids?"

A flush crawled up Stanley's neck. "You're lying just to make me look bad."

Judith cackled. "I never told nobody this, but Clyde Brown put his hands on me when I was a kid, and Petunia let it happen." Her nostrils flared, and she turned to Petunia. "Ain't that right, Petunia?"

Petunia froze, struggling to find the words to call Judith a liar. But she couldn't. Clyde *had* put his hands on Judith.

Cyrus and Trevor came up behind Judith. Sweat beaded on Cyrus's forehead, and he wiped it with a napkin. His jaw clenched as he stared at Petunia. "Did you allow a colored man to hurt my girl?"

Finally, Petunia found her voice. "Clyde didn't do nothin' wrong. He only kept Judith from hurting me. She's always been a bully."

Judith's mouth screwed up into a hateful sneer. "Liar!"

Adrenaline courses through Petunia's veins, and flames licked her skin. "I ain't no liar, Judith, and you know it! You was the one in love with Clyde, but he wouldn't have you."

There wasn't a person in the restaurant not staring at the spectacle. Some of the coon dogs down the road barking broke the silence, and most folks turned back to their meals.

Without a word, Judith backed away from the table and ran from the restaurant.

The table wobbled when Cyrus Cooper leaned both hands flat and got within an inch of Petunia's face. A whisper of a tone came out when he spoke. "Liars who try to ruin a good girl's reputation don't last long in this town."

Trevor Cooper's head flapped up and down and his lips pressed into a flat line. "Just wait and see what happens."

Stanley's browns pulled together, and his mouth set into a firm line. Slowly, he stood up and threw some money on the table.

"Let's go, Petunia." Anger vibrated from his voice, and his neck had blotchy red spots that ended at his hairline.

He drove Petunia home in silence. When they pulled up at Petunia's, he opened the passenger door and walked her to the steps. "Make sure you tell your mama we didn't go no place but the fish house."

Why would he act like nothing happened?

A yawn fell from Petunia's mouth, and she wrapped her hand across her face. "I'll tell her. Thank you for dinner, Stanley. It sure was good."

He inched closer to Petunia. "I'd be much obliged if you agreed to have dinner with me again."

The entire time he inched toward Petunia, she inched closer to the door. Verlon wouldn't want her dating the sheriff. Would he?

Shouldn't they talk about what happened before deciding on another dinner?

She rubbed her thumb back and forth. "I'm sorry about what happened with Judith."

"Don't pay that no never mind." His jaw clenched, and he inched a bit closer to where Petunia stood. "Just answer my question."

A forced smile crossed her lips, and she wrapped her hand around the doorknob. "How about you let me get back to you on that?"

The sheriff moved in between Petunia and the door causing her hand to drop. "All right, but don't wait too long."

The door creaked open, and Opal stood on the other side. She grabbed her chest when she saw Petunia and the sheriff. "Goodness. Y'all scared me."

Petunia stepped around the sheriff and closer to the door. "You going somewhere, Opal?"

Opal shook her head. "Nope, your mama asked me to check to see who was on the porch. She didn't want the boys getting woke up."

Petunia let out a shaky laugh. What would cause her to get so nervous all of a sudden? Maybe the fact she could see Mama's shadow through the window. That meant she would have questions. And what would she say about what had happened at the restaurant?

She needed to say something. Didn't she?

She glanced at the sheriff and smiled as she stepped inside. "Thanks again. Have a good night."

"You, too." He thrust his arm out, lightly grasping her wrist. "Oh and, Petunia? I think Judith may be right. Looks like you're awful chummy with these colored folks. I'd suggest you treat them like hired help instead of equals. Things could get ugly if you don't."

Heat tingled up her spine, and Petunia's body tensed. "Are you threatening me, Sheriff Keach?"

A dumbfounded expression flashed across his face, and he sucked his bottom lip inside his mouth, making a smacking noise when he let it out. "Of course not, Petunia. I'm simply warning you. People around town have been noticing you seem to be more than their employer. And some of them don't like it one bit." With that, he slowly walked to his car, whistling the entire way.

Petunia watched until he drove away, then stepped inside the house. What could he mean by things could get ugly? What things? That was a threat if she'd ever heard one.

Mama cleared her throat after Opal made her way up the staircase. "Did you really slap the doctor, Petunia?"

Oh boy. Now Petunia had a reason to be nervous.

Before she could get a word out, the living room window shattered. Shards of glass flew through the air, embedding in the wall. Petunia's first instinct was to shield Mama with her own body as her gaze landed on a brick. Why would someone throw a brick through the window? What kind of games were they playing?

Petunia moved away from her, and a sharp pinch tore through her side.

Mama's eyes grew wide as she looked Petunia over. "Don't touch it, Petunia. There's a big piece of glass sticking out of you."

Maybe slapping Dr. Thompson wasn't the bright-
est idea she'd ever had.

Chapter 43

The rag Petunia clinched between her teeth was the only thing keeping her from losing her mind. Her legs shook as pain near close to giving birth shot through her hip. A moan escaped her chest, and her jaw worked overtime.

"I'm sorry, Misses, but you need to be still if'n you want to be sewed up," Opal's voice grated through Petunia's nerves.

Mama held onto Petunia's hand and rubbed down her arm. "Everything's gonna be all right, my sweet girl. Mama promises."

A tugging sensation joined the pain in Petunia's hip as Opal finished the last stitch. "I'm just gonna put some witch hazel and alcohol on this. Hold on, it'll burn."

Like it ever stopped burning in the first place. How a piece of glass could do so much damage was a mystery. As was the identity of the person who threw that brick into the window. Itching to give them a piece of her mind, Petunia daydreamed of boxing their jaws. Or worse.

A banging on the front door snapped Petunia out of her trance. "Hold on, y'all, we don't need to open the door up willy-nilly."

"Open up, Petunia. It's me, Lloyd and Lonnie's with me."

Opal flitted out of the kitchen. The lock clicked out of place, and the three of them returned within seconds.

"What in tarnation's going on? Why is your window busted?" Lloyd's face went a shade whiter with the blood stains trailing down Petunia's skirt. "Whose blood is that?"

Mama shook her fist in the air. "It's Petunia's. Some blasted glass hit her when the brick came through the window."

Lonnie massaged his temples. "Brick?"

Petunia nodded and did her best to hide her quivering chin. "I guess I done made somebody mad."

Lonnie stopped at the broken window. He kicked a piece of wood out of his way. "Mildred's cousin heard the nurse talking about you slapping the doctor over Clyde getting hurt."

Petunia turned to face Lonnie and then winced when her side seemed to have a red wasp going at it. "Did Lloyd tell you about the awful thing that happened to Clyde by some men wearing sheets? That sorry no count doctor refused to come to help him. I was just letting him know I was unhappy with that decision."

Lonnie pulled a chair up to the table, a sorrowful expression lining his features. "Can y'all tell us what happened from the beginning until now?"

Petunia filled them in on the rest of the night's events. When she finally stopped talking, Lloyd raised his left eyebrow. "You really went on a date with Sheriff Leech? I bet MaryAnne a nickel you'd back out."

How big was that glass that landed on her side? Because it felt like the entire window. And the pain made her nerves stand on end. Doing her best not to sound mad, she corrected Lloyd. "Keach. His name is Keach, not Leech."

Lonnie snorted. "Nah, it ain't. Not to us, anyhow. We call him Leech."

"Well, anyhow, we ain't dating. I told him we could go as friends only," Petunia spoke through gritted teeth. "Why don't y'all quit interrogating me and get busy boarding that window up? And somebody needs to check on Clyde."

Lloyd made a face at Petunia. "You went to Chicago and came back talking like you got some learning. Using big words and everything."

Petunia poked her tongue out at the back of Lloyd's head as he walked over to the window. "Just hush, brother, and make yourself useful."

Chapter 44

Petunia put the car in reverse to back out of her driveway. She quickly found out the driveway was much longer with Opal in the passenger seat wringing her hands.

Her tires slid in the muddy tracks left over from an overnight rain shower as she maneuvered around Lloyd's truck. He and MaryAnne had stopped by to help their mama with Clyde and the boys while Petunia and Opal filed a police report.

Opal gripped the door handle like a ranch hand on a bucking horse. "Are you sure I need to be in the car with you, Misses?"

Petunia raised her hand to protect her eyes from the early morning sun. "Yes. We're reporting what happened, and you're a witness."

Opal rubbed the side of her head like she was trying to wipe something off. "What about Misses Dorothy? She's a witness, too. Can't you turn around and get her instead of me?"

Petunia checked the road both ways before turning onto the main road. "It'll be fine, Opal."

Opal turned eyes full of unshed tears on Petunia. "They ain't gonna believe me. It'll just make more trouble."

A thin line settled onto Petunia's lips. She couldn't believe the way Opal thought. "It's time to stand up to people, Opal."

Opal changed her tactics. "I ain't never been inside no police station."

"They're not really that fun," Petunia mumbled.

Opal sat up in the seat. "What did you say?"

Petunia would laugh if she didn't think it would make Opal mad. Or even more nervous. "Nothing important."

The police department must've been throwing a party with all the cars in the parking lot. Opal's shoulders tensed, and she shook her head back and forth.

"I can't go in there with all them people!" Opal's voice cracked with obvious fear. "Take me back to the house. Please."

A sigh left Petunia, and she put the car in reverse. "All right. We can go home. I'll bring Lloyd or Mama back with me."

Before she could get out of the parking lot, Sheriff Keach appeared in the window. "Hold up, there, little lady. What are you doing?"

Petunia left her foot on the brake. "Hi, Sheriff Keach. We wanted to file a complaint but decided to leave."

He leaned his head into the car and looked at Opal. "Well, who do we have here? Isn't this your maid?"

A couple of local men walked up to the car. The short one with a gap between his front teeth spit a stream of tobacco on the parking lot. "Looks like Miss Marshall done come to the police station with a colored woman in the car."

The taller one with a crooked nose cackled. "Yeah, she's sweet on 'em." He leaned closer to the driver's window. "Is that what it is? You still sweet on colored folks like when you was younger?"

Petunia gasped when the man got close. It was none other than Judith Cooper's older brother, Trevor. The shaved beard had thrown her off until he got up close.

After taking a second look at the other one, she shook her head. It was Trevor's cousin, Lionel Cooper. Another bully.

Sheriff Keach eyeballed the men. "Step back and let me talk to Miss Marshall. This is official police business now."

The men stepped back but lingered nearby. Petunia cut her eyes at them. What would they do if she hit the gas and broke their toes? They needed it. She'd bet her new dress Trevor had something to do with what had been happening. After the threat at the restaurant, he must've been the one to throw the brick.

Sheriff Keach plastered a fake smile across his lips. "If you can't tell, the good town folks have a problem with how you conduct yourself. Now, I have no problem with colored folks. As long as they stay where they belong. Are you staying where you belong, Miss Brown?"

Opal swallowed and nodded. When she spoke, her voice stammered. "I'm trying to, Sheriff."

"I hear you're living in the same house as Miss Marshall. And that your brother, Clyde, is bedding down in the barn. Is that true?"

Petunia leaned her head down, blocking his view of Opal. "Why don't you talk to me instead of Opal?"

His right hand rested on his gun holster. "I hope you're prepared for the fallout if you continue loving on colored folks. Y'all ain't kids no more where you can be buddies. She's a maid only. Do you understand what I mean?"

Petunia offered the sweetest smile she could muster. "Thank you for your advice, Sheriff, but

I'm a grown woman. I don't need you or anyone else telling me who I can or can't talk to. Do you understand what I mean?"

Lionel Cooper shook his head and stuck his tongue between the gap in his teeth. "I can't believe you let a woman talk to you like that, Sheriff."

Trevor Cooper laughed. "Maybe it's time for a new Sheriff. One with a backbone."

They walked to their rusty truck, laughing.

Sheriff Keach reached inside the car and grabbed Petunia by the nap of her neck. He leaned next to her and spoke low in her ear. "Don't say I didn't warn you. White folk running around with coloreds get dealt with."

Opal cried out with tears running down her face. "I promise I'll be good, Sheriff. Me and Clyde will move away from here. Just let her go."

The Sheriff spoke to Opal but kept a firm grip on Petunia. "You better keep your word and get out of here." He leaned so close to Petunia the sweat from his face covered her cheek. "And you better make sure she keeps her word, or something bad's gonna happen to you. You hear me, woman?"

Petunia strained to get out of his grip, but the pressure increased around her neck.

He smiled at her like they'd just shared a special secret. "I can be your best friend or your worst enemy. It's up to you. And after today, it looks like you gonna need a friend. Let me know when you're ready for that dinner."

The two men cackled as Petunia eased out of the parking lot. They spat on her car when she passed them by.

Trevor Cooper waved when Petunia slowed down to roll her window up. "We'll be seeing you real soon, Miss High and Mighty. Real soon."

Chapter 45

The following Saturday, Petunia loaded the boys and Mama up in her Lincoln Capri to visit Eddie and Gail. Opal and Clyde planned to spend the night with friends so they could try to find somewhere else to live.

A twinkle of hurt passed through her heart. Opal and Clyde were good people. They minded their own business, were hard workers, and cared about folks. And now they felt forced to move. Where could they go?

After their aunt passed, they didn't have any family to rely on. Their friends would try to help them, but what would come next? Petunia's chin hardened. She needed to try to help them, and she would.

Thankfully the past few days had been uneventful. Quiet. But Petunia could tell unrest lingered in the air. People didn't treat her the same as before.

She gritted her teeth at the thought of that leech of a sheriff trying to force people to do what he wanted.

Why? Who was she hurting? Nobody. She knew why Lloyd and Lonnie called him Sheriff Leech now.

If Verlon was here, he'd show that sheriff a thing or two. Lloyd would if she'd told him the whole story. She'd left the part about the sorry dog grabbing her out when she filled the family in on what happened at the station. She didn't want Lloyd getting in no trouble.

Martin and William were sound asleep before Petunia made it a mile down the road. Even the pothole she hit didn't cause them to stir.

A little later, Petunia grinned at Mama as she pulled next to Eddie's car. "I wish I could sleep like that."

Eddie came out of the house with Gail close behind. He opened the passenger door, and a grin split his face. "I'm so glad to see y'all!" He put his hand out to Mama. "Lemme help you out."

Even though Petunia couldn't see Gail's face, her voice floated into the car. "Eddie, will you come back for the boys after you get Dot settled? I need to talk to Petunia."

Dot?

Mama laughed as she settled the crutch under her armpit. "I can make my way, Gigi. Eddie, you go ahead and get the boys."

Gigi?

Petunia helped Martin out, and he took off running while Eddie grabbed William. Petunia propped her leg against the car. "What did you need to talk about?"

Gail glanced at Petunia. "I reckon I owe you an apology."

Well, that was unexpected. Petunia opened her mouth, but Gail held her hand up.

"Before you say anything, let me finish." Gail covered her face with both hands. "I've treated you something awful for the longest time, and I'm sorry."

The metal on the side of the car made a hollow sound as Petunia's foot tapped on it like a horse running on a track. She gawked at Gail a moment before finding her voice. "Don't give it another thought."

Gail's chest expanded, and she pointed at two metal chairs. They settled into them, and she turned to Petunia. "I promise I ain't never done nothing with your daddy. Me and your mama worked everything out this past week."

Petunia's mouth fell open. "Y'all did?"

A fluffy brown knee-high dog galloped up to them and jumped around like he was on a sugar high. Gail patted her leg and called him over. "Come here, Oscar, and settle down."

He settled in between the two women with what Petunia would call a smile on his face. Gail ran her hand through his fur before turning her attention back to Petunia. "We did. Me and your mama ain't getting any younger, and I didn't want one of us going to our graves before I could make things right."

Petunia ran her hand over Oscar's fur. It was surprisingly soft as he leaned into her touch. "I'm listening."

Gail crossed her legs and wiped at her eyes. "I'm ashamed. But I owe you an explanation, so I'm just gonna say it. I was jealous of Dorothy having all the kids while I had none. And when you was born, I was pregnant at the same time, but my poor baby didn't make it."

Petunia didn't bother to keep the tears from flowing. "I'm so sorry."

Gail shook her head and wiped under her nose. "I ain't looking for no sympathy, Petunia. I just wanted you to know I don't hate you."

This conversation hadn't gone the way Petunia planned. She swallowed, trying to figure out what to do. Hug Gail? Pat her hand? Just sit there and listen? "I thank you for sharing. That must've been hard on you."

"No harder than I've been on you your whole life." A bitter-sounding laugh left Gail. "You know I let my jealousy turn me away from my best friend? And I even let her believe me and Oliver had something going on. A lie." The laugh turned to a shoulder-shaking cry.

Okay. Petunia couldn't sit there without offering some sort of comfort. But would Gail want comfort from Petunia? Oh, forget it. Gail was getting a hug whether she liked it or not.

Petunia pulled herself out of the chair and wrapped her arms around Gail from behind. Gail leaned into Petunia's embrace. "Thank you for making this easier on me."

Eddie poked his head out the door. "Hey, you two. Me and Dorothy are starving to death in here. Y'all coming, or would you want to wait on Christmas?"

Gail clicked her tongue. "We're a coming."

A few hours later, darkness fell fast when Petunia and her mama decided to go home. The boys were asleep in the spare bedroom, and they agreed to let them spend the night.

It was nearly midnight when they pulled onto the main street in town. Petunia's eyes were as dry as sandpaper but making up with Gail had been worth it. Her heart sang a little tune, knowing she had one more person to call family.

Mama gasped when they got close to their house. "Child, what in the world is this madness?"

A cross the size of Petunia's car stood tall in her front yard. With flames blazing across the dark night.

Chapter 46

Even though a surge of ruby red clouded Petunia's vision, her heavy-as-stone legs wouldn't move. Tremors lit a trail to her heart and sunk deep into her bones.

Why was this happening? Who would do something like this?

Mama thrust her fist in the air. "This has to stop, Petunia. What if we had the boys with us? Huh?"

The boys?

That's all Mama had to say to get her legs moving. "Stay in the car, Mama. I'm gonna try to put this out."

She shook her head, concern marring her features. "Let's just go. You don't need to get out of the car."

Screams permeated the air from behind the house. Petunia's eyes popped wide. "I have to see what this is."

A figure stormed around the house, coming straight for their car.

Petunia put her hand on the door handle, and Mama screamed out, grasping Petunia's shirt. "Back out! Back out!"

Petunia's muscles went rigid, and she shifted the car into reverse with trembling hands. Before backing out, her realtor and neighbor, Woodruff Blevins, stopped and fell to his knees, holding his chest. Petunia slung the gear into park and hopped out of the car.

When she got near Mr. Blevins, she gasped. His face and clothes had black all over them, and his chest heaved up and down.

The heat from the burning cross hit her skin as she knelt beside him. Her voice came out in a near whisper. "Mr. Blevins?"

His head raised, and he looked at her through red-rimmed eyes. "You need to get away from here, Petunia. These people mean business."

She leaned on the ground beside him. "What people? Why are you so dirty?"

His shoulders sagged, and a low groan left his lips. "He's gone, Petunia. I'm sorry. There was nothing I could do. He was gone when we got here. They both were."

A sickness rose from her stomach and settled at the back of her throat. "Who's gone? Gone where?"

Mama hobbled next to where she and the realtor were. "Woodruff. Who in the world did this?"

His voice trembled when he spoke. "I didn't recognize them, Dorothy. They wore white dresses, and I couldn't see too good from the house. My son went after help."

Mama glared at him. "Now, that's a bunch of malarky. You're saying women did this?"

"No, Dorothy!" He scanned the area before lowering his voice. "It was that cult of men who go around hurting people!"

White dresses? Could it be the same white sheets Opal told her about when Clyde was attacked? Petunia's stomach bottomed out before what Mr. Blevins said sunk in. He's gone. He's gone.

Who was gone? She shot off the ground and ran to the back of the house with all her might. She thought she heard Mama and Mr. Blevins yelling for her to stop, but she couldn't. She *had* to see who was gone.

The shed Clyde called home had become nothing but black rubble. Someone who'd been badly burned lay on the ground beside the shed, holding what looked to be a sizzling bag of cotton. Petunia swallowed down the bile that kept coming up her throat. She had to see who it was. She had to help if she could.

A cry left her chest as she got close. It was Clyde. And she had no hope he was alive. Half of his body was burned so severely he was unrecognizable, and there was no breath in his body.

And the bag of cotton? Well, it wasn't a bag of cotton after all. It was a larger person who'd been completely burned from the chest down to his feet. A grayish hat that came to a point at the top covered the person's head, so she couldn't tell who it was. The only thing she knew for certain was that it was a man. Petunia closed her eyes and prayed, thanking God it wasn't Opal.

Falling to her knees, she lost her dinner. This couldn't be happening.

Headlights flashed down the driveway before two car doors slammed. Maybe they were coming back to finish them off. Even so, her legs wouldn't cooperate with her brain. Sobs racked her shoulders, and she wailed.

Strong arms pulled her up, and she turned to meet Lloyd's eyes. He pulled her close and rubbed her hair. "Oh, sis. I'm so sorry you had to see this. I'm so sorry."

Heat massaged Petunia's skin and her insides throbbed with adrenaline which got her legs to moving. "Why would someone do this?"

Lonnie and David Blevins burst through the back door, carrying Opal's limp body. "Hurry, we need to get her to a doctor."

Opal stirred in Lonnie's arms. "No. Please, no doctor."

Petunia's nostrils flared as she walked over to Lonnie. She rubbed Opal's hair and leaned close to her ear. "I'll kill ever last one of them, Opal."

Lonnie must've heard her because he stopped in his tracks and met Petunia's stormy gaze. "You most certainly won't kill nobody. What'll happen is you'll end up getting yourself killed and leaving your boys as orphans. Is that what you want?"

Well, that knocked the breath from her storm of rage. Her boys. She needed to slow down and think of them. Not her fury that needed to be let out. Not her sadness over what happened to Clyde.

At least she couldn't let her sadness and outrage overtake her good sense. Verlon wouldn't be happy if she put their boys at risk, even for a good cause like this.

But somebody needed to step up and hold whoever did this accountable. Who'd do it if she didn't? But she had to have help. Somebody who knew how to talk to folks. Somebody like a lawyer.

She'd hire a lawyer. That's what she'd do. She'd go to Tyronza, stay at Evelyn's bed and breakfast for a while, and look for a good lawyer.

Lloyd grasped her elbow and directed her toward the front of the house, where she parked. "We need to get you and Opal out of here, Petunia. Now!"

Petunia glanced at Opal and Lonnie. "Can Opal make it to Tyronza?"

He nodded. "I think so. She's been beat up real bad, but she should be able to make it. I don't think we have much choice, anyhow."

Petunia walked behind her mama. "I ain't leaving the boys. Let's meet at Uncle Edward's and figure things out from there."

Woodruff Blevins wiped his forehead with a napkin. "We wish y'all the best in life, and I'm real sorry this happened, but you ain't gonna be safe here no longer. We'll see to the bodies."

Petunia paused and turned toward the realtor. "Do you have any idea who the other person is?"

After clutching the collar of his shirt, Woodruff met Petunia's gaze. "I'm not certain who it is."

Even though it looked like Mr. Blevins was lying, Petunia opted not to bring attention to the fact. For now. "I appreciate you sending for my brother and trying to put the fire out."

"You're welcome, Petunia. Clyde seemed like a nice man. He helped me when I almost fell off my roof last month." He turned to his son. "Let's go on home, David. Your mama's probably worried herself sick."

Lonnie laid Opal on the ground and leaned close to her face. "Opal needs help. She ain't breathing."

Chapter 47

Lloyd sank onto the ground beside Opal and put his ear to her mouth. "She's breathing. Just barely, but she is."

Petunia's heart slowly started beating after Lonnie scared the life out of her. "Thank the Good Lord."

Lonnie grabbed Opal's legs and motioned for Lloyd to grab her shoulders. "Let's get her into the car and get out of here."

They all froze still when headlights flashed in the distance. The vehicle slowed down and crept into the driveway.

Who would be out at almost two o'clock in the morning? Unless it was the people who'd done this coming back to finish them off.

"It's Daddy," Lloyd grunted as he helped Lonnie get Opal into the back seat.

Petunia's spine stiffened when Oliver stepped out of his rusty Chevrolet Clipper. Oliver? Why would he be out this late? Or could he have something to do with what happened?

He slammed the door and ambled over. Pointing at the smoky cross, he shook his head. "What in the world is this cockeyed mess?"

Mama grunted before leaning against Petunia's car. "This here cross was burning when me and Petunia got home. Somebody done killed Clyde and hurt Opal."

"Killed Clyde?" He massaged his temples before setting his eyes on the cross. "I thought that cult went away a few years ago."

Petunia marched up to him and nearly screamed in his face. "What cult?"

Oliver stepped around Petunia and closed the distance between him and the cross. "A bunch of men used to go around hurting and killing people they didn't like. They always hurt mostly black folks, but they ain't been doing nothing for a long time."

Following him, Petunia's stern gaze landed on his face. "Are you a part of it?"

His unflinching gaze met hers. "You're whistling dixie trying to blame me for something I ain't got no part of."

Lloyd joined them close to the cross that had almost fizzled out to nothing but blackened wood.

"We need to go, Petunia. Quit trying to blame Daddy, and let's get out of here."

"You're right, Lloyd." Petunia's hand flew to her hip. "This is a lot to take in. I'm just trying to figure it out."

"I got a pregnant wife I need to get home to." Lloyd's eyes moved to the car their mama leaned on. "And Mama looks like she's about to fall out from standing around so long."

Well, that was a punch to the gut. May as well have called her selfish.

Petunia pressed her lips together as she looked at Mama. Her face softened, and she nodded. "You're right, brother. I'm sorry."

It took them thirty minutes to get to the Marshalls and another thirty minutes to explain what happened. Eddie had served as a military medic and checked Opal out while they talked through the night's events.

Thankfully, Eddie believed Opal would be okay after rest and healing. She'd been beaten, but amazingly nothing was broken.

After many tears and hugs, Gail packed a bag of goodies for the road. After putting a call through to James and Evelyn, Lloyd and Lonnie went home with an agreement to travel to Tyronza the following day and bring their families. At least Lloyd agreed. Lonnie hadn't been sure about leaving home.

Petunia, Mama, and the boys settled in the front seat while Opal slept in the back seat. The dark sky seemed to match Petunia's heart as she drove down the highway to Tyronza before dawn.

Oliver insisted on following Petunia to Tyronza to make sure they didn't run into no trouble.

But was he part of the trouble? Petunia couldn't get past the fact he showed up the same night everything happened. Could it really be a coincidence? Or was there more to it?

Guess that's what she'd have to find out.

Chapter 48

After what felt like an endless journey, they finally arrived in Tyronza as the sun began to peek over the horizon. The front porch of Evelyn's Bed and Breakfast was spacious and welcoming. It had two white columns that framed the porch, which was adorned with an array of colorful potted plants that seemed to sway gently in the morning breeze.

She was happy to say the place was nicer than she'd anticipated. Then she swallowed the thought. Thinking like that wasn't Christian-like. Why wouldn't Evelyn have a nice Bed and Breakfast?

Petunia's heart lifted when Evelyn and James came out the front door. Happy to put away those thoughts, she smiled at the duo. "Thank you both for allowing us to come here."

Evelyn hugged Petunia before leaning back to look at her face. "I oughta tan your hide. You'll always be welcome, sister."

A thicker dark-skinned woman came outside shortly behind James. He led her to the back seat and opened the door. "Do you think you can help her?"

She shook her head, and a tuft of gray hair slipped from her cap. "Let's get her out of the car and into my buggy. I'll need to take her home to see about her."

Swiveling her body, Petunia raised her hands. "Wait a minute, here. Who are you?"

The woman raised a gray brow at Petunia. "I'm Miss Betty, and I know how to care for folks. Your maid'll be in good hands."

Petunia moved her body in between Miss Betty and Opal. "This is Opal, my friend, not my maid. And I can take care of her just fine."

Miss Betty looked at Evelyn as if Petunia hindered her plan. "Misses Evelyn, did you need me or not? Cause I got other people I can be helping."

Evelyn grabbed Petunia's hands and pulled her over to where she stood. "Miss Betty is an excellent healer. She'll be able to devote time to help Opal. You got Mama and the boys to think of."

Oliver leaned his arm on the windowsill of Petunia's car. "Gal, you need to get yourself some shut-eye. Then make decisions afterward."

A rooster crowed in the distance, almost like it was trying to talk some sense into Petunia. She ogled

Miss Betty, and a tingle caused Petunia's nose to flare. "But I wanted to take care of her. I owe her that much. She's gonna need someone who loves her there to help her deal with everything."

Miss Betty's shoulders relaxed, and she approached Petunia. "I promise I'll help her. And you can come by anytime you want to. Misses Evelyn knows where I stay off Old Highway 63."

James piped up. "I'll take you there myself, Petunia. Let's get Opal the care she needs, and let you focus on figuring out what's next."

Petunia nodded. "Fine, but I'll be there to check on her in the morning."

Miss Betty chuckled and wagged her fingers in the air. "As long as it's tomorrow morning."

As Oliver helped James load Opal in Miss Betty's wagon, Petunia's head became light, and the bed and breakfast started spinning. Even in her current state, a thought struck Petunia, and she made her way to the wagon. "Wait. Do you have someone there to help get her inside?"

"My sons are there to help me." Miss Betty grabbed the reins and clicked her tongue rather impatiently. "Let me get out of here so I can see about her."

After getting everything unloaded and the boys tucked away in their bed with her mama, Petunia sat at the kitchen table with Evelyn sipping on a piping hot cup of coffee.

A sinking feeling cradled Petunia's guts like she used to cradle her boys. She smelled her cup before taking a drink. "Evelyn, I have a bad feeling."

"Don't go borrowing no trouble, sister. Let's pray everything's gonna turn out for the best." Evelyn went to the window when a car door slammed from the front yard.

"Who's out there?" Petunia joined Evelyn at the window and stretched her neck. "I can't see nothing."

Evelyn closed the curtain and sat back down at the table. "They must've parked on the other side. It's probably a customer."

Before Petunia reached the table, Oliver barreled into the kitchen holding a shotgun. "Sheriff Leech just pulled up." He looked right at Petunia before cocking the weapon. "Get ready for trouble."

Chapter 49

Under the circumstances, Petunia wouldn't be mad if Oliver shot that fathead, Sheriff Keach. What would make that man follow her all the way to Tyronza?

Nothing good, that's for sure.

Petunia probed Sheriff Keach's eyes as he walked in behind James. He raised both hands and landed a crooked grin on Petunia. "I come in peace. Will you hear me out?"

The weapon slackened in Oliver's hands but only a smidge. He glanced at Petunia with a question in his eyes.

She bit her bottom lip and looked hard at Oliver. For a split second, it was almost like Oliver cared about her. Like he was protecting her from harm, and she didn't know how to handle the emotions swirling inside. It was a lot easier to stay mad at him.

She turned her focus on Sheriff Keach. "Well? Go on, then. Speak your mind. But this better be good after you followed us this far."

Sheriff Keach removed his hat and held it to his chest. "I wouldn't have been able to live with myself if I hadn't come, Petunia. I owe you an apology for what happened."

Petunia's eyes narrowed to mere slits. "Are you admitting to being behind what happened, then, Sheriff?"

His breath hitched a little, and he immediately shook his head. "No, ma'am. I'm just apologizing for what happened at the station and also on behalf of the town. I don't like how they treated you one bit."

A memory of the Sheriff's hands on her throat caused Petunia to rise out of the chair and stand close to her daddy. "You don't like it? How do you think Opal feels? And what about poor Clyde? Seems to me you ain't much of a sheriff letting that go on in your town."

Oliver held the shotgun tight before looking Sheriff Keach up and down. "Or are you in on it?"

A pink hue spread up his neck, and Sheriff Keach stuttered when he spoke. "Listen here, I can admit I ain't perfect. But I sure ain't in cahoots with criminals."

Evelyn sat a cup of coffee and a cinnamon roll in front of Sheriff Keach before taking her seat. Always a good hostess. "Then why are you here?"

He took a sip of the coffee and nodded his head toward Evelyn. "Much obliged." He sniffed the cinnamon roll and cocked his head like it was the best smell in the world. "Frankly, Mrs. Hill, I'm here to see if I can help your family. I'm sorry for getting caught up in that mess. Real sorry."

Petunia's chin lifted, and she tugged a long strand of red hair behind her ear. "How do you plan to do that?"

Maybe she needed to chalk up how he acted at the police station to those men egging him on. Surely, he wouldn't have put his hands on her otherwise.

The sheriff swallowed the bite of cinnamon roll and washed it down with coffee. "I plan on finding out everything I can and then making arrests." He slapped the table. "These people must go to trial for two murders and attempted murder, at the very least."

Petunia cocked an eyebrow as she folded her arms over her chest. If this man was being honest, this would be good news. Should she be judging his heart? Maybe not.

Oliver kept his hand firmly on the shotgun as he leaned against the counter. "Do you know who the second fella was that died in the fire?"

Sheriff Keach's lip twitched right before a frown creased his mouth. "Not yet, Oliver. I plan on staying on top of it, in any case. Gotta push for justice."

Tossing the last of her coffee back, Petunia locked eyes with the Sheriff. "I plan on hiring a lawyer to help."

The Sheriff nodded his head. "That's a good idea, Petunia. Can I help you in any way?"

She tapped her nose and shrugged. "Not unless you know a good lawyer who lives within an hour's drive."

Pulling a pen and paper from his pocket, the sheriff grinned. "It just so happens, I had dealings with a lawyer from Harrisburg here a while back. Want his number?"

Making no attempt to hide her appreciation, Petunia's head flew up and down. "I sure do."

After giving Petunia the contact information for the lawyer and finishing his coffee and cinnamon roll, the sheriff got to his feet. "Would you call me if there's anything else I can do for you? And keep me posted on what happens with this here lawyer?"

Petunia stared at the number scribbled on the small piece of paper. "I sure will. And thank you for coming all this way to make things right."

He chuckled on his way out. "Not a problem, Petunia. I hope to see you again real soon."

Real soon? That sounded familiar. Petunia watched Stanley Keach's back as he left the room. That man was a sneaky one Petunia would have to keep a close eye on.

Chapter 50

Later that afternoon, Lloyd and MaryAnne pulled into the drive. Petunia and Evelyn had just returned from visiting Opal, so they stood on the front porch waving as Lloyd helped MaryAnne out of the truck.

Soft giggles floated through the warm afternoon air from the other side of the porch, beckoning Petunia's curiosity. Her eyes widened as she took in the lively scene. Oliver lay sprawled on the grass, his laughter mingling with that of the boys who energetically clambered over him like playful puppies. Nearby, Mama sat in her favorite chair, her eyes sparkling with delight as she clapped her hands, encouraging the playful chaos unfolding before her.

All four of them laughed like they were having a grand time. A slight pang struck her heart. Why hadn't he ever played with her like that? All she remembered him doing was yelling at her and getting onto her for something she had or hadn't done.

A longing she hadn't felt in years seeped into her bones as she stood outside his inner circle. Just like the skinny little girl with red hair, he'd always kept at a distance. The little girl who had cried herself to sleep because she thought something was wrong with her.

The one who would've given anything to have brown hair.

Lloyd screaming her name snapped her out of the fog she'd allowed herself to enter.

She marched around the porch. "What's got your feathers ruffled, brother?"

She didn't wait for him to answer. MaryAnne held her stomach as she doubled over at the front door. Oh. No. Surely, MaryAnne wasn't going into labor. They were too far from the hospital for that to happen.

Evelyn kicked into high gear and started belting orders to her and Lloyd. Looked like they would be delivering the baby themselves. Petunia stared at the door and tried to determine how much they'd hate her if she took off running.

Right on time, Petunia's stomach bubbled, and she pressed her hand on top of it. Hard. The thought of blood and all the other things that came along with giving birth was not appealing.

Lloyd grabbed her by the arm and walked to the bedroom where Evelyn had MaryAnne. "I need you now more than ever, sister. Please don't let me down."

How did he know what to say to guilt her into doing things she didn't want to? She'd rather eat a raw strawberry cake than do what was needed. But that didn't matter. She had to stick around and take care of her family. He'd do it for her.

All night long. That's how long it took to deliver the baby.

MaryAnne labored until she could hardly move her pinkie, and in the end, she gave birth to a baby girl.

With a head full of red hair.

MaryAnne insisted on naming her Carolyn Dorothy Hollings in honor of Petunia, Evelyn, and Mama. Petunia couldn't help but be impressed with the cleverness of combining Carol and Evelyn to come up with Carolyn.

After helping clean up Mama and baby, Petunia and Evelyn excused themselves and passed out in the same bed.

It was late afternoon when Petunia snapped awake to somebody hammering on something. She stumbled out of bed and started down the hallway with a cup of coffee on her mind.

She stopped when Mama's voice came from her room. "Ollie, I don't know what to say."

"Say you'll forgive me. I made a mess of things by letting my pride get the best of me."

"You know I'll forgive you. I love you more than anything."

Somebody blew their nose. Was it Mama or Oliver? It sounded like him, but she'd never seen him cry before Teresa's funeral.

"I've been a pain in the neck and then some."

Were they kissing? It sure sounded like it. Maybe it was time to stop eavesdropping and get that coffee.

Just as she started to walk off, Oliver spoke. "Do you think Petunia could ever forgive me?"

"She has a good heart, Ollie. All she's ever wanted was for you to show her some love and affection."

"Blast it, Dot! I wish I could go back and change things."

That did it. He wished he could change things? Like what? How many whoopings he gave her? How he always let the other girls get away with murder but not her?

Petunia stormed into the room, laughing maniacally. "You wish you could change things? Well, you can't! I've had to live my life knowing that you didn't think I was your child, that you didn't want me around. Do you really believe that saying you're sorry will suddenly fix everything?"

Her veins blazed with anger. She lowered her voice when Martin rolled over onto William from where they napped. Even with a lower tone, she put all the disdain she could muster in her next words. "Well, guess what? It won't."

With that, she slammed out the door and ran to her room.

Chapter 51

T he first order of business the following day was to meet the lawyer for Petunia's nine o'clock appointment. She slipped her fingers under her new sleeveless top's lacy collar. It was a stylish white with tiny black polka dots, but it sure was itchy. And not warm enough at all – September had started off cooler than average for small-town Arkansas.

"Ms. Marshall?" The secretary pushed her black-rimmed glasses up the bridge of her nose. "Mr. Beck will see you now. Follow me."

Petunia fell into place beside the woman who looked to be old enough to have witnessed the Civil War firsthand. After scolding herself for thinking ugly thoughts, she settled into a light green leather chair across from the lawyer.

An ink pen in his perfectly manicured hand tapped the desk repeatedly as he stared intently at some papers on the desk. Petunia took a moment to size him up since his attention was elsewhere.

She hated to admit it, but she liked what she saw. His tan complexion told Petunia he spent time outdoors. Brown hair tinged with a few pieces of gray above his ears lay perfectly cut and styled in the latest fashion.

Finally, he looked up from the desk and smiled. He had a tiny gap between his front teeth that added to his charming, good looks.

"Mrs. Marshall, I'm Richard Beck. Sheriff Keach was good enough to provide me with a copy of the reports from what happened." Deep brown eyes seemed to probe hers. "But I'd like to hear it from your point of view."

Petunia guessed he wasn't much on small talk. Fine by her. She filled him in on everything that had happened as the secretary plucked away on a typewriter. Petunia almost wanted to get up and slam the door. That pecking would drive her mad if she had to listen to it much longer.

She zeroed in on his lips to keep focused. Anything to take her mind off the banging coming from the other room. "Well, do you think you can help?"

He ran his top teeth over his bottom lip, and a flush stained Petunia's cheeks.

He cleared his throat, and his lips flattened. "Tell you what, why don't you let me do some digging, and I'll let you know what I come up with?"

"I'd appreciate that, Mr. Beck." Like a fool, her voice cracked when she spoke. Of course. "I want them to pay for what they did to Clyde. And to Opal and my family."

The typing stopped, and Petunia's head automatically eased from the pounding.

He shifted in his seat. "I understand. You've all been through quite an ordeal. If you don't mind me asking, what are your plans?"

Another blush crept up her cheeks, causing Petunia to fake a cough so he wouldn't notice. A fancy attorney wouldn't want no country girl. That would never happen.

And why she was thinking like that didn't make a lick of sense. She needed to keep her mind and heart on Verlon.

After pretending to tamp the cough down with a few sips of water, Petunia glanced at him. "We'll be settling near my sister in Tyronza for now. I'm not sure what'll come after."

After shuffling the papers on the desk around, he scratched his neck. "I'll be in the area next Wednesday. That should give me enough time to get some answers. How about I stop by?"

"I'd like that." There came the blush again. "You know to hear what you find out."

"Of course." He stood, letting her know the meeting was over.

What was she supposed to do now? Shake his hand? Wave as she slowly walked away? Run out of the office and never look back?

In the end, she settled on shaking his hand.

On the drive home, she couldn't stop thoughts of the attorney whisking her off her feet from entering her mind.

Just like always, an image of Verlon pranced around inside her head, causing her eyes to brim with tears. She had no business thinking of another man like that. It was too soon.

How many years would it take before she could look at another man without feeling guilty? Because these feelings couldn't continue too much longer. Or she'd be forced to take drastic action.

Chapter 52

By the time Wednesday rolled around, Petunia had worked herself into a mighty fine tizzy. Her mind raced as she meandered toward the stream in a small, wooded area behind the Bed and Breakfast.

One minute, she looked forward to seeing Mr. Beck. The next minute, she hoped he'd call instead of stopping by. Or hit a ditch and be forced to reschedule.

Running water caught her attention as she leaned on the wrap-around porch of her temporary home. Not that she wasn't thankful for James and Evelyn giving them a place to stay, but she wanted her own home. Like she had before everything happened.

Leaning by the bank, she dipped her hand in the water. She guessed she needed something else to worry about. Like raising two boys while dealing with finding a new place to live after running away from home like a scared little girl wasn't enough.

He was probably involved with somebody else, anyway. Most dreamboats on all the shows Petunia watched on television were already taken. Or they were looking for a certain type of dame. The kind that Petunia wasn't.

Her gaze drifted down the stream, and she paused when a deer stepped out of the woods. A few steps from the water, it froze in place and met Petunia's excited gaze.

That deer looked about how Petunia felt. Stuck in a situation without many options. At least she hadn't married Lonnie. That would've been a nightmare with everything that's happened. A wave of relief passed over her shoulders that Lonnie had enough sense to say no. He and Mildred had tied the knot over the weekend. Petunia planned on going but figured her presence would make for an uncomfortable wedding. Especially since Judith was the Maid of Honor.

Evelyn's loud voice interrupted Petunia's private moment with the deer. "Petunia, can you pick Opal up this afternoon? Mrs. Betty says she'd be ready to come home today."

The deer jumped and, like a streak, ran back into the woods. Petunia's lips formed a thin line, and she inwardly sighed.

Evelyn came to a stop by the water's edge. "There's a whole family of them out in those woods."

Petunia turned a smile on Evelyn. "It had the sweetest little face."

Evelyn nodded and linked her arm with Petunias. "Did you hear what I asked?"

Petunia laid her hand on top of Evelyn's. "Sorry, my mind was on the deer. I heard, and I can go pick Opal up."

Raising her brow, Evelyn led Petunia down the stream. "It looked like you were deep in thought. What's on your mind, sister?"

"Well, I've decided to find another lawyer," Petunia answered with a small smile.

Evelyn stopped so abruptly that Petunia almost tripped over her own feet. "What did Mr. Beck do wrong?"

Petunia shrugged and stared into the woods. A flash of movement caught her attention, and she pointed before turning to Evelyn. "Did you see something move in the woods?"

Evelyn squinted and shielded her eyes with her hand. "I don't see nothing. Not even the deer. What are you talking about?"

Nothing seemed out of place when Petunia looked back into the woods. "Maybe I was imagining things."

Evelyn responded with a wink and a sideways grin. "I think you was trying to change the subject."

Petunia's face fell, and she removed Evelyn's hand from her arm. "I don't know what you're talking about."

Evelyn grabbed Petunia's arm and laced her own through it. "I think you like the attorney more than you want to."

Would pushing Evelyn into the stream be wrong? Petunia almost did it, but she figured that wouldn't be very sisterly of her.

Petunia took off toward the front of the house. "I ain't looking at that man like that. He ain't even that nice looking."

A laugh broke from Evelyn's chest. "Liar! I've seen him before, and he sure ain't no hairy knucklehead. You better keep him around. At least as your attorney."

Massaging the back of her neck with her free hand, Petunia nodded. "I reckon you're right."

A branch cracked at the edge of the woods.

Petunia and Evelyn spun around, as a shadowy figure emerged from the woods. Unblinking eyes raked over them for what felt like minutes. Dressed in a black toboggan that concealed all but his piercing eyes, he stood motionless, his gaze fixed intently on them. After what felt like an eternity, the figure abruptly turned on his heel and dashed away, disappearing the way he came.

Chapter 53

J ames closed the door and entered the front room behind Lloyd. He shook his head and took a seat in the only recliner in the room. "We didn't see nobody out in the woods."

Lloyd sat beside MaryAnne on the loveseat and smiled at the baby sleeping in her arms. "It was probably a hunter just messing with y'all."

Petunia glanced at Mr. Beck as a chill entered her chest. She shook it off. "Well, that was downright mean of whoever it was."

Martin trotted up to Petunia, holding a wooden boat Oliver had made him before taking off for who knew where. She pulled him onto her lap and hugged him close, even though he squirmed like he was determined to get away from her.

"It sure was." Evelyn added with a fist shake, barely missing the side of Petunia's face.

Petunia set Martin down in time to duck the fist that came close to clocking her upside the head.

She landed a dirty look on Evelyn. As she turned, she took inventory of the darkness passing over Mr. Beck's face. "You all right, Mr. Beck?"

He crossed his legs and sat straighter on one of the two high-back chairs, showing off his shiny black dress shoes. His face relaxed and he attempted to smile. The edges around his face softened, and Petunia gulped.

"I'm fine. I can't tolerate men who get pleasure from scaring women."

Evelyn slightly elbowed Petunia and jiggled her eyebrows. Thankfully, Mr. Beck seemed too busy wiping something off his shoes to notice.

Lloyd leaned forward. "What did you find out about Clyde's death, Mr. Beck?"

An expression Petunia would call fake understanding replaced the earlier darkness on his face. "I'm sorry, but his death was ruled an accident."

"An accident? That can't be right." Petunia's voice turned into a shriek with the last three words. "We heard it was that blame group of murderers that call themselves the KKK."

Mr. Beck wiped something else off his shiny black shoe. Whatever he kept wiping off, Petunia couldn't see it. "Mrs. Marshall, those criminals have been disbanded."

When Petunia furrowed her eyebrows, he continued. "They don't meet anymore. You know, they
got shut down years ago."

Petunia managed to keep a straight face, even
though her hand itched to punch something. He
thought she was stupid. Arrogant man.

James rubbed his stubbly chin. "Then who was it?"

Mr. Beck shifted in his seat and met James's gaze.
"Sheriff Keach believes it was a group of people
trying to scare your family out of town."

"But why would they do that?" Petunia tried to
keep her voice from rising but failed miserably.

Mr. Beck didn't seem to notice that Petunia was
getting worked up. "Sheriff Keach seems to think
it's because of jealousy. He said to tell you there's no
longer any danger if you good folks want to return
to your homes."

Lloyd sprung to his feet and moved by the fireplace. "No, sir, we will not. My family will be staying right here in Tyronza, where they're safe."

Mr. Beck raised his hands in front of his face,
palms facing Lloyd. "I'm just relaying what I was
told, Mr. Hollings. Of course, you're free to stay
here."

Petunia opted to ask a question instead of punch-
ing the wall. "Did they find out who the other man
was?"

He scratched his chin and shifted in his seat. An almost guilty look crossed his face. "They're not releasing that to the public as of yet."

Lloyd's body swiveled and his gaze landed on Mr. Beck. "We have the right to know. And I expect you to tell us who it was, Mr. Beck."

Mr. Beck seemed to consider Lloyd's words as he stared into the fireplace. Finally, he scooted to the edge of the seat and nodded. "You're right, Mr. Hollings. But I need you all to give me your word you won't share this information."

After gaining agreement from everyone, he scratched his right brow and sighed. "The other man was Lionel Cooper."

That was all Petunia needed to hear. There was no doubt in her mind that Cyrus and Trevor Cooper were involved. Probably Judith too. "I knew it was them Coopers doing all this."

James glanced at Evelyn. "If you all don't mind, I'll ask that you excuse Evelyn and me. We have guests coming in this evening and need to get ready."

After they left, Lloyd ran his hands through his hair. "Petunia don't get too worked up right now. Let the police handle it. We got us a place here. Let's forget about that town and try to live in peace."

Petunia cut her eyes at Lloyd. When he noticed the dirty look, she landed on him he shrugged.

"Great news." Mr. Beck's eyes landed on Petunia and stayed long enough to make her squirm.

Tugging loose hair behind her ear to hide her red cheeks, Petunia met the attorney's gaze and tried to forget about the Coopers for a minute. "It was perfect with three houses already situated."

The phone ringing interrupted their conversation. Mumbled voices came from the front entrance, where the only phone was located.

"Mama," Evelyn screamed as she ran past the front room. Lloyd made haste to follow Evelyn.

Petunia wanted to fall behind Lloyd, but her legs wouldn't cooperate. A possum ran over Petunia's grave was a saying she'd grown up hearing the older folks say. She'd never quite understood what they meant by it until this moment. A feeling she'd never experienced walloped her, and that's the only way she could describe it.

William, wailing like somebody was trying to murder him got Petunia's legs moving. She ran down the hall as fast as possible, joining the rest in Mama's room.

Mama held her hand over her mouth, crying out Oliver's name while she had William in her lap.

Petunia scooped William up and ran her hand down the back of his head. "It's okay, baby, Mama's here." She peered at Evelyn. "What's all this ruckus about?"

Evelyn choked up when she opened her mouth, so James answered. "That was the police out of Alabama. Oliver's been in a bad car wreck."

Chapter 54

When Petunia entered the kitchen a few days later, whiffs of bacon and eggs lingered in the air. Lloyd had left for Alabama that morning with plans to bring Oliver home. Not that Petunia cared.

A hunting party checked into the Bed and Breakfast, so James and Evelyn were much busier than when they'd arrived. Which suited Petunia just fine. Anything to keep her mind off Oliver and Mama's situation.

Her stomach gurgled, and she looked over Opal's shoulder. "That smells so good."

Opal ran some water in the sink, rinsing her hands off. "Yes, it sure does, Misses."

Petunia snuck a piece of bacon off the plate and slipped it into her mouth. "Have you had breakfast yet?"

Opal shook her finger at Petunia. "Oh, no, Misses. I wouldn't do that before you've had yours."

Petunia sighed and moved closer to Opal. "I don't want to hear that nonsense talk, Opal. You're a guest here. And my friend."

Opal lowered her gaze to the floor. When her mouth opened, no words came forth. She just shook her head back and forth.

Evelyn moseyed into the kitchen. "Petunia's right, Opal. You're our guest and friend. Petunia would say Daddy didn't do much right, but she can't deny he taught us kids we show everybody the same respect no matter their skin color."

A worried expression skirted across Opal's face. "Y'all are the best folks I ever met, Misses Evelyn. But I done caused enough trouble. And now that Clyde's gone…" Tears brimmed in her eyes as she choked up on the last few words.

A few men in hunting gear walked through the hallway and grabbed cups of coffee on the way out. They glanced at Opal, but none of them said anything or asked questions. Which was good for them. Petunia was not in the mood for onery men worrying about somebody's skin color.

Petunia watched the men until they vanished from view before meeting Opal's gaze. "I need to tell you something," she said, her lashes glistening with unshed tears. "You're worth it."

A faint smile flashed across Opal's face. "That's what Jasper says."

Petunia and Evelyn looked at one another, and Petunia put her hand on her hip. "Who's Jasper?"

Evelyn clasped her hands together and leaned her backside against the sink. "Miss Betty's youngest son."

Understanding dawned on Petunia, and her eyes grew wide as an egg. "Are you sweet on him, Opal?"

Opal's teeth flashed white and straight as joy emanated from her. "We sweet on each other."

For a moment, Petunia forgot her troubles and grasped Opal's hands, forcing her to jump up and down with Petunia like they used to when they were kids.

MaryAnne walked into the kitchen holding baby Carolyn. "Well, ain't y'all a sight."

"Opal has a sweetheart." Petunia laughed and held her arms out for the baby. "Come to your favorite aunt, cutie pie."

MaryAnne handed her over and went straight for the coffee.

After breakfast and cleaning up, Petunia headed to her room to wake the boys. She paused outside her mama's room and smiled. Mama sat with her only foot halfway propped on a chair, asleep, with her mouth hanging open.

She couldn't be comfortable in that position. Petunia tiptoed into the room and moved Mama's leg where it was better propped up.

She turned to leave when a piece of paper on Mama's chest caught her attention.

Oliver's name stood out. Maybe it was news about the wreck. Should she read it? It was lying right there for anyone to see. It couldn't be too private. Plus, if it was about the wreck, Petunia deserved to know. Right?

Right.

Leaning close to Mama, she stood still for a moment. Pushing the guilt of reading her letter aside, she eased it off her chest and settled on the bed next to the window.

Hello Dorothy,

Thank you for calling to tell me about your marriage to Ollie. Over the years, I've wondered why he refused to marry me many times. Even after our first son was born almost twelve years ago, he still had one excuse after another. I finally decided he didn't want to marry a widow and decided to be happy with what he offered. Which hasn't been much. He comes and goes as he pleases, and I always thought it was for his job. What a fool I've been! Maybe in the back of my mind, I knew all along, but I can't worry about that now. I have to do what's right and give him up.

He's your husband to keep and not mine to take. I beg your forgiveness for what I've done these past twenty years. The next time he comes, I'll be sending him back home to you. Our boys will learn to live without their father, which will be my penance for what I've done.

Forgive me,
Pauline Adams

Was it possible to hear blood blistering to a boil in your head? If it wasn't, then Petunia needed to see a doctor.

She reread the letter while clenching her jaw so tight, her bones should've broken. She crumpled the letter in her hands and then raised herself off the bed, only to find Mama awake. And her usual kind face held nothing but fury.

And it was directed at Petunia.

Chapter 55

Mama held her hand out. "Give me the letter back."

Petunia squeezed the letter into a tight ball and didn't make a move to give it to her mama. "How long?"

"I ain't no mind reader." Mama said as she worked to raise herself out of the chair. "How long what?"

"Don't act like you don't know what I'm asking. How long have you known that man has another family?" Petunia continued to smoosh the letter into the smallest ball possible.

Mama's shoulders sagged when she got close to the bed. She threw the crutch to the side and lowered herself beside Petunia.

When she spoke, it was a whisper. "I found out a few months after you moved to Chicago."

Petunia's knuckles stretched white as she pressed the letter in her hand. "Does anyone else know?" She held her breath, waiting for her to answer.

"Nobody." Mama's head hung, and tears landed on her leg.

Some of the fury deflated, and for a moment, Petunia reverted to that young girl in their old barn holding Mama as she cried. She held her arms out and hugged her with all her might.

No matter how much she wanted to snap her cap, Petunia had to keep calm. It wasn't Mama's fault she married a louse.

Mama blew her nose on a rag she pulled from her pocket. "The first time he left me was a few months after you were born. Said he needed time to hisself. Then he said he found a job somewheres else."

Petunia found she needed to blow her own nose. Just when she thought Oliver couldn't get any worse in her sight. Wrong.

"And he has other children? Are you sure you can believe what this woman says?"

Mama nodded and wiped underneath her eyes. "He admitted it to me, child."

Petunia's hand went to her chest. "Why'd he say he did it? Or did he say?"

Mama shrugged, and her mouth slid into a frown. "It don't matter. What's done is done. It's in the past now."

"What's done is done?!?" Petunia's hands flew up to her temples, and she ran her hands through her hair, pulling hard. "Are you saying you've forgiven him for this?"

"I think it's best to work through our problems, child. We just had a misunderstanding, is all."

Petunia's face drew into a hard line. Could it be her fault that he cheated?

He was mad over her red hair. He must have been trying to hurt Mama over thinking Petunia didn't belong to him.

Why did everything have to boil down to her hair color?'

Maybe it was time to dye it black. It would fit better with her life.

Evelyn rushed into the room. "Mama, Lloyd's on the phone. I think he's got news about Daddy."

If only Evelyn knew what Petunia just found out.

Petunia opened her mouth, but before she said anything, Mama spoke one word. "Please."

"Fine." Petunia handed her the crutch that had slipped to the floor and helped her off the bed. "Come on, Mama, let's get to the phone."

Mama smiled directly after saying hello. "Oh, Ollie. What happened? Are you all right?"

The color drained from Mama's face, and her body slumped into the wall. "I hate to hear that. I do." She listened for another minute before continuing. "It don't matter, Ollie. Just bring 'em here."

Bring who here? Petunia's hands itched to jerk the phone out of Mama's hand and tell that two-timing snake off. And she would if not for Mama. She'd been hurt enough. No need for Petunia to add to it.

Mama's head cocked, and a look of determination crossed her features. "They can share a room, can't they?"

Oh no. This couldn't be good. What could Mama mean by that?

"Then it's settled. We'll be seeing you tomorrow."

Mama hung the phone up and leaned her head against the wall.

Petunia sighed. "You may as well tell us what's happening, Mama."

"Pauline Adams lost her life in that wreck. Ollie's bringing your brothers here to live with us."

She may as well have stabbed Petunia in the gut with the fireplace poker. That would've been preferable.

Chapter 56

A slight breeze entered through the open windows and ruffled the curtains in the front room at the bed and breakfast.

Martin and William made zoom zoom sounds from the floor where they played with their toy cars Ralph and Hazel had sent them.

Seeing them there tugged at Petunia's heart. She'd give anything for Verlon to be able to see their boys. Martin, with his red hair and Verlon's face, and William, who looked so much like Verlon, it was uncanny.

Hopefully, they'd be in their new home soon. She hated the car wreck had caused a delay. Not that she'd complain. A woman lost her life and now two boys would have to live without their mama.

Her brothers. Even thinking about it caused her head to throb. What Oliver had done wasn't their fault, so she better make sure not to treat them like it was. He wouldn't have wanted her no matter if they existed or not.

She sensed more than felt Evelyn's presence in room. "What do you think about what that man did to us, Evelyn?"

A long sigh came from behind Petunia. "I'm at a loss. But what he did was to Mama. Yes, we're hurt, but the one who has the most right to be upset is her."

Petunia's chin titled slightly to the right and she folded her arms across her chest. "I know that but that don't stop it from hurting."

After tugging one of Petunia's arms away from her chest, Evelyn hugged her closely. "I'm sorry, I wasn't trying to make light of what Daddy did. I know you're hurting."

Petunia's face softened, and then she hugged Evelyn back. "Can you believe we have two more brothers?"

A black car came to a stop in front of the house. "Not really. But it looks like we're about to meet them."

Petunia pulled the curtains back farther and then turned to Martin and William. "Boys, run get your granny real fast."

Mama hobbled into the room with MaryAnne following close behind. "So, they're here, then?"

Car doors slamming answered her question, but Petunia nodded anyway. "I reckon so."

Evelyn lit out the front door and down the steps and then wrapped Oliver in a hug. "I'm so glad you're okay, Daddy."

Lloyd unloaded the trunk before making a beeline for MaryAnne.

A burning sensation filled Petunia's chest as she watched Oliver and Evelyn. Had Evelyn lost her marbles? That man had been living a double life. He was a liar and a cheater. Worse than that even. And here Evelyn was treating him like nothing happened. Pathetic.

And Mama? Well, she was just as bad. She tapped her one foot until Evelyn stepped away, and then she wrapped her arms all around him. He pulled her close and they hugged like nothing ever happened.

Made no sense to Petunia. Instead of focusing on them, she moved her attention to the two boys with identical sandy blonde hair standing behind Oliver. The first one looked to be ten years old, while the littlest one appeared to be about six or so.

The older boy's dirty face had a look of fear on it that struck Petunia's heart. Maybe it was the streaks on his cheeks left behind by tears that did it. Whatever it was, Petunia wanted to make things better somehow.

She held her arm up and motioned. "Come here, young men."

The older boy met her eyes briefly before putting his head down and taking a hesitant step in her direction. He stopped before getting close enough to touch.

Petunia leaned on the ground and looked at him at eye level. "I'm Petunia. What's your name?"

After wiping his nose on his shirt sleeve, he whispered his answer. "Benjamin Hollings, ma'am."

"Nice to meet you, Benjamin." She glanced behind him. "And who's this here you have tugging on your shirttail?"

Before Benjamin could answer, the little boy walked up to Petunia. "My name is Patrick Hollings. Are we going to be living here with you?"

Benjamin shook his head and rolled his eyes before he chuckled. "This ain't no house, Patrick. This is what Daddy called a bed and breakfast."

Even though Patrick turned to Oliver, his innocent face penetrated Petunia's heart. "Well, where will we be living then?"

As bad as Petunia wanted to clock Oliver in the head, she refrained. It looked like he'd already been walloped with a big stick. His eyes were black, and his nose had a bandage across it.

Instead of walloping, she met Oliver's pained gaze with as much care and concern as she could muster. "We got a place you're all welcome to stay for as long as you need."

Oliver swallowed, and when he tried to speak, a sob came out instead. He swallowed a couple more times before nodding. "Thank you, Petunia. For everything."

As he walked away, Petunia ogled him hard.

Be dogged if he wasn't crying again.

Chapter 57

Their new place turned out to be perfect in Petunia's eyes. She grabbed Opal's hand and dragged her out the door and to the back porch. A lake stretched out in the distance as far as the eyes could see.

Petunia bounced on her toes and giggled like she used to before the days of picking cotton took over her life. "Look at this view, Opal. We can fish for days."

Opal stared across the yard as she hugged herself. "This is a beautiful place. I just love it."

Benjamin and Lonnie's son Jonathan came around the other end of the wraparound porch. Lonnie and Mildred had dropped Jonathan off for a few days so they could go on a proper honeymoon in Memphis.

It took Petunia some talking, but Lonnie had finally agreed to buy her house on a payment plan. He paid her what he could afford every month. Petunia figured that would help Lonnie with Jonathan while taking care of the promise she'd made Teresa. All Teresa had wanted was for her son to be cared for, and Petunia would always be there for him.

"Aunt Petunia," Jonathan said as he barreled up to Petunia and wrapped his arms around her legs.

She hugged Jonathan closely before turning to Benjamin with a smile that only got bigger when Mr. Beck appeared behind him. "Hello, there, boys. Mr. Beck, what brings you here?"

Mr. Beck tugged at his plaid necktie and waited until Benjamin ran past him and down the steps before answering.

"I wanted to let you know that I've been unable to get anywhere on the case. They've ruled Mr. Brown's death an accident, and they won't change their minds."

Even though a September wind stirred on the ground, a heat the likes of mid-July traveled up Petunia's body. "I shoulda known nothing would come of it."

Mr. Beck leaned on the railing on the other side of Petunia. "At least you can say you tried."

At least you can say you tried? Would they throw a person in jail for slugging a lawyer? Luckily for Mr. Beck, Opal spoke up before Petunia made her mind up.

Not that she really wanted to slug the man. She might mess up that pretty face of his. And that would be a shame.

A slight tremor laced Opal's tone. "Mr. Beck, nothings gonna come of it. But I thank you for what you've done all the same."

He nodded his head and met Petunia's gaze. "I'd suggest we consider our business dealings done. Does that suit you, Miss Marshall?"

"I reckon so." She shifted her body towards Opal. "If Opal agrees."

Opal's head bounced up and down like Petunia's insides the last time she rode Sampson. "Oh, yes. I never dreamed you'd hire no lawyer for the likes of me. You've done too much."

Petunia looked Mr. Beck up and down. She wished she could feel something more than a passing attraction. Then again, maybe not. Verlon's kisses burned her memory and kept her pillow wet at night. How would another live up to him?

Could you have more than one perfect person for you in a lifetime? How likely was it to happen once, much less twice?

Was living life alone any better? It's not like she needed money to live on. She could just live with herself and the boys and be fine and dandy.

Sheriff Keach stepped around the porch. "Now, let's not go getting ahead of ourselves, Mr. Beck."

Mr. Beck narrowed his eyes at the same time, and his back stiffened. "Afternoon, Sheriff. I was just leaving."

He tipped his hat at Petunia as he disappeared around the porch.

Sheriff Keach watched him leave with a hardened face. Which was odd to Petunia. Hadn't he been the one to recommend Mr. Beck? Why would he do that if he didn't like the man? Because there was no mistaking that fact.

He got his face under control, and his lips lifted into a smile that didn't quite reach his eyes. "Howdy, Petunia."

Petunia bestowed the same smile on him. "Sheriff. What brings you this far from home? Again?"

His lips turned downward, and he wiped his forehead with a white handkerchief. "I rode this way with Eddie and Gail."

Petunia clapped her hands together. "Eddie and Gail are here?"

His lips turned into a grin. "They were talking with your folks when I came around the porch." He paused, and his grin turned to a frown. "I'm afraid I have to deliver some bad news."

Petunia's chest tightened like the last girdle she wore. "What bad news?"

He looked away, and Petunia craned her neck to see his face. He was either a good actor or something bad had happened.

His tone became dull when he spoke. "Judith Cooper is dead."

Petunia's hand flew up to her mouth, but it didn't prevent a sob from escaping. "Dead?" She grabbed Opal's arm to keep steady.

He took out a pack of Winston cigarettes and fumbled with the package until he got one out. He lit it with a match and took a deep drag.

"David found her yesterday shot in the head. Dead as a doornail." He coughed before taking another drag from the cigarette. "I don't have a sister, but I can't imagine finding a family member dead like that."

"Do they know who killed her?" Petunia glanced at Opal. She stood there staring unblinkingly at Sheriff Keach.

He threw the cigarette down and smashed it under his boot. "She killed herself. Left a note that said something about losing the love of her life and not wanting to go on without him."

Petunia blinked a few times as the conversation she'd overheard between Clyde and Judith played through her mind. Judith told him she loved him. Could it be Clyde she didn't want to live without? It must be. Even though Judith had treated Petunia horribly, she vowed then and there that she'd take that secret to her grave.

She started to hightail it to the front yard but stopped in her tracks. She couldn't leave Opal alone with that man. He may have apologized and acted like he was a good person, but something was off.

"Come on, Opal."

Right around dusk that evening, the entire family, plus the Sheriff, sat outside around a fire playing musical instruments and visiting.

Miss Betty and Jasper, her son had picked Opal up before dinner. Opal and Jasper seemed to be meant for one another.

A solid black sedan with tinted windows pulled into the driveway. Oliver stood and set his harmonica down.

Two military men stepped out of the car and approached the group. The shorter bald one spoke. "We're looking for a Mrs. Carol Marshall."

Petunia shot off the log she used as a chair. "I'm Petunia, er Carol Marshall. What can I do for you?"

His face never showed emotion as he gave the news Petunia had been praying for. "Private First-Class Verlon Marshall is alive and in an undisclosed location receiving treatment. Expect him to arrive home before the month is out."

Everything started spinning. The log. The fire. The military men.

When Petunia was a kid, Teresa had talked her into rolling down a hill in a barrel. She had thought it was gonna kill her.

It ended up knocking her out when it came to a stop by hitting a tree. She's lucky nothing had been broken.

Right now, Petunia may as well have been back in that barrel.

Chapter 58

The roller coaster that used to be Petunia's brain jumped from one thought to another. Taking a sip of her coffee, she forcefully slowed her mind down. The news from the night before had thrown her into shock.

Verlon was alive! That's all she remembered the military men saying. And at the moment, that's all that mattered.

He was alive!

Opal shook her head and smiled before sipping her own coffee. It had taken Petunia the longest to get Opal to sit with her at the same table.

The day Opal sat down with her had been when Petunia knew Opal regarded her as more of a friend than an employer. Which made her happy.

Right now, they were the only two awake in the house. After everything settled down last night, Mama and Oliver took the boys to their house next door. And amazingly, the baby hadn't woken MaryAnne and Lloyd up yet.

Edward and Gail had opted to stay at the Bed and Breakfast along with the Sheriff, so the place was quiet.

Verlon.

He. Was. Alive.

Petunia's foot tapped so fast under the table that the coffee in her cup jiggled. "Oh, Opal! Can you believe it? I gotta figure out where he is so I can go to him."

A grin appeared on Opal's face. The one she kept reserved for those times she was really happy. "I'm so happy for you, misses."

Could a heart thud so hard and fast it explodes? Cause if so, Petunia had to find a way to calm herself. She sure didn't want to kill over before seeing Verlon again.

"I just can't wait to see his face."

Opal got real still and reached across the table to grasp Petunia's hand. "Now that I know you gonna be in good hands, I need to tell you something."

Uh oh. Whatever Opal had to say must be serious. Petunia's leg slowed down from its tapping. "What's that?"

That big smile returned, and Opal's eyes fell to the napkin bunched up by her coffee cup. "Jasper asked me to be his wife."

Petunia stood up so fast that her chair fell over backward. "Opal, congratulations!"

A grin the size of her fist settled on Opal's face, and she smoothed her curly hair behind her ear. "We plan on having the wedding the day after tomorrow. But we can do it later on if you want."

Petunia's wheels started turning with grand ideas for the ceremony. Everyone deserved to be as happy as she was. "No way. That's as good a day as any, and we can have it right here."

Opal picked her fork up and laid it down a couple of times. "We settled on the date before knowing your husband was alive."

This news was just what she needed to keep her mind occupied while waiting for Verlon. "Well, that's not a problem. You and Jasper's wedding won't hinder Verlon from coming home, and it'll give me something to do while I wait for him to come home."

A knock coming from the front door interrupted their celebration. Petunia pulled the curtain back. "Looks like Uncle Edward's car."

Opal headed through the door. "I'll let them in, misses."

Petunia let the curtain down and yelled after Opal. "Okay, but we have some celebrating to do, Opal."

A couple of minutes later, Edward, Gail, and Sheriff Keach filed into the kitchen. Opal excused herself to finish up her housework.

Petunia raised a brow at Opal but left it alone. One of these days, Opal would understand she was more than a housemaid to Petunia.

"Morning, folks. Help yourselves to some coffee and a muffin."

Later that evening, Petunia hummed the tune to Johnny Cash's song Ring of Fire as she loaded a few bags of groceries. She planned on baking Opal a special wedding cake.

The trunk closed with a thud. When she turned around, she ran into Cyrus Cooper's chest. A chill traveled down her spine as she backed away.

Cyrus gripped her wrist, and his mouth quivered when he spoke. "You're the reason Judith is gone."

Another chill sliced through Petunia, settling in her chest as she shook her head.

His grip tightened, and he moved so close to Petunia that a stench like rotten food burned her nostrils.

"The way I see it is you owe me, and you're going to pay one way or another."

Adrenaline surged in her chest as she pushed Cyrus away and grasped the door handle. "Stay away from me. I'm sorry about Judith, but that has nothing to do with me."

He placed his hand on the door, stopping her from opening it. "Oliver promised I could marry you. You need to honor that promise, or you'll regret it."

As she said a silent prayer to remain calm, her fingers clutched the handle. She pulled on the door with her free hand. "You'll be sorry if you don't leave me alone."

A maddening sound close to a laugh erupted from Cyrus. "I like 'em feisty. Just wait. I ain't done with you."

Petunia's spine stiffened. "Is that a threat?"

He licked his lips and smiled like they were sharing a special secret. "I been keeping an eye on you, and it seems to me like you been careless."

Her heart thudded hard against her ribcage. "It was you in the woods that day, wasn't it?"

He grinned and shot up a brow. "I guess you'll never know. Just keep them boys close. I'd hate for something to happen to one of 'em."

That did it. Heat swam across her chest, and she slammed the palms of her hands against his torso, shoving with all her might.

He stumbled backward but quickly gained his balance. His hands balled up into fists, and he took a step toward her.

"Ma'am, are you all right?" A man leaving the grocery store stopped.

Cyrus stepped back, and she slipped inside the car. She landed a smile on the man and nodded before backing out and putting her foot on the gas.

Two days later, the melon and pink sunset gliding across the lake made for a stunning backdrop to the wedding reception to honor Opal and Jasper. The September breeze added the perfect touch to ensure the attendees weren't too hot as they celebrated.

Petunia stood in between Ralph and Hazel, clasping Hazel's hand. They'd flown into Memphis the day before to wait on Verlon. The three of them had a happy glow they had missed the past few years.

Regardless of the people standing around the reception, Petunia stepped away from her in-laws and hugged Opal. "I'm so happy for you, my friend."

Opal threw a hand across her mouth and spun around. The white dress reminded Petunia of a lily as it wrapped around Opal's body.

"I never thought I'd be this happy after we left home."

A shrill of delight left Petunia. This moment would forever be etched in her memories. Two friends just being happy. No matter what color their skin happened to be.

"You deserve all the happiness in the world."

Opal's new mother-in-law, Miss Betty, sauntered over and plopped a hand on her right hip. "You really meant what you said that day we met."

Cocking her head, Petunia met Miss Betty's gaze. "Pardon?"

Miss Betty pointed at Opal, and her lips turned upward. "When you called Opal your friend. You really meant it."

Petunia's eyes moistened as she stared at Opal. "She is my friend."

Jasper picked up a guitar and belted out a song. Oliver joined him with a harmonica.

Benjamin came running across the lawn in their direction. "Petunia. A snake done bit your mama!"

Chapter 59

The road to the Baptist Hospital in Memphis seemed to continue for a thousand miles. Oliver sat in the back seat with Mama while Lloyd drove the car. How she'd ended up being the one going with them was beyond Petunia.

Lloyd kept glancing in the rearview mirror. "How's she doing, Daddy?"

Oliver held onto Mama even though he looked half asleep. One of his eyes was swollen shut but had faded to a light gray over the past few days.

Petunia's nostrils flared but one look at Mama made her swallow all the mean words she wanted to say. "Mama's doing the same. Just keep your eyes on the road."

After leaving the hospital, the drive home had a happier feel than the drive there. The snake hadn't been poisonous. She was given some cream and sent home. She had to be the luckiest human.

The next day, Petunia strolled along the water's edge, skidding rocks on top of the water. Her mind rolled through her upcoming reunion with Verlon. How would it go? Would they kiss right away, or would he look at her as a stranger?

And why wasn't he home yet? Was he hurt too bad to travel? No, that couldn't be it. Speaking of people going home, she still couldn't figure out why Sheriff Keach hadn't returned home.

What was his purpose?

Surely, he didn't think he and Petunia had a chance to be together. Verlon would be home soon, and all would be right in the world.

She'd never have to look twice at another man again.

Even though the sun had risen, the moon hung in the early morning sky. It looked a lot like a milky white hunk of cheese. Petunia could see why some people said that about it.

"Howdy, gal." Oliver picked up a rock and watched it jump across the water before he turned to Petunia. "I got something to say to you, and I hope you'll hear me out."

Petunia stared straight ahead like the water had her in a trance.

Oliver took a long breath and tugged on the strap of his blue jean overalls. "I've done you wrong your whole life, Petunia. I ain't thinking I can make up for it this late, but I'm hoping…."

His voice caught, and he cleared his throat.

Her body tilted slightly in Oliver's direction, and she met his eyes. Part of her wanted to tell him off and walk away. But the other part…

A tiny part had to know what he was going to say.

His chin quivered as he continued with his speech. "I'm hoping you'll be able to forgive me. To let me be a part of your life like I shoulda been all along."

"I don't know what to say." A hot liquid shimmied around Petunia's throat, and she tugged on her ear-lobes. "Why did you always love the other kids but not me?"

He swallowed, and his gaze darted across the land-scape. "I was full of hate thinking your mama done cheated on me. I took my meanness out on you instead of believing her."

She grabbed a chuck of her red hair and raised it to the side of her head. "All because of my hair? Is that really the reason?"

He took two steps toward her, stopping short of standing beside her. "Nah, it ain't because of your red hair. It's because I was jealous and let it drive me to do things I shouldn't have. It's my fault, Petunia, not yours. I done asked the Good Lord to forgive me. Now I pray you will."

She let her hair drop to her shoulders as she met his pleading gaze. Her voice cracked when she spoke. "I…"

Oliver rubbed his jaw and kicked at a rock. "Why don't you take some time to think about what I said?"

She tossed another rock over the water, and it sank without skidding. A sting pierced her arm, and she killed a mosquito, wiping the blood it left behind on her pants. She swallowed hard and allowed her body to relax. "I reckon it won't hurt me none to think about it."

His face lit up as he turned to walk away. "That's more than I would've hoped for. I'm gonna get home to tend to your mama."

She rubbed her arms and jumped when a train's whistle pierced the air in the distance. "Let me know if y'all need anything."

He grinned and shook his head. "I swear that woman can't be put down. She's done took on a horse and now a snake. I hate to ask what's next."

Petunia surprised herself when she giggled. "She's a tough one, that's for sure."

He stuck his hands in his pockets. "Can the boys come over later?"

A lizard ran across the grass by Petunia's foot. She moved over to the left to make a hundred percent sure it didn't touch her.

"I don't mind. As long as you can peel Ralph and Hazel away from them for a few minutes."

"Thank ye, Petunia. I'll send Benjamin over to fetch them later on." He paused and swiped at a mosquito buzzing around his head. "Don't stay out here too long. The skeeters have sniffed us out."

He walked off whistling like he was happy as a lark. He was already trying to look out for her. This couldn't be right.

Maybe he had something up his sleeve. Or maybe, just maybe, he really wanted to be forgiven. Could she deny that request? Was it in her power to say no and still be right with God?

Petunia raised her eyes to the sky before bowing her head. A prayer for God's will to be done seemed the most appropriate thing now.

The prayer turned out to be much more than what she intended. She dropped to her knees on the damp ground, tears streaming down her face as she poured her heart out.

"Dear Lord, please be with my family. Help my heart to be more open and forgiving to Daddy. I pray for Your will to be done in all things. Thank You for allowing Verlon to be found alive. I love You, Lord, and beg for Your forgiveness for all the times I've failed. In Jesus Name, Amen."

Petunia wiped her nose with the sleeve of her shirt, and a still calmness entered her heart.

"That was a beautiful prayer."

Her heart dropped to the damp ground she sat on before she bolted upright.

Verlon stood there with a lopsided grin and his arms open wide. His eyes caressed her. The eyes she'd spent many sorrowful nights dreaming about.

A sob left Petunia, and she wasted no time jumping into Verlon's arms.

Her heart plummeted like a stone to the damp earth beneath her as the weight of her emotions surged within her. In an instant, she sprang upright, her breath catching in her throat. There he was—Verlon—standing before her with a lopsided grin that seemed to light up the dim surroundings.

Petunia's heart sang with joy at the sight, memories flooding back of the countless sorrowful nights spent dreaming of those very eyes. The overwhelming rush of emotions became too much to bear, and a sob escaped her lips.

Verlon opened his arms, and without a moment's hesitation, she leaped into his embrace. He tenderly pressed his lips against her cheeks, moving slowly to her forehead and then to the tip of her nose. When his lips met hers, a flood of goosebumps covered her skin.

With a groan, Verlon gently lifted Petunia off the ground, cradling her in his strong arms. With a soft smile on his face, he carried her toward the house.

Chapter 60

They didn't get far before Hazel and Ralph bombarded them. How Petunia would love to be in a bubble with just her and Verlon. Even though that line of thinking was selfish, she couldn't stop herself.

Wiggling out of his arms, she nodded in his parents' direction. "Go on and hug your parents. They been missing you, too."

Ralph and Hazel wrapped Verlon in a hug.

He pulled Petunia in, and he met her eyes through tears. "Where's our boy?"

"You mean boys?" Petunia whispered in his ear.

He stepped out of the group hug and turned his head to the left. "I can't hear out of my right ear. What did you say?"

Petunia tented her hands together and settled them in the crook of her nose. "I said we have two boys."

His brows scrunched together, and he looked from her to his parents. "I don't guess I still heard you right. Did you say you have two boys?"

Almost like their ears were burning, Martin and William hopped around the side of the house.

Petunia nodded in their direction. "There they come now."

Verlon followed her line of sight, looking like he saw a ghost. Ralph pointed at William and seemed to sense what Verlon thought.

"Little William Ralph looks just like you, son."

Verlon's tone came out filled with wonder. "How is that possible?"

Petunia raised her voice so he could hear her better. "I was pregnant when you left for Korea. We just didn't know it."

As Verlon leaned on the ground, a laugh left him. The boys stopped a few feet in front of him with curious expressions.

After their reunion, they took the rest of the day to fill Verlon in on everything that had happened since he'd gone missing.

The days following Verlon's return blurred together for Petunia. Her life turned into a fairytale. She never would've dreamed Verlon would be home. Really home.

Then he wasn't.

After leaving to get a haircut, two days had passed without him coming home. She lowered herself onto the sofa and punched the cushion. She'd scream but would hate to wake the boys up at almost midnight. Petunia tried to file a police report and was told he was a grown man and to give him some space.

Stupid cops.

She considered calling Sheriff Keach for help. But that would be desperate.

Desperate times called for desperate measures. Before she could decide, the front door creaked open, and Verlon tiptoed inside.

Eyes so green they could cut glass met eyes full of sorrow. She shot off the couch. "Where in the world have you been?"

He sighed and tried to walk past her. She grabbed his shirt and made him stop. "I asked you a question, and I expect an answer."

He wouldn't look her in the face. The floor apparently held something of great interest. "Petunia. Please don't do this."

"Don't do what? Ask my husband where he's been the past two days?" She let go of his shirt and gagged. "You stink to high heavens. What is that?"

"No telling. I'm going to take a shower." He left the room as quickly as he came in.

What was all that about? Could he be cheating like Daddy had? But how would he even know who to cheat with? He had only returned home a couple of weeks ago.

Her hands balled into fists that she dropped to her sides. That wasn't it. Something else had to be going on. She just had to figure out what.

The water running seemed to make her blood boil even more than it already was. She paced across the floor while waiting for Verlon to finish his shower. He owed her some answers. And she would not be going to bed without them.

Twenty minutes later, she had to eat those words. Verlon lay snoring in the guest bedroom.

She guessed it was time for Verlon to meet the old Petunia. First thing in the morning.

Chapter 61

Petunia stomped out of the kitchen as fast as she could, carrying a bucket of ice-cold water. She'd teach Verlon to disappear for days and then sleep in the guest room. She wouldn't be treated like that.

She stood by the bed, watching him sleep for a few seconds. He looked so peaceful. She almost changed her mind. Almost. Before deciding against it, she lifted the bucket and poured the water on Verlon's head.

He shot off the bed and pinned Petunia against the wall with his forearm covering her throat. He had a wild look about him like Petunia had never witnessed. After a split second, he shook his head, and water landed on Petunia's face.

She pulled at his arm and bucked against his sturdy frame. "Get off of me, Verlon."

After blinking several times, he backed away and sat on the bed.

Petunia brought trembling hands to the base of her neck and pressed her spine into the wall as far as she could. She eyeballed Verlon through a narrowed gaze.

He sat with his head in his hands for what seemed like forever. Finally, he raised bloodshot eyes and looked Petunia in the face.

"Petunia?" An expression of confusion flitted across his face. "What's wrong with you?"

She kept her hands wrapped around her pulsating throat. "You really don't know?"

He stood up and took a step towards Petunia. Her stomach clenched, and she scooted into the corner of the wall.

Pausing, he tilted his head. "What's going on? Are you scared of me?"

Pushing aside the fear that had taken over her mind should've been easier than it was. But she had to do it for Verlon's sake. For her marriage.

"I…"

"Wait a minute, did I hurt you?" He wiped at the tears pooling in his eyes. "I did, didn't I?"

Her spine relaxed a little, and she stepped in his direction. "You didn't mean to."

He turned and punched the wall. "I was afraid this would happen."

Her breath hitched a tiny bit. "It's fine."

"No, it is not fine." His head dropped.

Footsteps sounded down the hall. "Verlon? Petunia? Everything okay?"

Hazel. How could Petunia have forgotten about them being there? They might not be in this situation if she had calmed down before throwing ice water on Verlon.

"Sorry, Hazel. We're fine." Petunia yelled through the closed door.

"Are you sure?" Hazel pecked on the door like they weren't already talking.

Petunia moved closer to the door, poised to press her body against it. She didn't need Hazel questioning why Verlon had a wet head. "Positive."

"Okay then. I'm gonna make breakfast." Her footsteps faded the further she got away from them.

Petunia waited with her ear against the door until she was sure Hazel was out of earshot. "Where have you been? We've been worried sick these past two days, Verlon."

He raked his fingers through his hair and grabbed a t-shirt from the foot of the bed. "I'm sorry, Petunia, but I needed some space to clear my head."

She inched closer to Verlon and sat beside him on the bed. "But where did you go?"

Even though his body tensed when she got near, he remained beside her. "I camped out in the woods behind the Evelyn's place."

He could've just punched her in the gut. "Why didn't you say something?"

A pained look passed his face, and he raised his hand toward Petunia, only to let it drop before he touched her. "I didn't plan it. It just happened."

"Well?" Her fingers worked on pulling a rip in a tiny hole she'd found in her nightgown. "Did you get your head cleared?"

"I did." His nod seemed final to Petunia. Almost like he'd made a big decision without asking for her input. "Things are real clear now."

She folded her hands in her lap to keep from tearing a bigger hole in her gown. Her stomach settled down, but she couldn't shake the weird feeling in her belly.

Trying not to cry, Petunia met his dark gaze. "Good, so we can get on with our lives?"

Thunder rumbled, shaking the windows and floor, and Petunia's hand flew back to the hole in her gown.

"You can." His broad shoulders tensed, and he nodded. "Petunia, we're getting divorced."

Chapter 62

Verlon held Petunia's gaze briefly before walking out of the room. She sat on the bed for a moment listening to the blood rushing around her head. Things were not about to end like this. There was no way she was losing her husband after all she'd been through.

Not after waiting so long for him to come home.

No way.

Not on her life.

Hazel had pancakes and sausage on the table when she reached the kitchen. Ralph sat with his cigar propped between his fingers, reading the newspaper, mumbling over somebody getting away with murder.

Verlon stood at the window looking outside.

He swiveled his body and shivered. "There's a storm brewing."

Did he really think he could say what he did and pretend nothing had happened? It seemed to be the case. Boy, was he mistaken.

Petunia poured a cup of coffee and moved close to Verlon. Her right arm touched his left arm as she stared out the window.

"You have no idea what kind of storm's coming." Petunia clenched her jaw to keep her lips from quivering. She needed to keep her head on straight for the boys.

He whipped his head around, and Petunia watched his Adam's apple bobble. Good. He had every right to be nervous.

Ralph laid the newspaper down and cleared his throat. "Is everything all right this morning?"

Pressing a finger to her lips, Petunia shrugged and cast a glance at Verlon. "I don't know. Verlon, is everything all right this morning?"

Verlon's forehead creased, and he lowered his voice to a whisper. "Let's not do this right now."

Hazel sidled up next to Petunia, a worried expression marring her features. "I knew something was wrong. What is it?"

Ralph's voice came out harsh. "Is that band of racist varmints starting something again?"

Petunia let out a soft laugh. "Not at all. Ask Verlon what's wrong. He can tell you." She elbowed him almost playfully. "Can't you, Verlon?"

His expression turned stony, and he pressed his lips together in a thin line.

Hazel touched Petunia's arm, and a sigh escaped her lips. "What is it, dear? Please tell us."

Ralph stood up and joined them at the window. "We can't help if we don't know what's wrong."

As the storm roared outside, a storm raged inside Petunia's heart. Maybe she should've slowed her racing heart down before speaking, but her feelings overruled her good sense at the moment.

She let out another laugh, this time a loud one, and she elbowed Verlon a second time. "Oh, it's nothing serious. Verlon wants to divorce me, is all."

As soon as she said the words, she burst into tears.

Hazel gasped and started saying something to Verlon. None of the words made sense to Petunia.

Verlon stomped out of the house. The car door slammed, and he walked back inside a few minutes later, holding a few papers.

He handed the papers and an ink pen to Petunia. "I didn't want to do this now, but since you've forced me, there you go."

Her vision clouded as she tried to make sense of what she held.

Ralph took the papers out of her hands and exploded. "Do you have any idea what you're doing to your family?"

His face turned stony, and his voice came out still and even. "Yes, I do. I'm keeping them safe."

Safe?

Petunia's heart jumped. This was about him. Not her. "What do you mean, Verlon? We're safe with you."

A bitter laugh escaped Verlon's lips. "Don't you see? I'm not the same person you married. I refuse to put my family in harm's way. Even if it means protecting you from my own self."

"No." One word played over and over in Petunia's head.

"Sign the papers, Petunia. Protect yourself. Protect the boys." With that, he turned on his heel and stormed out of her life for the second time.

But this time, it seemed way more personal.

Chapter 63

Rain pelted against the windshield as Petunia drove down the gravel road. After reading the divorce papers, she discovered Mr. Beck was the one who put them together. How dare he do that to her family.

She'd show him. These stupid divorce papers would be ripped and thrown in his face. She would not be signing them.

The pothole came out of nowhere and caused her car to slide to the right. She took her foot off the gas with her heart beating out of her chest. Better slow down, or the papers wouldn't matter. Nothing would.

A few minutes later, she eased down the main drag in Harrisburg. The lawyer's office was on the square by the courthouse, and thankfully, there were plenty of parking spots.

She glanced inside the barber shop and waved. Daddy sat in the chair, prepped for a cut and shave. He waved at her before leaning his head back.

Verlon stepped out of the store next door before opening the door to the barbershop. He paused and stared at Petunia. She scowled and turned away.

She guessed Verlon was keeping an eye on the lawyer's office to make sure she signed the divorce papers. Well, she had news for him and Mr. Beck both. She'd make them eat those papers before she signed them.

The secretary's desk sat empty as Petunia entered the lawyer's office. Voices drifted down the hall, so she took a seat. She'd wait her turn to give him a piece of her mind.

She sat straight up in the seat and cocked her head. She knew that voice.

"I've already put my life on hold for you. I even hired another secretary at my own expense just to get closer to the woman! What else do you want?"

"You didn't need to be marrying your secretary anyway. I told you I want Petunia Marshall to pay for what she did to me!"

"You never did tell me what she did to you. I think I deserve to know."

"*She made me the laughingstock in town! I can't even walk down the street without somebody snickering and saying Petunia left me for colored folks.*"

"*I don't think I can do much more to help you.*"

"*Well, I'll be talking to my Mayor about what you stole from him. You'd rather be dead than help me?*"

"*Of course not! But I only took a little off the top! The more I think about it, the more I think he won't do anything as serious as have me killed.*"

"*Do you enjoy living in fear, Mr. Beck?*"

"*This has gone on long enough. I must ask you to leave.*"

"*I ain't going nowhere. Now, you **will** finish what we started. Get that girl divorced!*"

"*Then what? She's divorced…oh well.*"

"*Then I'll marry her and be a rich man! Plus, I'll get to spend the rest of my life showing her what it means to have a real man!*"

"*All this because she embarrassed you? It seems extreme to me.*"

"*She would rather be with them coloreds than me! She coulda had it all, Mr. Beck! But I wasn't good enough for her! Even though she's never been nothin' but a crummy dame with a trashy family!*"

A sledgehammer couldn't have stopped the gasp that left Petunia's lips. She bolted out of the seat and across the room. She pulled on the doorknob, but

Sheriff Keach made it to her before she could fully open the door, leaving it open a crack.

He picked her up and carried her into the room, kicking and screaming.

"Well, well, well. Look who we have here." Sheriff Keach snarled and then shoved her close to Mr. Beck.

"You sleazy snake!" Hot spasms of fire traveled up Petunia's spine, and she lunged at Sheriff Keach.

He unholstered his gun and pointed it at Petunia. He screwed a long, black piece on the end of it. What in the world it was, Petunia couldn't say.

Mr. Beck grabbed her shirt and pulled her next to him. "Let's not get out of control, Sheriff. There's no call in pulling a gun on anybody."

The sheriff waved the gun toward the stairs. "Get on up them stairs. It looks like you two lovebirds will fight over Petunia's husband."

Petunia dug her heels into the carpet. "We ain't lovebirds, and I ain't going up no stairs."

He cocked the gun. "Do it!"

Mr. Beck pulled Petunia up the stairs with him. He whispered so the sheriff couldn't hear. "Let's do what he says and try to overpower him when we get upstairs."

Once they reached the top of the stairs, Mr. Beck put his body in front of hers. "Think about what you're doing, Sheriff."

"I have, Mr. Beck. Too bad your love shoots you. She *is* known for her bad temper, you know." He raised the gun and shot Mr. Beck.

Red crimson spread across his white button-up shirt, and a shocked look crossed his face. He gripped Petunia's arm as he fell to the ground.

The scream that left Petunia pierced even her own ears as she fell to the ground alongside Mr. Beck.

Chapter 64

Could life move in slow motion? Like a black-and-white picture show? She would've said no if she'd been asked that before this moment. Impossible. But now, she would have to say yes.

Sheriff Keach loomed over her, steadily waving the gun. "Get up off the floor, Miss Marshall, before I shoot you."

It was odd how he threatened to shoot her as casually as inviting her to Sunday dinner. He had to be a lunatic.

She somehow managed to get to her feet but couldn't take her eyes off the red stain on Mr. Beck's shirt. She had to help him.

The sheriff grabbed her hair and pulled her across the floor. She flailed her arms like a wildcat fighting a bear, but it did no good. He let go of her hair long enough to open one of the doors at the top of the stairs.

That was plenty enough time for Petunia to run. She swiveled on her toes and headed down the stairs, only to have him grab the back of her neck and drag her back to the room.

Did she somehow attract crazy people? First, the nutjob in Chicago, now the looney tune sheriff. Had she done something she needed to make amends for? If so, she would do whatever it took.

She dug her nails into the doorframe and held on for dear life.

The sheriff cackled and then hit her hand with the butt of that long gun. "You're quite a handful, aren't you, Miss Marshall?"

How the sharp pain moved from her hand to her shoulder so fast was beyond Petunia's comprehension. Her entire right side went limp as the throbbing increased. "I'll kill you!"

"How do you expect to do that, little lady?" One last pull and she landed on all four in another office.

If only she could find a letter opener.

The sheriff kicked her side before leaning close to her ear. "You gonna kill me with your bare hands?"

Pounding footsteps sounded from the stairs. The sheriff turned away from Petunia right before someone tackled him.

Petunia coughed and sat up, holding her aching side. That man had feet like a horse. She blinked several times to believe the scene in front of her. Daddy had the sheriff in a headlock, beating the side of his head.

Verlon gently helped her to her feet and put her hand around his neck.

How did they get in there?

The sheriff slung Daddy into the wall and turned the gun on her and Verlon. "You bunch of hicks think you can outdo me? I don't hardly think so."

He pointed the gun from Petunia to Verlon and tilted his head to the left. "Let me see…who do I want to shoot first? The trollop or her husband?"

Verlon pushed Petunia behind his body. "I guess you have no choice but to shoot me."

His lips curled into a snarl. "That'll do just fine."

Before the sheriff pulled the trigger, Daddy took off at a dead run and wrapped the sheriff in a bearhug before they tumbled down the stairs.

Verlon grabbed Petunia's hand and raced down the stairs behind them. One look told Petunia the sheriff hadn't made it. His neck looked twisted, and his unblinking eyes stared straight at the ceiling.

Daddy sat there with the sheriff's gun in his hand, pointing it at the dead man.

Verlon let go of Petunia and stepped over the sheriff. He took the gun out of Daddy's hand and laid it on Mr. Beck's desk.

Mr. Beck!

Petunia limped up the stairs, followed by Verlon, but it was too late to do anything for the lawyer.

She sobbed and leaned into Verlon. "Thank you for saving me, Verlon. How did y'all know to come in here?"

Verlon rubbed Petunia's head. "Oliver noticed the door had been opened a crack right before we heard a faint scream."

As soon as they got down the stairs, Petunia wrapped Daddy in a hug. "Thank you, Daddy."

He kissed the top of her head before leaning onto the desk.

Hours later, after giving their statements to the police and informing the rest of the family about what had happened, they gathered around a fire outside Petunia's home to celebrate the fact that none of them had died. Verlon gestured for Petunia to join him on the porch.

He cleared his throat and leaned on the rail. "I'm glad you're safe, but nothing has changed. I still want a divorce. I'm not the same person I was before, and I wouldn't be able to live with myself if I hurt you."

Squaring her shoulders, Petunia met his gaze with a hard one of her own. "No. I'll agree to separate, but I don't want our boys being raised by divorced folks."

He stared at the lake and nodded before turning to Petunia. He pulled her close and kissed her mouth. "Fair enough. Goodbye, Petunia."

Chapter 65

Petunia realized that the best way to take her mind off Verlon was to focus on her own life. She needed to understand what would truly make her satisfied.

Over the past few months, she had come to the surprising conclusion that she didn't need much at all. Volunteering to help those in need, especially the elderly, provided a significant sense of purpose and filled the void in her life.

One of the people she helped owned a café off the beaten path. Robert and Jan Lamb had lived in Tyronza all their lives, and they knew everybody. When Robert suffered a stroke, the community stepped up to help by taking turns helping Jan at the café.

Petunia and Opal were some of the volunteers. Opal helped Jan with the cooking three days a week while Petunia took care of the baked goods.

The small café had a few people still scattered across the room, left over from the lunch rush. It was one of the only places to eat where whites and blacks freely mingled and had quickly turned into a favorite place for Petunia and Opal to meet even before they got to know the owners.

Miss Jan weaved in and out of the tables, stopping when she came to where Petunia and Opal sat. "Howdy, ladies. Petunia, I had ten orders for your Lemon Cake this week. You think you can get them done?"

Pushing her chair back from the table, Petunia rose and hugged Miss Jan. "Evelyn ordered some muffins for the Bed and Breakfast, but I can get 'em done."

Miss Jan plopped a wrinkled hand on her hip. "Don't bite off more than you can chew, young lady."

A customer that looked old enough to be Miss Jan's grandpa walked into the café and settled in at the table next to theirs. Miss Jan turned to the man and waved. "I'll be with ya in a minute, Horace."

"I can get them done, Miss Jan. Don't you worry," Petunia said before shoving in a bite of Pecan Pie and groaning.

Miss Jan's mouth quirked up, and she turned to the next table.

Petunia sipped her sweet tea and smiled at Opal. "I'm so glad to see you're feeling healthy."

Opal's eyes brightened, and she patted her round belly. "I'm better than ever. Jasper is such a good man, and we can't wait to meet our little one. We gonna name him after Clyde, you know."

Petunia sipped her sweet tea and smiled at Opal. "What a sweet way to remember Clyde. I'm happy for you, Opal."

With tears brimming in her eyes, Opal looked at Petunia. "I don't know how to thank you for all you did for me and Clyde."

Leaning forward, Petunia reached for Opal's hand. "You don't have to thank me, Opal. You and Clyde brought a bit of happiness to my childhood. I'll never forget what y'all did for me when Judith tried to kill me."

Opal's face took on a look almost like she'd been transported back to the days of their youth. "You was always so good to us. I sure wish Clyde was here to see us now."

Petunia's eyes burned with unshed tears. "He'd be so happy for you, and I know he'd love Jasper." Her nose flared as she fought back memories of the night Clyde was killed. "I still can't believe the new sheriff found out that Judith Cooper's family was behind everything that happened."

An uncharacteristic snort left Opal. "Those Cooper's was always mean as snakes, so it don't surprise me none."

Petunia tilted her head and then shrugged. "Yeah, they sure was. At least David and Cyrus Cooper are going to court next week."

"Now that's something I can't believe. White men going to trial for what they did to us." Opal clamped her mouth shut like she regretted what she said. After taking a sip of her tea, she continued, "I'll pray for their souls."

A wide smile parted Petunia's lips with the thought of Opal praying for the Cooper family. That was one thing she'd always loved about Opal and wished she could be more like. "I admire you, Opal."

Petunia should've known Opal wouldn't want to be admired. She didn't even reply to that comment. "I'd like to be there when they go in front of the judge."

A swirl of excitement swished around in Petunia's belly. "You do?"

"I do. Will you go to court with me and Jasper? We can take our own car."

"Of course I will."

The corners of Opal's mouth quirked into a small smile before she leaned her elbows on the table.

"Now that we got that settled, are you ready to make things right with Verlon?"

A tightness tugged at Petunia's heart. "I'm beyond ready. I just don't know that he is."

Laughter from the next table echoed off the walls. Opal looked at the group and grinned before turning back to Petunia. "You never will know unless you try."

Petunia rubbed the moisture around her glass of tea before screwing her lips up. "I know."

After finishing their pie and sweet tea, they said their goodbyes and agreed to meet the following week to drive to Des Arc.

Chapter 66

Despite the long drive from Tyronza to Des Arc, Petunia talked Lloyd into driving out to the place where they grew up. Opal wanted to show Jasper where she lived, and Petunia wanted to see Eddie and Gail.

The long road reminded Petunia of the many times she walked down it running errands for Mama. That version of Petunia seemed to have lived a thousand years before. It was almost like she couldn't wrap her head around the change in her. If anyone would've told her then that she'd be living the life she had now, she would've called them a liar.

Opal hung her hand out the window and pointed. "The Coopers live down that road."

Petunia shuddered. "That brings up lots of bad memories."

After they drove around showing Jasper everything they could, including their old fishing spots, they stopped by the Marshalls.

An hour later, Lloyd looked in both directions before pulling onto Main Street, headed in the direction of the Prairie County Courthouse. A slight flutter hit Petunia's stomach as she glanced at Opal. Opal's expression was taut, and it was hard to tell if she was nervous or angry. It had taken a lot of talking to get Opal to agree to ride in the same vehicle with Lloyd and herself.

Jasper shifted in the front seat and held his hand out to Opal. Her face softened as she took his hand. "Don't be nervous, Opal. We gonna get through this together."

She clutched at her shirt collar and turned her head to look out the window. "I know we are, I just don't know about being in this town."

Petunia's face paled when Lloyd pulled down the road to the Courthouse. A mob of men stood in the middle of the road, yelling out to free the Coopers. Several of them held homemade signs saying the same thing. She sat up in the seat and rested her arm beside Lloyd's headrest. "Maybe we need to keep driving, Lloyd."

He turned to Jasper. Jasper let out a long breath. His eyes darted all around and then he threw his hand up. "We done come too far to turn back now."

After giving one nod, Lloyd slid into one of the only two available parking spots.

Opal clutched her side and rubbed beads of sweat off her brow. "I don't know if I can do this."

"Why don't you two stay in the car? Me and Lloyd can go in and see what happens." Petunia grabbed the door handle.

"I gots to be strong. For Clyde." Opal opened her door and stepped out before Jasper could make it around to open the door for her.

Heads held high, the foursome marched down the sidewalk and up to the crowd in front of the Courthouse.

One man shook a fist at Opal. "Lookee here. If it ain't the culprit behind Cyrus and his good son getting arrested."

Another man shouted as they walked by, "Y'all got some nerve showing up here."

Lloyd yelled over the commotion for them to keep walking. Lloyd elbowed their way through the mob until they finally made it inside.

The all-white jury sat stone-faced as the Prosecuting Attorney finished his closing statement. Petunia's body broke out in a sweat as she took inventory of the jurors' expressions. Sadly, they'd missed almost all the court proceedings, but at least they would be there to hear the verdict.

Trevor Cooper turned and met Petunia's gaze. He elbowed his daddy, and they whispered something before Trevor mouthed, "you'll pay," to Petunia.

The nerve of that crummy piece of filth to threaten her. While Petunia was busy having a staring contest with Trevor Cooper, the judge dismissed the jury to deliberate.

Less than an hour passed before they filed back into the courtroom.

Judge Simpson looked over his reading glasses and addressed the jurors. "Ladies and gentlemen of the jury, have you reached a verdict?"

A skinny man that looked to be wearing a toupee stood up and answered, "we have."

"What find ye?"

"We find the defendants not guilty."

Almost everyone in the courtroom applauded and shouted with joy.

Petunia grasped Opal's hand. It was clammy even in the heat. "I'm so sorry."

Jasper stood and helped Opal out of her seat. "Let's get on back home."

Judge Simpson banged his gavel as Lloyd led the way out of the courthouse.

Once outside, the mob shouted and thrust their signs in Opal's face. Jasper took her hand and did his best to get through.

Petunia elbowed her way past a few men. One of them grabbed her hair and pulled her next to him. "I'm Cyrus Cooper's friend, and you better believe he's gonna be coming after you."

Lloyd shoved the man back and glided her away from the man. Her scalp almost came off he jerked her hair so hard.

Once past the crowd, a thud hit Petunia's shoulder, and she cried out. Someone had thrown an egg. Another egg came flying and hit Jasper on the side of his head. Then another hit Opal's back. They took off running and got in the car, soaked in eggs.

Several men chased after the car, throwing eggs as Lloyd backed out. Opal cried, Petunia fumed, and Jasper and Lloyd both looked ready to fight.

Petunia held Opal as her body shook. Opal pulled back and wiped her eyes before she whispered. "They got away with killin' Clyde."

The agony coming from Opal about did Petunia in. She was ready to turn around and flog Cyrus and Trevor.

Since it wasn't up to Petunia, they sped down the highway until they reached a creek outside Cotton Plant. Lloyd pulled over and they washed off the best they could.

No one said a word the rest of the way home.

Chapter 67

The next day, Petunia received her first threatening phone call. Within three days, she'd been called ten times. The caller disguised his voice and told her he'd be seeing her real soon every time he called.

So far, she'd kept the phone calls to herself. She didn't want to upset anyone just yet. Not with Opal being pregnant and all. On top of that, they'd formed a pact that they wouldn't talk about what happened.

They hadn't even told her parents, and Verlon was still staying far away from her. You'd think she had the plague or something. Ralph told her he thought Verlon just needed a little time to deal with what had happened in Korea.

On top of volunteering, she'd made it a habit to stop by Opal's daily to check on her. The worry Petunia carried almost choked her with the idea of something happening to Opal. And that's where she was now. Enjoying lunch with Opal.

She picked up a pimento cheese sandwich and took a bite. A smoky flavor burst inside her mouth, and she smiled. "Opal, this is so good."

Opal licked her fingers and wiped the rest on a napkin. "My mother-in-law gave me this recipe. It's my favorite." She patted her stomach. "And I think little Clyde loves it as much as I do."

Jasper stepped through the front door and took his boots off. "Hi, Petunia. Opal, I need to spend the night on the water. I got some fishing that will take all night."

Opal shifted in her seat and rubbed her neck. "All right then."

A thought struck Petunia, and she landed a mischievous look on Opal. "Why don't you come to spend the night at the house? You can keep me company since Verlon has the boys this weekend."

Opal tapped on her chin. "If you're sure I wouldn't be no trouble."

Petunia's face lit up. "No trouble at all. I'm looking forward to it." She took another bite of the sandwich before licking her lips. "Especially if you bring a few of these sandwiches for a late-night snack."

A little later, after she and Opal had eaten their fill of sandwiches and lemon cake, Petunia poured two glasses of sweet tea. She handed one to Opal and took one with her to the couch.

Opal sat her glass on the side table and went to the window. She pulled the curtain back and stared outside. "Jasper is supposed to come by to say goodnight before he gets on the water."

Almost like she'd conjured him, Jasper pulled into the drive. Opal slipped out the front door and met Jasper beside the car. Petunia disappeared into her bedroom and pulled out a pair of pants and her old work boots.

The front door thudded closed, and Opal hummed a tune as she walked through the house. Petunia slipped the pants and boots into a paper sack and then peeked out the bedroom window in time to see Jasper's tail lights going in the opposite direction from the fishing hole.

Petunia's eyes narrowed to slits. Where could he be going? That way led out of town. Why would he lie to Opal?

Shortly after Opal drifted to sleep, Petunia slipped out the front door with her sack of items and drove in the same direction Jasper had gone.

A couple of hours later, Petunia traveled down the dirt road that she'd spent many days walking on as a youth. Sure enough, Jasper's car sat behind the Coopers' barn. What was he up to?

Petunia pulled down the road and parked her car behind some bushes. She quickly changed clothes and crept toward the Coopers, careful to keep her eyes on the trees for animals. Stars littered the sky, providing plenty of light for her trek.

Thirty minutes later, a pain blasted through her lungs as she threw her body behind the Magnolia tree. She clung to the tree, laboring to get her breath and calm her breathing. Sweat clung to her scalp, leaving a cool sensation that almost stung. She needed to keep running, but her body wouldn't cooperate.

Instead of making haste to get out of there, she traced her fingers over the initials someone had carved into the tree. JC and CB. It had to have been Judith Cooper and Clyde Brown. How did Cyrus Cooper not know his daughter loved Clyde? Or did he know and choose to ignore it? To cover it up? That answer would go to the grave with him.

The full moon and stars cast an unearthly tint across the horizon. The night would be peaceful if not for the flames consuming the burning house.

Even though Petunia stood far off from the flames, the heat almost lovingly stroked her face. Smoke mixed with singed chicken feathers permeated the air and assaulted her senses.

Two horses barreled out of the barn and disappeared into the night as Petunia watched with wide eyes. Jasper rushed out behind them, carrying a cat.

Jasper's dark skin had a blue glow to it as he sat the cat down and leaned against the barn. Banging and screams of horror came from the burning house, echoing throughout the night. *"Please open this door!"*

His rigid body stood motionless for at least a full minute as he stared at the flames consuming the front door of the house. Then it was almost like his brain registered what was happening, and he moved closer, reaching his hand toward the only window. The glass exploded, and he pulled his hand back, holding it next to his side. He stood another second before backing away from the fire. His head lowered, almost like he was saying a prayer before he lumbered away from the house and fled into the night.

By the time Petunia returned home, it was almost dawn. She headed to the backyard and threw her paper bag into the trash barrel. She stared into the distance with a blank expression before striking a match and watching a fire for the second time that night. What had Jasper been thinking about going to the Coopers? Did he not realize he would've been killed if he'd been caught?

After the fire burned out, Petunia sat on her porch swing, listening to the cicada's chirp. She could swear a whole army of them had moved into her backyard, but she would never complain. She loved the way they sounded. In sync like a family unit looking out for one another. The world could take a lesson from these little creatures. They'd been singing to her all night long.

The screen door closed, and Opal moseyed over to the swing and crawled in beside Petunia. "You sure are up early."

Petunia bit her bottom lip and shrugged. "Yeah, I had a lot on my mind."

Opal kicked Petunia's foot. "How about some coffee?"

Petunia kicked Opal's foot back, and they laughed in unison. "I'd love some coffee. Then why don't we grab a couple of poles and go out back to catch some fish?"

"That sounds good. Maybe I can find another cat."

Petunia groaned. "Oh boy, I forgot all about Buford, the cat. I wonder what ever happened to him."

"I talked Mama's friend into taking him when we got sent away. Last I heard, he was still doing good."

"Well, what do you know." Petunia stood and walked around the porch. "Let's get that coffee."

Later that afternoon, they'd caught enough fish to have a cookout. Their entire family sat around laughing as they worked on cooking their dinner.

A knot of dread hit Petunia's stomach when the phone rang. After taking the call from Lonnie, she made her way outside. Might as well tell the family all at once.

She raised her voice. "I have some news." Everyone turned to look at her, and she swallowed a lump down before continuing. "That was Lonnie on the phone. He called to tell us that Cyrus and Trevor Cooper died in a house fire last night."

Gasps of shock and surprise came from all around her. From everyone but one person.

Chapter 68

A few weeks later, Petunia stared at the baby in her arms as she settled onto the sofa at Opal's. She rubbed his hand and grinned when he grasped her finger. "To be such a little thing, baby Clyde has a grip on him."

"Yes, he sure does." Petunia had never seen Opal smile so widely. Happiness agreed with her. She nodded at Jasper. "He's strong like his Daddy."

Jasper's lips edged up at the corners as he pulled Opal close. "I think he's strong like his Mama." A scabbed-over cut stood out on Jasper's arm.

Petunia chewed on her lips as she contemplated the cut. "What happened to your arm, Jasper?"

His brows drew together, and he frowned. A look Petunia couldn't quite describe crossed his face before he answered. "I got cut by a fishing hook."

The screen door banged against the house and Petunia sucked in a quick breath. That's when it hit her. He must've been cut the night of the fire when the window blew out. Her face softened and she snuggled baby Clyde close. "I bet that had to hurt."

His chest expanded like he'd been holding his breath waiting for Petunia's reply. "It hurt like fire."

Petunia cooed at the baby. "Speaking of fire, did you know Lonnie told me the new sheriff tried to say somebody set the fire that killed Cyrus and Trevor Cooper?"

The wind kicked up a notch, causing the screen door to slam against the house again. Jasper rubbed the back of his neck before making his way toward the front door. "Well, ain't that something. I better get out here and care for the animals before the storm hits."

Opal watched Jasper leave before she shook her head. "He gets really nervous talking about those hateful men. I wonder…"

Petunia stopped Opal from saying it. "Don't you dare say what I think you're gonna say. We need to make a pact right here and now that we won't bring up Cyrus, Trevor, or even Judith Cooper no more."

Pressing her fingertips to her temples, Opal rubbed in a circular motion for a minute. "But do you think Jasper…" Opal stopped midsentence, and her shoulders shuddered. "You know what, Petunia? I think you're right. Let's not bring those people up anymore."

After placing a kiss on little Clyde's hand, Petunia angled her head. "How's Miss Betty doing?"

"She's tickled pink to have little Clyde. He's her first grandbaby, you know."

Jasper came in through the back of the house and poked his head into the living room. "It's about to storm. You better get going before it hits."

Petunia stood and handed the baby to Opal. "I'll see you later this week."

"All right." Opal's expression turned mischievous. "I want to hear all about your visit with Verlon."

Petunia cringed. "What visit?"

A smirk the size of Chicago crossed Opal's face. "The one you need to make tomorrow."

Petunia sighed, and her hand flew to her hip. "Now that you're a mama, you sure are bossy." By her amused expression, anyone would know she wasn't really put out with Opal.

Opal let out a giggle that followed Petunia through the front door. "Just go see him."

BREAK

The following day, Petunia eased her Rocket 8 Oldsmobile into the parking spot in front of Verlon's house and laid her head on the steering wheel. She glanced at the bowl sitting in the front seat and grimaced. This was a terrible idea.

Maybe Verlon wouldn't want to see her. After all the trouble with the sorry Sheriff and attorney, maybe he wouldn't want to deal with Petunia. Even though both men could no longer cause trouble, what if Verlon blamed her for what happened?

Perhaps the past few months had given him enough time to find someone else. Someone better.

She ground her teeth and grabbed the bowl, quickly stepping out of the car. Marching up to the white screen door, she knocked three times on the metal part of the screen.

Her heart beat into her throat. After waiting for a second, she turned on her heel and walked toward her car. She reached the door, but her trembling hands couldn't open it fast enough for her liking. This most definitely was not a good idea.

The door to the house swung open so hard that the metal around the screen banged into the wood. Verlon stood there with a stunned expression. "Petunia?"

She spun around and rested her eyes on him before taking a few faltering steps in his direction. His hair had grown out, giving him a boyish but attractive look.

Once she got close enough to touch him, she took the lid off the bowl. "Do you want this banana cake or not?"

Verlon grinned. "Why sure, Petunia. I'll take it."

She handed the bowl to him and smiled. "I never told you, but it nearly killed me to offer you the cake at the church potluck that day long ago."

His grin doubled in size. "I know it did. Why do you think I gave it back to you?"

She cocked her head. "I thought you just didn't want it."

"Nope. I wanted it really bad." His gaze bore into hers. "But I wanted you more."

Holding his gaze, Petunia inched toward him. "What about now? After all that's happened, could you possibly still want me?"

He looked into the bowl and licked his lips. "This cake looks awful delicious. But the way I see it, there's enough cake for both of us."

A sob escaped her lips. "I wondered if you'd moved on. Benjamin and the boys won't tell me nothing about their visits with you."

He shrugged. "None of the boys have a problem informing me about your life. Benjamin says you spend your days helping your mama and volunteering at the homeless shelter."

"That little traitor is gonna hear from me." She scrunched her lips into a circle and then smiled. "Thank you for including my brothers, by the way."

He waved his hand in the air. "I enjoy spending time with them. And I'm thankful Benjamin told me. It gave me hope knowing you hadn't run off and left me for nobody else yet."

A spasm rocked her stomach so hard she put her hand across it. "Hope?"

The rim around his eyes held unshed tears. "Hope we would one day reunite. I just called Daddy and Mama yesterday and told them I was well enough to do whatever it takes to win you back."

She took a step closer to Verlon and raised her face to his. "You did? I thought for sure you'd tell me to get lost. What happened to change your mind?"

He wrapped his hand around her waist, tugging her so close an ant couldn't have squeezed between them. "I've spent the past six months dealing with my issues left over from the war."

Her voice came out raspy as her heart tripped over the beats in her chest. "And have you dealt with them?"

"It's been a struggle. Then my buddy Guy came by for a visit. Turns out he lives a few towns over." A smile skated across his lips as he lowered himself onto the sofa. "Petunia, Guy was the best man I've ever met. Kindhearted, and he kept me grounded on top of everything else he had to deal with."

She sat beside Verlon and turned her body in his direction. "Would you tell me about how you met him?"

"Guy was part of the 24th Infantry Division deployed to Korea from Japan. Somehow, I ended up as part of this group of men, also known as the Victory Division. Without Guy there to help me, I don't know what would've become of me."

"I'm thankful you had someone like Guy to lean on." She tugged at her bottom lip, pondering how to ask the one question to which she had to know the answer. "How'd he help you change your mind about divorcing me?"

He shot off the sofa and ran a hand through his hair. "Guy was in the same war as me. We fought side by side, and he still found love."

"Oh?"

He sat beside her and clasped her hand in his. "He told me he's engaged to a woman named Jane. Petunia, he's not allowing what happened in Korea to ruin his life. So why am I?"

Petunia didn't know this man named Guy, but she said a silent prayer of thanks for him.

"I still have my bad days, Petunia. I can't lie about that. What happened to me can't simply be forgotten. But I've come to an understanding." He scrubbed the bridge of his nose and underneath his eyes with both hands. He dropped his hands to his waist and fixated his sweet blue eyes on Petunia.

She caressed the side of his face. "Care to tell me what you're thinking?"

He grasped her hand as it lingered on his face and kissed her palm. "I have a choice. I can let my past ruin my future or move forward to the best of my ability. Are you willing to take me as I am? Damaged, but in love with you more than ever?"

Tremors ran down her palm, and she remembered how she had felt before their first official date. Like she'd eaten rotten hog slop. Well, that had nothing on what her stomach did now. "Only if you'll take me as I am."

His fingers trailed down her neck as he gazed into her eyes. "Always. I wouldn't change a thing about my Petunia."

Static moved from the place his fingers touched, settling into her bones. She stood on her tippy toes, leaning her body into his, just like their wedding day so many years before. "I love you, Verlon."

Verlon's lips met hers, and her knees no longer held her up. She sighed deep within her heart. Not a sad sigh. A sigh of happiness. Of finally finding the place she'd longed to always be. Home. That's what Verlon was. Home.

Epilogue

July 1973

Petunia held onto her belly and moaned. "Verlon!"

He squeezed her hand. "I'm here, baby."

"Baby! I can't be having no baby!" She got out between gasps for air. "I'm almost forty years old. What were we thinking?"

"Everything is going to be just fine." Verlon rubbed her arm. "I promise."

"No, it ain't. We have grandchildren." A pain shot down her side, and her eyes rolled back into her head.

"That just means the little one will have someone to play with." His soothing voice was not helping her. If only she had a piece of banana cake. She'd gladly smear it into his face this time.

Or eat it. Why'd she have to go and think about banana cake? Her stomach rumbled, and she grasped his wrist. "Verlon. I need you to listen to me. RIGHT NOW."

"I'm listening to you, Petunia."

"I need you to go get me a piece of cake. I don't care what kind. Any. Even strawberry. MaryAnne keeps cake for Lloyd. Go get some from her or Opal."

Dr. Hagen butted into her private conversation. "Now, Petunia, you can't have anything to eat. You're in labor."

She ground her teeth together. "I DON'T CARE! I've been here all day."

A cramp shot through her abdomen, and she banged her head into the hospital bed. "She's COM-ING!"

Dr. Hagen mouthed something to the nurse, and the rest happened faster than she could blink.

A few hours later, Petunia smiled at Verlon and their new baby girl, Sherry Francis. He held her close to his heart, cooing at her. The look on his face caused Petunia's heart to tighten.

Contentment spread through her chest. "What are you over there whispering to our daughter?"

"I'm telling her about her brothers and little nephews." His face almost glowed as he stood up and walked close to Petunia, reaching out to push a few hairs off her forehead before planting a kiss there. "And how lucky she is to have such a strong and brave Mama."

Petunia wiped under her nose with a tissue from the table. "And Daddy."

Little Sherry screeched a cry that would've had a rooster getting up early. Verlon chuckled as he handed her to Petunia. "I think she's hungry."

Petunia settled her in for a feeding, and a peacefulness traveled over her like never before. "I love you, Verlon. My life with you has been everything and more."

Tears pooled in the corners of his eyes. "And I love you. Thank you for never giving up on me."

As Sherry continued eating her dinner, Petunia squeezed Verlon's hand. "I never will."

He leaned in for a kiss that should've been old by now, but it was as sweet as that first one they shared on their wedding day.

As he lingered near Petunia's lips, he held onto Sherry's fingers. He stood up with one of the goofiest grins Petunia had ever seen and motioned toward the door. "I think I better let our folks in here. Your daddy's been chomping at the bit to meet his granddaughter. And I'm afraid he might throw his walker through the window if we don't let him in!"

Petunia's teeth nipped at her bottom lip, trying not to laugh too awful loud. "I'm surprised Ralph and Hazel haven't knocked the door down with their canes!"

A broad smile spread across his face. "And your Mama's in her wheelchair sitting right outside the door. She hasn't left that spot since you went into labor."

A few days later, Petunia stuck a piece of mint gum in her mouth and grinned at Opal. "Can you believe the two little girls who used to dream about growing up and marrying good men made it to this point?"

Opal smoothed the back of her hair that she'd recently cut beneath her ears. "Some days, I have to pinch myself."

"Me, too. Life sure has been good to us."

Opal lowered her voice and leaned across the table close to Petunia. "I know we ain't talked about this in a long time, but I wish I knew for sure that Jasper didn't set the Cooper's house on fire. He won't talk about it."

Sherry's loud cry came from another room, and Verlon hollered from the kitchen that he'd take care of Sherry so she could visit with Opal. Petunia met Opal's gaze. "Jasper didn't do it, Opal."

Laughing almost nervously, Opal narrowed her eyes. "How could you know that?"

Petunia shrugged, and a partial smile nipped at her lips. "I'm sure they made plenty of enemies over the years. Maybe they had the wrong person whipped."

"I reckon so." Opal said as she burrowed her gaze into Petunia's. After what seemed like an eternity, Opal fluttered her lashes and a ghost of a smile appeared. "I hear that Des Arc has been one of the best towns to live ever since that day."

"I bet." Petunia replied, a crooked smile lighting her face. "The people there were always wonderful besides a few bad apples."

"Yeah, but that's anywhere." Opal angled her body so she could grasp Petunia's hand. Moisture gathered on Opal's lashes. "Thank you, Petunia. For everything."

Later that evening, when the sun hung low on the horizon, Petunia curled up on the same swing she'd sat in after the Coopers died. She stared into the distance and allowed her mind to drift back to that night. She could still smell the smoke and feel the heat on her face. She searched her memory for any small detail she could've missed that night. Had Jasper seen her?

Could he have known she hid behind the Magnolia tree? Had the screams been too much for him? He'd run like he was racing a cheetah. But not Petunia. She'd traced those initials on the tree until the fire died to embers. Then she'd stood there until there was nothing but cicadas singing a song of deliverance.

Just for her.

Thank you for taking the time to read *Petunia 1949*. If you found it enjoyable, I would be grateful if you could leave a review. Your feedback truly makes a difference!

Acknowledgements

I can't begin to list everyone who's given me a hand with this labor of love I call Petunia 1949.

Thank you to my dear family for putting up with my constant talk about life seventy years ago. I appreciate you all for listening, reading, giving me advice on cover design, and more! I love y'all!

To Miss Jane – thank you for allowing me to use Mr. Guy's book from Korea. I appreciate you so much! You are such a huge encouragement to me!

I owe so much to my two "Vickies" for reading, giving a lot of feedback (even when it hurt), and reading it all over again. The input you've both given has been invaluable.

To my editor, Stephanie – you still rock!

To my readers – THANK YOU ALL! I appreciate you and would love your feedback. I truly want to grow as a writer, and I need to know what you think! You can share your thoughts by leaving a review, rating, emailing me, or following me on Facebook at writingleahbrewer.

I love my people. Each and every one of you.

Love,

Leah

about the author

L eah Brewer is a multi-genre author who focuses on writing clean books that anyone can read. She was born and raised in Des Arc, Arkansas, before moving to Northeast Arkansas when her children were young.

She spends her spare time with her husband, Mark, their grown children, and granddaughter, Charlotte. If she's not on a beach, she's dreaming about when she can be!